T0193759

Oh, Susannah

Ruth Callick

authorHOUSE®

AuthorHouse™
1663 Liberty Drive
Bloomington, IN 47403
www.authorhouse.com
Phone: 1 (800) 839-8640

Published by AuthorHouse 05/02/2018

ISBN: 978-1-5462-4067-9 (sc)
ISBN: 978-1-5462-4066-2 (hc)
ISBN: 978-1-5462-4065-5 (e)

Library of Congress Control Number: 2018905295

Print information available on the last page.

This book is printed on acid-free paper.

CHAPTER ONE

"Brock?"

Abner Brockman, Brock to anyone who knew him, gave a start and opened his eyes, barely able to turn his head as he lay in the hospital bed. His eyes focused on his friend and partner, Cade Candlewood.

"I got here as soon as I heard," Cade told him, hiding his shock. Brock was bandaged from head to foot with tubes sticking everywhere. "Shotz, Brockman. If I had thought Marlett would –"

"Wasn't…Marlett," Brock whispered painfully.

Cade stared at his partner. "Wasn't –?"

Brock closed his eyes and swallowed. His hand slowly made its way up and under his pillow. He brought out a half sheet of paper, and after a quick glance at it, handed it toward his partner. "Woke…this morning… with that…in my hand," he told him.

Cade's eyes skimmed the note, and then with a "Dear God!" he read it again.

Hello Brockman-

Feelin bad? Saw your partner's car blow up last night. Too bad he didn't live through it. Heard he was a close personal friend of yours. Rough losing a close personal friend, isn't it? I should know. You killed mine.

Tit for Tat, Brockman

"Must…have thought Erickson…was you," Brock said.

"Any ideas?" Guilt was choking Cade. If he hadn't gone…If it hadn't had been for his grandmother's funeral…

"No," Brock whispered. "I've been…racking my brain." Brock raised his eyes to his friend. "You might…want to lay low…for a while."

"Does the chief know?"

Brock managed to shake his head, "Hasn't…been in yet. Cade…"

"I'll see that he knows, and I'll take care," he assured his partner.

Brock closed his eyes in relief.

Guilt again shot through Cade as he watched the pain flit across his partner's face. Brockman was more than a partner, more than a friend to him. They were comrades; closer than most brothers. Too close for him to have let this happen to him. He cursed silently and stared down at the note in his hand.

Who?

The why was self-explanatory; revenge. Cade glanced around the room, looking for the telephone. There wasn't one. That would have to be remedied. Now.

"Brock?"

"Yes?" He didn't bother to open his eyes.

"I'm going down the hall to find a phone. I'll see that one is put in here today."

Brock barely nodded his head and Cade strode purposely out of the room. The telephone he found immediately at the nurse's station and pulling rank, used it to call in to their chief, explaining the note and his gut feeling that this wasn't going to be the end of it. Brock's room would be secured.

He hung up the phone and smiled devastatingly at the nurse behind the desk. "We need a phone put in Room 308 immediately," he told her. "We're also going to need –"

"Mister?" he was interrupted as a younger nurse grasped his arm and shook it.

He whipped around, staring at the frightened, upset young woman. "What is it?"

"Your friend," she cried, "In room 308. He's says he needs you now. He's quite agitated. He –"

But Cade was already running, the nurse running after him.

"I'm sorry! All I did was deliver a letter! If I knew it would upset him like this..."

"Brock?"

Cade was in the room and by his bed in seconds. His heart caught in his throat. Brock lay clutching another note in his clenched fist, stringing curse after curse. The look on his face was a mixture of anger and terror... and of total helplessness.

"Brock!" Cade called again, more forcefully.

The curses cut off and Brock focused on him. "Susie," he choked out. "He's after Susie!"

"Susannah?" Cade whispered. He grabbed the note from Brock's hand and read:

> *Are you hurting, Brockman? I sincerely hope so. I did my best to make you as uncomfortable as possible short of killing you. But I don't want to kill you. Yet. I want you to feel as helpless as I did when you made it impossible for me to protect my sister. You heard they terrorized her in that prison, didn't you? Tortured her? Raped her time after time?*
>
> *Tit for Tat, Brockman*
> *Terror -- Torture -- Rape*
> > *bye bye*

"Cade!"

"Where's Susannah living?" Cade interrupted tightly. "Brock!" he demanded, "Where did Susie move to?" God in Heaven! He'd tear the man limb to limb himself if he touched Susannah!

"Trendex," Brock managed, shutting his eyes, "221 Trendex. In...Langley."

Cade was out of the door and down the hall before Brock realized he was gone. His first call was to the Langley police. Assured that they would put Brock's sister under protective custody immediately, he made his second call to the airport. The third was again to their chief.

"I leave in forty minutes," he told Brock coming back into the room. "Don't worry. Susannah should be in protective custody by now. I'll call as soon as I have her."

CHAPTER TWO

Susannah Brockman gave herself one last critical look in the mirror mounted near her front door. Golden brown eyes stared back at her. Her rich, brown hair tumbled just past the shoulders of her trim, 5'4" frame in soft waves. She readjusted her bangs.

"Come on, Susannah!"

Susannah grinned as she grabbed her purse and headed out the door. She pulled her door shut and locked it then carried her duffle bag down to her friend's car. Becky Weaver already had her trunk open. They plopped in the duffle bag then climbed into the car. Susannah glancing back, waved goodbye at her neighbor who was just picking up her newspaper. "See you in three weeks!" she called out.

Diana Heber grinned and waved them off.

Susannah turned back to her friend. "My phone died a terrible death this morning. Got yours?"

"Yes. What happened to yours?"

"Who knows? It simply won't turn on. Think Gloria will be ready?" she asked as she slipped on her seatbelt.

"Not likely," Becky returned with a slight giggle as she pulled out of Susannah's drive. The girls, Gloria included, were heading out of state. Gloria's family was having a family reunion and both Becky and Susannah had agreed to drive her home, taking a traveling vacation as they did so.

They would be gone three weeks; three glorious weeks of vacation. They planned to take their time driving Gloria home for her family reunion, exploring the countryside as they went then doing more exploring as they drove back home to Langley after it was over.

Susannah had welcomed the vacation. She had thought fleetingly of visiting her brother but had dismissed it just as quickly when Becky and Gloria had suggested this traveling vacation.

It would have done little good to visit her brother anyway. He was on a hard case at the moment, one that would take up most of his time; time he wouldn't have to visit with her.

Besides, spending time with Brock would also have meant spending time with Cade, something she didn't want to do.

She flushed with the thought of Cade Candlewood; of how she had embarrassed herself thoroughly, throwing herself into his arms and practically begging him to make love to her. She had been barely eighteen at the time, and deeply in love with Cade.

Cade, already twenty-three then, had refused her point blank. His rejection had been brutal and painful, and had hurt terribly. And she had never forgiven him for that in the passing years.

Not that she was vocal about it. Cade Candlewood was her brother's closest friend and it would hurt him to know that there was a rift between her and Cade. So she avoided her brother's best friend whenever it was possible. When it wasn't, she attempted to be civil for her brother's sake. The fact that her brother and Cade lived several states away and were both working in a special division of some security branch of the government, helped keep her run-ins with Cade to a minimum. The two men were generally busy with this case or that case, keeping visits short and far between.

The arrangement was fine with Susannah. Though she missed her brother, he was generally bossy and over-protective and still treated her as a kid when he was around despite the fact that she was now twenty-four. And Cade? Well, Cade treated her just the same which was insulting.

And more than enough reason to look forward to this trip with both Gloria and Becky.

Gloria, to their surprise, was ready and waiting when they drove up to her apartment. "Too excited to see home again," she said ruefully, handing them her bags. They packed them in the trunk beside their own and then headed out.

"This is going to be great," Becky stated in contentment as she headed her car onto the freeway.

"Where are we heading first?" Gloria asked from the backseat, hardly able to contain her own excitement.

"Grandon," Becky replied, having been the first one to pick a destination. "Where we'll pop over and visit the Pioneer museum."

"I thought we agreed to tour the Border Gardens?" Gloria asked in surprise.

"We did," Becky returned, "right after we tour the museum."

"Well," Gloria said, "Just so we get to indulge in one of their outside garden teas." It was a well-known fact that Gloria loved gardens; gardens of any kind. She could, in fact, sit enjoying one for hours which is why it had been her choice of Border Gardens.

Susannah looked to Becky. "Did you get the reservations for tonight?"

"Oh, yes," Becky returned. "We have reservations at the Prairie Cabins, just outside of the small town of Prairie Town."

"A cabin?"

"It's an inn, Glory," Becky corrected her with a giggle, "One with all the modern conveniences despite its name."

"It better be," Gloria grumbled good-naturedly.

But the worry of the Prairie Cabins dissipated as they went on. All three of them were in high spirits as they eventually reached Grandon. It was almost noon, and they stopped for a quick lunch before they traveled through the large city looking for any sign of the museum. They eventually found it at the south end of town.

The museum was like a trip back into the old west; pioneer life, to be exact, for there were a host of artifacts from the era, from covered wagons, to washboards to homemade furniture. There were also diaries and journals and a multitude of pictures depicting the old lifestyle of the pioneers.

The girls took their time going through it, taking pictures and marveling at the lives their early ancestors had lived. "I don't think I would have made it," Gloria stated on a sigh. "Having to grow all your own food and worry about Indian attacks or having to walk miles just to visit a friend."

"I think the hardest would have been the food preservation," Becky added. "I can't imagine life without a refrigerator."

"Or having to make your own clothes," Susannah said knowing she couldn't sew a straight line if her life depended on it.

Becky giggled. "It means we just aren't pioneer stock."

"In that case, let's leave this all to the past and go sit and enjoy a modern garden," Gloria suggested with a hopeful grin.

"All right," Becky said handing her the keys, "Let's head over to your Gardens. You're driving."

"Great!" Gloria said happily. "Someone give me directions."

Once again settled in the car, Susannah reached onto the dash and grabbed the map and the itinerary all three of them had formed. Susannah herself had taken the time to write up all the directions from highway to highway for each of their destinations. She had also taken the time to plot them onto the map.

"Take the freeway west to Lexton," she instructed Gloria. "Then we'll veer down 83."

"Will do."

It took another two hours to reach the gardens. Hot and tired from the long drive, they sat down and enjoyed a late afternoon tea before touring the gardens themselves. Though neither Becky nor Susannah were garden enthusiasts, they were amazed at the gardens regardless. Border Gardens covered several acres of meandering paths winding around a shallow creek and through trees and bushes and flowers; flowers of every type and color and fragrance.

"It's so beautiful," Susannah said with a touch of awe as they walked around the meandering paths.

"Definitely," Becky agreed, "I wonder how long it took to develop all this."

"Well, the brochure says it was started about twenty years ago and they're still developing it," Susannah returned.

"How can they add to it?" Becky asked in surprise. "It's perfect already!"

"I'll say!" Gloria murmured as she snapped another picture. Both Susannah and Becky grinned at each other. Gloria was definitely enjoying the gardens. She was roaming through it all, taking her time in order to see everything as well as taking lots of pictures of the expansive garden and the variety of flowers it held.

Not that Susannah and Becky didn't take snapshots of their own though theirs were more of the gardens as a whole rather than individual flower arrangements growing throughout. It was close to six o'clock before they finally headed back toward the entrance.

"Anyone hungry?" Becky asked.

"Not super hungry," Gloria answered.

"Well, we could have a light supper here, or go on and eat when we get to Prairie Town," Becky suggested.

"Well, in that case," Gloria said her face brightening. "I'm starving! Let's eat here."

The girls ate at the outdoor restaurant there at the gardens then headed down the highway to Prairie Town, where they checked into their motel for the night.

"Wow!" Becky said looking around. "It really does look like one of those old cabins!"

Prairie Cabins indeed looked like a set of cabins. Though totally surrounded with logs on the outside and wooden walls on the inside, the buildings were fashionable and up-to-date with all the amenities one expected in a modern motel. Gloria gave a sigh of satisfaction.

Susannah grinned at her. "I take it you're happy with it?"

"Perfectly," she said. "Come on, girls. Let's get settled!"

CHAPTER THREE

Cade Candlewood waited impatiently for the seatbelt sign to go off. Though the plane had been a direct flight and had taken barely an hour, he knew time was of the essence. Thank God the Langley police had listened; had understood. They would have Susannah in custody by now. But he wanted Susannah in *his* protective custody! Only then would he feel her safe from that monster after her. His eyes glued anxiously to the sign above his head. It finally blinked and went out.

Cade grabbed his bag and stood, impatiently pushing his way through the throng of other passengers disembarking. He ignored the cries and insults that were sent his way.

Two uniformed police officers and a plain-clothed detective were waiting for him just outside the plane. Cade made a bee-line for them. The detective stepped up. "Agent Candlewood?"

"Do you have her in custody?" Cade asked immediately.

"I'm afraid we have a problem with that," Detective Alcott answered with a heavy sigh.

"What?" Cade's heart froze. "What do you mean a problem?"

The detective took his arm and began leading him out of the airport, the officers behind them. "I think we'd better take you to the house so you can see for yourself."

There seemed nothing out of the ordinary when they pulled up to Susannah's small house. The lawn had been recently mowed; the flower beds were clean and he could see Susannah's car parked in her carport. And the house itself looked quiet; peaceful...until Cade walked through the front door that was held open for him.

Susannah's home had been totally demolished. Everything she had owned was strewn on the floor, broken or ripped apart. Clothes, knick-knacks, phone, photographs, books, CDs and DVDs, dishes, food; everything. Not one item appeared to have remained intact. The television and stereo system had been destroyed. The cabinet doors ripped from the cupboards. Her mattress cut in pieces with a knife. The furniture broken. Even the toilet seat had been ripped off.

A sickening dread filled Cade as he took it all in. The detective stepped up. "The only thing he didn't seem to damage was her car," he informed him quietly. "We believe he may have been afraid of being seen if he attempted it."

"Forget the car!" Cade bit out. "Did you find Susannah?"

Jeremy Alcott slowly shook his head. "But I don't think he did either," he said. "According to the neighbor, your girl apparently left with a friend yesterday morning for a three week vacation; female friend. Destination unknown."

Cade's heart jumped. "She see her leave?"

"Oh, yes, about 8:00 am. Even waved goodbye. Reported that both girls seemed happy and excited as they left. Overheard them say something about picking up another friend along the way."

"So when did this happen?" Cade asked his hand sweeping to the destruction.

"Apparently yesterday afternoon. Mrs. Heber, the neighbor, said a man showed up around two stating that he was Miss Brockman's brother. She told him what she told us, that your girl had left with friends on a vacation. The man questioned her about where, and she told him she didn't know. Mrs. Heber thought he had left after that, but wasn't sure as she herself had left for a hair appointment. I have a feeling that he took the time to do this as a message for your girl."

"So do I," Cade said tightly, knowing exactly what the message meant. He fought down the terror that tried to grip him and began scanning the papers on the floor for any indication of where Susannah had been headed; any receipts or reservations. Names of places. Anything.

The terror began climbing back up in him as he found little. No personal phonebook. No itinerary. Nothing but a torn piece of paper with the word Gardens printed on it. Had that monster already found the information he was seeking? He turned back to the detective. "Do you –?"

He stopped as he caught sight of a corner of what looked like a brochure sticking out from under the broken bookcase, a ripped apart book hiding most of it from view. He shoved the book aside and picked up the colored paper, his heart hammering. It was definitely a brochure; a rather new looking brochure.

Bristel Falls. The brochure showed a colored photo of the falls; a description and a map of how to get there. A small surge of relief sifted through Cade. Susannah loved visiting waterfalls; any kind of waterfalls. He pocketed the brochure and turned to the detective. "Alcott…"

"Jeremy?" a new voice interrupted.

"Over here," Alcott called out, turning to the two men just entering the house. He waved Cade over. "Gentlemen, Agent Candlewood," he introduced him. "These are two of my best detectives, Cashe and Cortner," he explained. "They've been trying to find out where Miss Brockman and her friends were heading."

"And?" Cade's eyes had gone immediately to the two detectives.

Detective Cortner pulled out his notebook. "According to her co-workers, she was going on a traveling vacation with two of her friends, one which had a family reunion to attend somewhere in New Mexico. Near Santa Fe, one co-worker believed. The girls were going to take the scenic route there and back, leaving yesterday and returning in about three weeks."

"Any names?"

"Just a Gloria, though no one could give me a last name." He took a heavy breath. "But there's more," he added looking up at Cade. "Apparently a man identifying himself as Miss Brockman's brother appeared at her jobsite asking for the same information."

"*Oh, God,*" Cade breathed. The monster was most likely already after Susannah. "Any idea whose car they're traveling in?" he asked.

The detective's head shook. "Unfortunately, no."

"Any description of it?" he asked shortly.

Alcott sighed. "It isn't much help. The neighbor said it was white. She wasn't sure of the make or model, but she thought it looked a lot like one of those newer sports models advertised on television. The man's car, according to her, was small and dark. Foreign, she thought, but couldn't tell us anything else."

"So noted." Cade's mind reeled. There was no way to put an APB out on either of the cars. And that monster after Susannah already had close to a whole day's head start! He looked up at Alcott. "You said Susannah's car was untouched?"

Again the detective nodded. "As far as we could discern."

"Thank God," Cade muttered. He glanced around then headed for the closet. Susannah, he knew, always kept an extra set of car keys hidden. And he knew just where…if they hadn't been already found.

Moving several things out of his way and saying a short prayer, he leaned into the hallway closet and reached up, his fingers feeling the small wall space just above the door. Relief filled him as they came in contact with a set of keys. He grasped them in his fist.

"I'm taking her car," he stated, already heading for the door. The detective was on his heels. Cade pushed the front door open, then in afterthought turned to the man. "Got a pen?" he asked hurriedly as he pulled one of his cards from his back pocket.

Alcott took a pen from one of his officers and handed it to Cade. With a nod and a brief thanks, Cade wrote down his cell phone number. "Have an APB put out on Susannah Brockman and friends. Call me if anyone locates the girls, or if you get anything else."

Alcott, assuring Cade that he would keep in constant contact as well as secure Susannah's home, saw him into Susannah's car. "If we get anything at all we'll be in contact. Just let us know if you're able to find her yourself…and good luck," he added with a salute.

Cade barely acknowledged it as he started the car and backed it out of the carport and into the street. His eyes went to the brochure he pulled from his pocket. Bristel Falls. It was a place to start.

CHAPTER FOUR

Susannah woke just as dawn was breaking. She slipped out of bed and into the small cabin bathroom, shutting the door. She might as well shower and dress while she had the bathroom to herself. It would save time later, not to mention be easier than having all three of them trying to get ready all at once.

Both Becky and Gloria were awake and talking when she finished and made her way back into the main cabin. "You're up early," Becky greeted her.

"Only way to have the bathroom to myself," she said with a wry grin. Two pillows were tossed at her simultaneously. She tossed them back. "Come on, girls. Up and at it! We want to get to the Bristel Falls sometime today!"

"All right, already!" They both giggled, climbing out of the beds. They were well aware of how eager Susannah was to see the falls, any falls for that matter!

The girls showered and dressed in turn and after packing the car, all three of them headed over to the restaurant for breakfast.

"We still need to stop for gas," Becky reminded them when they headed for the car a short time later.

"There's an Ace Station up on the corner," Gloria said.

"Good enough." Becky slipped behind the wheel as the others climbed into the car with her. They drove the short block to the service station where they all three piled out yet again.

"I'm going to go on in and pick up some gum and a bottle of water," Gloria announced, "Anyone else?"

"I'll come with you," Susannah said.

"Bring me a water and a candy bar or two," Becky called out, placing the gas nozzle into her car and starting it.

Gloria and Susannah headed for the station's store.

To the girls' surprise, the store was more than what they expected a small gas station store to be. It was more like a gift shop. Both Susannah and Gloria roamed around it several minutes before two squabbling children drove them to find their purchases. Susannah was just pulling out several bottles of water from the refrigeration unit when something hit her hard on the leg. She turned to find the boy who had been squabbling with his sister tossing yet another box from the shelf down the aisle. Checking her leg, she stood and glared at the boy. He merely stuck his tongue out at her and disappeared down another aisle pushing past yet another customer. With a shake of her head, Susannah took the bottles of water up to the counter where Gloria was waiting.

"If I get my hands on that kid I'm going to spank the daylights out of him!" she muttered at her friend.

"Susannah Brockman, you wouldn't dare!"

"Well, you're right, I wouldn't, but it would serve him right!" Susannah said with a giggle. She was unaware of the male customer that had swung abruptly around at the sound of her name and was now staring intently at her from the aisle while both she and Gloria began paying for their purchases. He disappeared a moment later.

"Come on," Gloria groaned the moment their purchases were made. Still giggling, she pulled Susannah out the shop door and down the steps only to find both herself and Susannah knocked to the ground by a hard, male body that seemed to ram them. Packages and purses flew from their arms.

It took Susannah a moment to regain her equilibrium. She pushed herself up from the ground to find the man who had run into them picking up their purchases that had gone flying. He wasn't a large man, but lean and wirily with an indistinguishable tattoo on his upper right arm. About thirty, maybe thirty-five, she guessed. His hair was slicked back and he was wearing faded jeans and a sleeveless dark shirt.

Having tossed their purchases back in the bag, he threw the bag at Gloria then threw her purse at her as well. "I suggest you girls watch where you're going!" he snapped, his hard eyes intent on Susannah. He bent and picked up her purse.

Susannah shuddered as she eyed him. The man looked ruthless and tough and there was a mean, malevolent look to his eyes. "I'm sorry," she returned quietly, her eyes going from him to her purse, then back up to him. "I'm afraid we didn't see you."

"So I noticed," he sneered, rubbing his arm.

Again Susannah's eyes went to her purse. For a moment, she was afraid he was going to just take off with it. To her relief, he didn't, though he did fumble with it for a moment or two before he let it fall purposely from his hand. He eyed her another moment then turned abruptly and walked away, leaving her purse where it was.

Susannah immediately retrieved it. It was partially unzipped and she quickly took stock of her valuables. They all seemed present. She turned to Gloria.

"You okay?"

"Yeah. But I'm afraid our candy bars are in pieces. What a creep!"

"No kidding," Susannah returned. Her eyes scanned in the direction the man had retreated in but he had disappeared from view. "I suggest we get out of here."

"I'm with you!"

They joined Becky at the car, and after brushing themselves off, climbed in. Becky slid behind the wheel. "What happened?" she demanded as she started the car. "I look over to find the two of you on the ground."

Gloria plunged into an explanation. "The man was nothing but a creep!" she added. "He acted like it was our fault when he was the one who ran into us!"

"Let's just forget it," Susannah said, wanting to put the episode behind her. "I have no intentions in letting him ruin our vacation!"

"Right!" her two friends said together.

"Straight ahead to Bristel," Becky added, easing her car out of the parking lot, "And to the Bristel Falls."

"Where we'll have lunch," Gloria said stoutly.

By the time they reached Bristel, all three girls were back in high spirits, the incident with the man behind them. They excitedly followed the signs to Bristel Falls, just east of the small city. Once parked, they left their purses in the trunk of the car and began the mile hike to the falls themselves.

"You would have to choose a place we had to walk to," Gloria said as they trudged on.

"It's a measly mile jaunt," Becky retorted.

"So I would have preferred a measly half mile jaunt," Gloria said and giggled.

"It will be worth the walk," Susannah assured her friends with a grin. It was.

"Oh, wow!" Gloria commented when they finally joined the array of other tourists already at the falls. The falls were beautiful and quite different from the other falls any of them had seen in the past. Instead of billowing down in a single current of water, Bristel Falls seemed to seep out in fractured layers from the bright, green-laden hillside to cascade in thin veils downward 126 feet into the waters below. The waters shimmered in the sunlight as they flowed downward. Rainbows danced in the rising clouds of mist that rose.

"It's like a piece of paradise," Susannah murmured as she took it all in. The falls were everything she had wished for; hoped for: beautiful, peaceful, cool...

"Calm and serene," Gloria said in evident awe.

"So beautiful," Becky added on a breath, "Oh, Susannah. You were right. It was definitely worth the walk! I've never seen falls such as this!"

Susannah merely smiled, her eyes still on the veils of cascading water.

They spent almost an hour at the falls, sitting on the large boulders at the edge of the water, taking pictures, and just enjoying the picturesque view. Becky eventually stirred.

"I think we best get going if we plan to make it to Lone Tree Ranch for lunch."

"You sure we can't go to lunch now?" Gloria asked.

Becky shook her head. "Nope! We're eating at the Chuck Wagon. Come on gang!"

Susannah with a sigh stood and joined her friends as they began to amble back down the long path to the parking lot below. They retrieved their purses from the trunk and climbed into Becky's car.

"Got directions?" Susannah asked as she slipped behind the wheel.

"Right here," her friend said with suppressed excitement. "Just stay on 83. It's only about forty-five minutes down the highway."

"Sounds good to me," Susannah said and started the car. Lone Tree Ranch had been Becky's choice; a taste of a dude ranch as she put it, with horses, bunk houses, and, most probably, handsome dudes.

"You really think we might meet some guys?" Gloria asked with growing excitement.

Becky giggled. "We can only hope."

"And dream," Gloria said. "Tall, strong, handsome men with–"

"Cowboy hats and boots –"

"And great personalities and easy smiles –"

"And wonderfully warm kisses." Gloria sighed.

"And with our luck, a host of women vying for their attention," Susannah said with a laugh. The laugh was cut short as Susannah caught sight of the small car coming quickly up on them; too quickly.

"Ladies…"

It was a far as she got before they were all jolted as the small black car bumped into them, then backed off.

"What was that?" Gloria cried out as Susannah slowed to keep the car on the road.

"The car behind us," Susannah answered tightly, her eyes flickering again to the rear view mirror.

Both Becky and Gloria turned around and stared. The car, they noted, was still too close for comfort. "Well, slow down and let him pass if he's in that much of a hurry," Becky said a little nervously.

"I am," Susannah muttered having slowed even further. But instead of speeding up and going around them, the driver again moved forward with a small spurt of speed.

"He's going to ram us again!" Becky cried out.

The words had barely escaped her when the car behind them rammed into them again, this time with a slightly harder bump. Susannah hung onto the wheel as she struggled to keep control of Becky's car. She pulled over to the side and brought it to an abrupt stop. The small car behind theirs spurted around them and drove off with a burst of speed.

"Susannah! That's the man who knocked us down this morning!" Gloria said as they watched him pass.

"I think you're right," Susannah said as she watched the small black car speed away. Despite the cap he was now wearing, she was sure it had been the same man. She watched until he disappeared from sight before she opened her door. "Let's go see what damage he left."

All three girls climbed out and looked at the back of Becky's car. Surprisingly, there was little visible damage. Only a minor scrape on the back bumper.

"That man's a creep!" Gloria stated again. "How dare he ram our car like that!"

"I'll agree with you there," Susannah said. Her eyes went down the road where the small black car had disappeared, then flickered back to Becky. "Maybe we should report this."

Becky glanced at her bumper then back to the girls. "Do you think we really have to? It's not like he did much damage."

"True, but…"

"And it's not that we could give the police much information. None of us got his license plate."

"That's because there was mud smeared all over it," Gloria stated.

"I didn't see one at all," Becky said in surprise.

"Not on the front," Susannah said, "But Gloria's right, the rear license was there, just with mud hiding most of it."

"So all we can tell them is that some man wearing a cap and a dark sleeveless shirt with cutoff sleeves and driving a black foreign car with no license in the front bumped into us and then drove off."

Gloria's head shook. "I thought it was a dark blue car."

"Black," both Susannah and Becky said in unison.

"No," Gloria said with another shake of her head. "It could have been foreign, but it was definitely blue, a dark blue maybe, but blue."

Becky looked to Susannah. "So now we're not even sure of the car's color."

"That's the way the police are bound to take it," Susannah admitted. She herself had no doubts. It had been a small foreign car and definitely black.

"If that's the case, we might as well just forget it and go on to the ranch," Becky said. It was evident she had no inclination in wasting time talking to police who weren't likely to believe them anyway when they could be spending the afternoon at the guest ranch. "After all, it isn't as if he *really* tried to run us off the road…"

"True." Susannah sighed feeling the incident needed to be reported regardless, yet not wanting to go against the other two girls. It was evident neither wanted to spend the time talking to the police. Besides, the girls were right. The man really could have hit them a lot harder if he had seriously wanted to do them damage or run them off the road.

"Then we can go on to the ranch?" Becky pleaded hopefully.

Susannah gave in. "I don't see why not. It's likely he just wanted a little revenge for running into us this morning," she acknowledged.

"And now that he's had it, it isn't likely he'll bother us again."

"Not the way he took off," Gloria said stoutly. "He's probably long gone by now. Besides, I'm starved! Let's hit the road, girls! The chuck wagon awaits us!"

Susannah, with a rueful shake of her head, climbed behind the wheel and once more started down the road. Though none of them voiced it, they each kept watch for the small, dark car and its creepy driver.

CHAPTER FIVE

"There it is!" Becky said pointing to the sign reading *Lone Tree Guest Ranch.*

"Wow!" Gloria whispered as Susannah turned and drove in through the gates and down the winding drive. "This place is huge!"

It was indeed. A vast, well-kept lawn spread out in front of them. Beyond that a large four story building stood; a building that looked as if it were bent into three sections.

"The main lobby and activity centers are there in the middle," Becky informed them, "That section off to the right is for the guest ranch guests, and the left is for the guests just passing through."

"Like us," Gloria said.

"Like us," Becky repeated looking longingly at the right section of the building.

Susannah grinned knowing that Becky had wanted to spend more than one day and night at the ranch. She didn't comment however, but asked instead, "I take it we need to go to the main lobby to check in?"

Becky nodded. "They'll direct us from there." Her eyes wandered. "I wonder where the stables and horses are."

"Most likely behind the buildings," Susannah said as she found an empty parking space in the large parking lot in front of the main building and brought the car to a stop.

Gloria giggled. "Well, let's hope so, though I'm going to find that chuck wagon before I go look for them."

"Sounds like a plan," Susannah said, "*After* we check in."

Gloria merely groaned.

The three of them walked into the main lobby impressed again at the size of the place. The lobby was large and decorated in a rustic, western motif. The walls were painted in swirls of pastel blue and white looking very much like the wide open skies. Long, narrow planters of prairie grass grew along the base of the walls. Cactus and small evergreens grew here and there in other planters. The furniture, both chairs and benches, were wooden though many held soft looking pillows to add to their comfort. Off to the side was a large marble statue of a black stallion rearing on its hind legs in the center of a fountain.

Becky was drawn to the fountain and the stallion immediately. "Isn't it magnificent?" she said, staring at it.

"I have to admit it looks like the real thing," Gloria commented eyeing it. "Are horses really that big?"

"Yes," Becky answered, "Some really are. Come on, let's go check in."

The service desk like the furniture was polished wood. The three girls checked in at the desk, and then were shown to their room. The room to their satisfaction was large and also done in a western motif. It held two beds, a table with two chairs and a wooden rocking chair.

Susannah slipped into the rocking chair immediately, loving how comfortable it was. "Girls, this is wonderful," she said letting her hands run up and down the smooth arms.

"It might be wonderful," Gloria complained, "but it doesn't put food in my belly. Come on, let's go get our things from the car and then find that chuck wagon!"

"I'll second that," Becky said.

Susannah reluctantly came out of the chair. She followed her two friends down to the parking lot. Though the other two headed directly to Becky's car Susannah found herself pausing, her eyes sweeping the parking lot for the small, black car. A grain of relief filtered when she didn't see it. She joined the girls and with their bags retrieved they dropped them off at their room and headed for the restaurant.

"You really meant the Chuck Wagon," Gloria said as she caught sight of the name of the restaurant.

"What else would it be called on a dude ranch?" Becky retorted with a laugh.

The girls took their time eating their light lunch, giggling and laughing and eyeing the young men that wandered past. "Shall we follow them?" Gloria asked with a mischievous grin.

"Nope!" Becky said coming to her feet. "We need to go sign up for that moonlight ride before it's too late."

"That's where she expects we'll find the real hunks she was talking about," Susannah whispered to Gloria.

"Let's hope so!" Gloria said with a giggle.

The grounds in the back of the building overwhelmed the girls as they stepped out onto the patio. They were amazed at the size and openness of the ranch and how well-taken care of it was. A large swimming pool was just off the back patio to the left, and tennis courts could be seen off to the right. Further down in front of them, past the massive yard, a large stable stood with surrounding corrals. And beyond that wide open spaces.

"This is awesome," Becky said as she tried to take it all in. "It's even bigger than I had envisioned."

"Bigger?" Susannah teased her.

"Yes, bigger!" Becky retorted. "Come on, let's find the stables where we need to register for that ride. The lady behind the desk said it was the main stables."

"Which should be that one right there," Susannah said pointing to the large stable building standing between the two big corrals.

The girls made their way over and tentatively walked in. They all stopped in awe. The stables were huge; huge and clean and surprisingly cool inside. There was a small office off to the side as they entered and further down they could see two rows of stalls lining the walls, several housing horses. A young man sitting behind the open window of the office pulled their attention around. "Could I help you?" he asked.

The man himself appeared about their age, give or take a year or two. He was tall, slim, fit, and very good-looking. He was wearing a cowboy hat pushed back and a warm, interested smile.

"We're trying to find out where to sign up for the moonlight ride," Becky said with a flush.

"Right here," he answered, his smile turning into a grin. "All three of you?" His eyes had gone to Susannah.

"All three of us," Gloria confirmed with a bright smile of her own.

The man, Wes Anderson, he informed them with another warm smile, picked up his pencil. "Okay, I'll need your names, and 78 dollars from each of you."

All three girls stepped up and gave him in turn their names and the required fee.

"Have you girls ridden before?" he asked, glancing up from his paper work.

"I've ridden all my life," Becky told him. "And both Gloria and Susannah ride off and on."

"So all three of you should know your way around a horse."

Gloria giggled. "As long as the horse isn't too excitable."

"Or too big," Susannah added with a wry smile.

"I'll see to it," he said, his twinkling eyes again on Susannah. "The ride begins at 8:30, so if you can be down here at the stables a half hour early, we'll see that you all have appropriate mounts."

"Thank you," all three girls answered.

"We'll be here," Becky added.

The girls left the cool stables and meandered over to the large corral. "Well, he definitely had his eyes on you," Gloria teased Susannah.

"For all of two minutes," Susannah retorted. She had noticed the interest she had been receiving but put little stock in it. The man worked for the ranch and most likely had rules about fraternizing with the guests.

"Ah, but two minutes could turn into an evening of fun," Gloria said mischievously.

"Right," Susannah said joining Becky at the corral fence. Becky's eyes were on the horses in the corral itself.

"Look at all the beautiful horses," she said dreamily.

Gloria and Susannah exchanged amused glances. Any horse to Becky would be beautiful. "Do you think these are the horses we'll be riding tonight?" Gloria questioned aloud.

"More than likely," Susannah said, glancing around. "I don't see any others."

"Except the few that were in the stables," Becky added, "but I doubt if they're for guest use."

Gloria glanced up at the hot sun. "It's getting kind of hot out here. What do you say we change and go check out the pool?"

"Sounds good to me," Becky said glancing at the pool area, and at the host of young men who seemed to be there. "Susannah?"

"Sounds good to me," Susannah echoed having no objections. It was indeed getting hot.

The girls headed back to their room, changed and went and joined the multitude of other guests at the swimming pool. Susannah, eager to get in the water, plopped down her towel on a nearby lounge chair and made her way to the pool's edge and dove in. Cool, silky water immediately caressed her skin.

"Heaven," she said on a contented sigh. She dove back under water and swam the length of the pool, then coming up for air, swam back in the other direction all the while dodging swimmers. Becky and Gloria were just diving in she noted but let them be. They had a tendency to play more than swim and Susannah wanted to get her laps in before she relaxed.

Unfortunately that wasn't as easy as she had hoped. The pool was crowded, making lap swimming near impossible. She had to constantly dodge around the other swimmers as she swam from one end of the pool and back again. She finally gave up and joined the other two girls.

"Isn't this just super?" Gloria asked happily, lightly splashing Susannah.

Susannah grinned, her eyes going to Becky. "I figured the two of you would have a horde of guys zeroed in by now."

"We do," Becky whispered. "See those two hunks over there; the ones just getting ready to dive in the pool?"

Susannah glanced over in the direction Becky had indicated to see two similar young men standing by the edge of the pool. Both were tall and dark-haired, and even from a distance, good-looking.

"Gloria and I've sort of zeroed in on them."

"Well it looks as if they've sort of zeroed in on the two of you," Susannah commented noting the looks the two were sending their way.

"We hope so." Gloria said and giggled. The giggles gave way to surprise. "Oh, wow! They *are* heading our way!"

"Then I'll leave the two of you to your fun," Susannah said with a laugh. She swam off again, trying once more to see if she could swim her laps. Again she found it a struggle and gave up. Instead of rejoining the girls who were now happily conversing with the two good-looking guys that had made their way over, she climbed out of the pool and settled in her lounge chair. Her eyes wandered back to Becky and Gloria, noting that they and their two handsome guys had become engaged in some sort of game with a nerf ball. She watched them for a while, and then closed her eyes, letting herself relax.

Her eyes opened awhile later as water splattered over her and she heard Gloria's giggle.

"Have fun?" Susannah asked as both her friends dried off with the hotel's towels they had brought out and sat down.

"Oh, yes! You should have stayed and joined us."

"Hey, I can count," Susannah returned.

"You still should have joined us," Becky said. "Not that we don't appreciate your…counting efforts," she added with a laugh. It was helpful at times when Susannah was out of the competition.

"Oh, Susannah." A happy sigh escaped Gloria as she plopped herself down on her lounge chair. "They were so perfect! Tall, dark, handsome, and so very nice! And *they* have signed up for the moonlight ride, too!"

"I see," Susannah murmured, hiding her grin.

"And we're having dinner with them at six," Becky said, settling on her own lounge chair. "Or rather they're joining us for dinner," she corrected herself. "You, too," she added before Susannah could make any excuses.

"You sure you want me around?"

"Yes!" both girls cried out at the same time. "It would be no fun without you," Gloria went on to express, "As long as you don't mind them joining us?"

"Not at all," Susannah returned coming to her feet. "Look. I'm going to go swim to the other end and back and then what do you say we head back to our room to take it easy until we need to get ready for dinner?"

"Sounds good to me," Gloria said settling back. "We'll be here waiting."

With a grin at Becky, Susannah turned and walked back over to the pool's edge and dove in. There were less people in the water now and she had no trouble swimming her lap then one more before she hauled herself out of the water and rejoined her friends. All three of them walked leisurely back to their room.

"So tell me about these hunks," Susannah ordered curiously.

"They're brothers," Gloria happily told her.

"Twins," Becky said, "Ian and Isaac Severin."

"Isaac's mine," Gloria stated.

"They're here with their parents and little sister," Becky continued. She suddenly sighed. "But they're leaving tomorrow, too. I guess they've already been here a good ten days."

"That's too bad," Susannah commented lightly.

"Not that we're not leaving ourselves," Becky acknowledged. "At least we'll see them on our moonlight ride."

"Not to mention, at dinner."

"Then enjoy them while you have them," Susannah told her friends.

"That we will," Gloria returned, "That we will."

The girls relaxed in their room for the rest of the afternoon. At least until it was time to get ready for dinner. Then came the indecisions. Did they dress for dinner? For the ride they would be taking later? Or what?

"What do you think, Susannah?" Gloria implored.

"Well, considering we'll have to come back here at least for sweaters or sweatshirts before the ride anyway, why not dress for dinner?"

"Wonderful thought!"

Though they had brought no dresses with them, they decided on wearing one of the light, summer outfits they each had brought along for Gloria's family reunion. Taking the time to shower and fix their hair before dressing, they barely made it to the dining room by 6:00. To both Becky and Gloria's relief, Ian and Isaac were there waiting for them.

The twins greeted the girls warmly, acknowledging Susannah as she was introduced. Susannah found them just as nice and thoughtful and fun as the girls had told her. Though their attentions were centered on Gloria and Becky as they joked and told stories through dinner, they had made it a point to include Susannah. Susannah found she was enjoying herself just as much as her two friends were. Eventually dinner was over.

"How would you girls like to take a walk around this wonderful place?" Ian asked as he picked up the tab and placed a tip on the table.

"We would love to," Becky agreed for them all. Her eyes went to Susannah in afterthought. "Sue?"

Susannah shook her head. "Not this time around," she said smiling at them. "I've got other things to do."

"You're welcome to come," Ian assured her as he pulled Becky to her feet. Gloria was already on her feet, her hand encased in Isaac's.

Susannah smiled with a shake of her head. "Thanks. You guys go on and have fun. Just meet me at the room at 7:30."

"We will," Gloria promised. "See you later."

But before they could take their leave, another tall male was suddenly standing at their table. Wes Anderson. He was in a clean shirt and jeans and it was evident from his wet hair and smooth skin that he had just showered and shaved. He greeted them all with another warm, youthful smile, his eyes going to Susannah. "They deserting you?" he asked. It was impossible to miss the hopeful look in his eyes.

"It's beginning to look like it," Susannah said with a smile of her own. She flashed the girls a look to find Becky giving her a thumbs up as Ian led her away.

"Do you mind if I join you then?" Wes asked bringing Susannah's head back around.

"Not at all," Susannah returned.

"Thanks." He smiled and slipped into the seat that Becky had vacated. Almost immediately a waitress was beside their table. Wes ordered a steak dinner and turned to Susannah. "Would you like some dessert?"

"I would love a dessert," she told him. "Hot fudge sundae?" she said looking up at the waitress. The waitress with a smile and a nod disappeared. Wes turned back to Susannah.

"You're…Susannah. Right?" he questioned hesitantly.

"Yes," she acknowledged.

"Staying long?" he asked.

Susannah shook her head. "We're only here for the night."

"I see," he returned with an inaudible sigh. "I hope you're enjoying the ranch anyway?"

"Very much so," Susannah said. "It's a magnificent place. Have you worked here long?"

"Every summer since I was sixteen. My uncle owns the place," he added with a shrug.

"Convenient," Susannah commented. "Have you always worked in the stables?"

"More or less. Are you looking forward to the ride tonight?"

"Actually I am," Susannah said in return. "How long a ride will it be?"

"Three hours, more or less. About an hour out, an hour rest around a campfire, then an hour back."

"Sounds like fun," Susannah said. "Do you go along?" She looked up as a hot fudge sundae was placed in front of her. At the same time a steak dinner was placed down in front of Wes.

"Actually I do," Wes answered as he cut into his steak, "Though I'm not in charge of it. I simply ride up and down the line making sure the guests are having a smooth ride."

"As well as enjoying themselves at the campfire?"

He grinned. "Of course."

Susannah found she liked his grin; liked the man despite his youthfulness. He was pleasant and thoughtful and had an easy manner. He was, Susannah found as they talked, twenty-three, a mere half-year younger than she was. He worked here at his uncle's dude ranch during the summers, and during the rest of the year spent his time attempting to record western songs, teaching riding at a local riding school, and finishing up at the State University.

"I'll be graduating this coming year," he told her. "I should have two years ago, but, due to family circumstances, I had to take some extra time off, so..." He stopped and shrugged. His eyes went to his watch. A sigh came out of him.

"Well," he said, coming to his feet. "As much as I've enjoyed this, I'm afraid my dinner break is over and I need I get back to work. It's my responsibility to see that the horses are saddled and ready for the ride tonight." He stopped and looked down at her. "You wanted the large, spirited stallion, right?" he asked tongue-in-cheek.

"As long as he's small and not *too* spirited," Susannah corrected with a grin.

He laughed. "I'll see what I can do. See you soon."

Susannah watched him go with a contented sigh. His warm smile reminded her of someone, but she couldn't place who. Picking up her small purse, and after leaving a tip on the table, she walked over to the cashier to find that her dessert had already been paid for. Surprised, yet not surprised, she meandered out of the dining room.

Having nothing better to do, Susannah wandered through the small shops inside the grand hotel. She didn't purchase anything, most items of interest were too expensive, but she enjoyed the looking. Eventually however, she found herself on the spacious, back patio. She bought herself a large lemonade and settled in one of the loungers. A contented sigh escaped her as she glanced around the expansive ranch. Becky had been right, the place was heaven; large, spacious, and relaxing.

She let her eyes roam, watching the other guests as they indulged in their variety of activities. The tennis courts seemed to be full; the swimming area busy. Others seemed to be milling around enjoying the horses in the corral. She caught sight of Wes moving around the corrals, then further down, Becky and Ian. Gloria was nowhere in sight. Her eyes went back to the swimming area where some sort of contest was going on at the diving end.

She watched for a while, marveling how some could dive with such artistic perfection. She didn't know what made her pull her eyes from the divers, for she suddenly found herself glancing around at the other guests on the deck around her. Her heart seemed to stop as she caught sight of a man in a dark blue T-shirt disappearing into the hotel; a familiar, lean, wirily man.

"No," she breathed. "It couldn't be." But Susannah was up on her feet and after him to be sure.

But there was no sign of him inside. She passed several men wearing dark blue T-shirts, but none was the man she had thought she saw. Unable to leave it at that, she meandered out the front of the hotel, her eyes scanning the parking lot. There were several black cars but none was the small black foreign car she was searching for. A sigh of relief escaped her. She must have been wrong thinking she had seen the man who had accosted them.

After all, the man couldn't have followed them. He had been ahead of them. There had been no sign of him or his car along the road or in the parking lot when they had arrived, just as there was no sign of it now.

Feeling much better, she ambled to their room to find both Becky and Gloria already changing for the moonlight ride.

"You're late," Gloria teased her. "It's already 7:34."

"Got caught up in something," Susannah said as she began to change back into her jeans.

"Like daydreaming about a certain cowboy?" Becky teased.

"Among other things," Susannah allowed, deciding to say nothing about who she had thought she had seen. After all, it hadn't been him so why upset the others with the thought of him? "I was strolling the shops," she said instead.

"Buy anything?" Gloria asked, with sudden interest.

Susannah shook her head. "No, too pricey," she told them. "But it was fun looking."

"I'm sure it was." Gloria said. Gloria loved to shop and rarely missed an opportunity to do so.

"How was your walk?" Susannah asked.

"Nice," both girls answered at once. "Very nice," Becky added with a wide smile. "I just wish we had arrived a week ago."

Gloria giggled. "I'll agree with that! Now, come on, girls. Let's finish getting ready and get over to the stables.

"Alright," Susannah said smothering her laugh.

CHAPTER SIX

All three of them finished dressing and feeling presentable, headed down to the stables. Both Ian and Isaac were there waiting for them, along with a younger girl.

"This is Deborah, our little sister," Ian introduced her.

"I prefer Debbie," Deborah told them with a sour look to her brothers. Debbie was twelve. She was tall and slim, with long, brown hair she wore in a ponytail, and sparkling blue eyes. She turned instinctively to Susannah as her brothers immediately turned to Becky and Gloria. "Are you going riding, too?" she asked, adjusting the western hat on her head.

"Yes I am," Susannah replied sending the girl a smile.

"Do you mind if I ride with you, then?" she asked, casting an irritating look at her brothers.

"Not at all."

It took just under a half hour for everyone to get mounted for the evening ride. Wes, she found, had found her a decent-sized pinto to ride. Though it was smaller than most of the other horses, it was too big to consider a pony. "Just what you ordered," Wes told her with a grin as he helped her on. "Not too big and not too spirited though she's not exactly dormant either," he added. "I think you'll like her."

"Does she have a name?"

"She does," he said pushing back his hat. "She's been named Hot Fudge Sundae. Of course, we simply call her Sundae."

"She's perfect," Susannah told him, pleased with the mare. Hot Fudge Sundae was a deep, rich brown and white pinto. She appeared alert and ready to go.

"Glad you approve." He turned to Debbie. "Give me a sec and I'll be right back with your Candy Bar."

"Candy Bar?" Susannah questioned as Wes disappeared in the direction of the corrals.

The girl grinned up at her. "Candy Bar, the name of the horse I always use. Like Sundae, Candy Bar is a pinto only she's a lighter brown than Sundae and has more white. She and I have a connection."

"I'm sure you do," Susannah said. "I take it this is Candy Bar coming?" she asked catching sight of Wes leading over another small, brown and white pinto.

"Yup! That's Candy Bar," Debbie returned, running to meet Wes and her horse. Susannah watched as she easily slid into the saddle with very little help from the groom. Adjusting the white cowboy hat on her head, she rode over to Susannah.

"Isn't she perfect?!"

Susannah laughed. "Quite perfect. We'll make a perfect team, you riding Candy Bar and me riding Hot Fudge Sundae."

Debbie laughed. "Come on. Let's go join everyone so we don't get left behind!"

Susannah followed Debbie over to the meadow where everyone seemed to be assembling for the ride. Becky and Gloria were already there, each sitting on their own mounts talking to Debbie's brothers as they waited. Becky, she saw had been given a large, buckskin stallion, and Gloria, a slightly smaller roan mare. Neither really cared she surmised, for both had their attention on the two guys with them. With a shake of her head, she and Debbie joined them.

A few minutes later Greg Dotson, the 'trail master' as Debbie called him, gathered their attention and explained the rules and the ride itself. It was just as Wes had explained to her earlier. They would be riding the trails for just over an hour then stopping at a campfire where there would be food and singing, before they continued on their return ride back to the ranch.

"It's fun!" Debbie said to her as they lined up behind both her brothers and Susannah's friends. "I went on it last week, too!"

Susannah grinned at her enthusiasm. "I'm sure it will be," Susannah said. Her grin turned into surprise as Wes rode up just as they were starting out and plopped a white, western hat on her head.

"Goes with the territory," he said and with a salute, moved on up the line checking on the other guests.

"I think he likes you," Debbie said with a giggle, her eyes following the man.

"I think I like him," Susannah said.

"I like him, too." Debbie sighed then flashed Susannah a smile. "I know he's way too old for me, but he's really nice and really good looking and besides, a girl can dream, can't she?"

"A girl can definitely dream," Susannah returned stoutly. Not that all dreams came true, she admitted bitterly. Sometimes they turned around and bit…hard! She pushed Cade's image from her mind and turned her attention back to Debbie. "I understand you've already been here a week," she commented.

"Ten days, actually," Debbie said. "I wish we were staying longer, but we've got to go home tomorrow."

"I know what you mean," Susannah said glancing around. "I wish we didn't have to go either. It's so beautiful here."

"Not to mention fun," Debbie added. "Especially the riding horses bit."

Susannah grinned. "I had a feeling you felt that way."

Debbie laughed. "Oh, I do, I do."

"Do you ride back at home?" Susannah asked curiously.

"I sure do," the girl told her. "We have riding stables not too far from where I live. That's where I learned to ride."

"You ride often then?"

Debbie shrugged. "Not as often as I would like," she admitted on a sigh. "I usually get to ride about once a week. That's all my allowance will allow."

"Money does factor in," Susannah agreed, hiding her smile.

"Money does factor into what?" Wes asked as his horse pulled up beside Susannah's.

"Everything," she answered. "How's everyone doing?"

"Just fine," the man replied with a lop-sided smile. "How are the two of you doing?"

"Great!" Debbie said.

"Just great," Susannah echoed with a giggle. Her eyes swept the wide open countryside. "It's so beautiful here," she said. "You must never tire of it."

"Actually I don't," Wes admitted. "I'd stay all year round if I had a choice."

"Well, no one promised us a bed of roses when we were born," Susannah said.

"That's for sure." Wes laughed and his eyes went to Debbie. "I hear you and your family are leaving tomorrow."

"Yeah," Debbie muttered. "Not that I want to go."

"Maybe you can come back next year," he soothed. "You, too," he said to Susannah with a hopeful smile.

"Maybe we can," Susannah returned though she doubted it.

"I'm sure going to try!" Debbie stated adamantly.

"I'm sure you will." Wes grinned then with a slight salute to them both, he urged his horse forward and rode off taking time to stop and talk to other riders up and down the line. He came back every few minutes and spent time joking and talking to both Susannah and Debbie before he was off again.

Susannah was well aware that the man was interested in her, but was pleased that he seemed to pay just as much attention to Debbie as to her when he was around. In fact, he didn't seem to leave any of his guests out. He was interesting and informative to everyone he stopped and talked to.

The sky began to darken as the sun began its final descent. Dusk came then faded into darkness as they arrived at their resting place. A camp fire was already blazing away and a chuck wagon was seen open and ready for them. Susannah dismounted with a relieved sigh. She felt stiff and sore, not having been riding in months.

"Got a few kinks?" Becky teased her as she and Debbie joined the two couples already tethering their horses to the posts available.

"You could say that." Susannah said sourly taking care of her own mount.

"Where'd you get the hat?" Gloria asked eyeing the cowboy hat.

"From a friend," Susannah admitted with a small smile.

"Actually Wes gave it to her," Debbie spoke up. "I think he likes her," she added.

"I think so, too," Gloria murmured, exchanging grins with Becky.

Susannah groaned. "Come on. Let's go get something to munch on."

"I'm for that!" Debbie said.

The six of them meandered over to the chuck wagon and armed with a drink, a hot dog on a stick, and a bag of chips, they joined the rest of the guests already sitting around the campfire. Debbie immediately stuck her hot dog into the flames and Susannah followed suit. She loved hot dogs roasted in open flames. The more roasted the better.

"Need a bun for that?" Wes inquired, sitting himself down beside her.

"Nope," she answered, taking a tentative bite of it right off the stick.

"I see." He grinned as he pushed back his hat. "Having fun?"

"Oh, yes."

"So am I," Debbie said. "Are you going to sing tonight?" she asked.

"We'll see," Wes replied. "But if I do, I expect you to sing along. You, too," he added with a grin to Susannah.

"I'll try," Susannah said.

"You do that," he returned coming to his feet. "But right now, I've got things to do."

Susannah watched as the ranch hand walked over to the chuck wagon and joined the other ranch hands. What he had to do became evident as all five ranch hands retrieved ropes from the wagon and practiced a moment before they all spread themselves around the fire. As if on cue, all five began twirling the ropes, first along-side themselves, then over their heads.

For the next twenty minutes they were all treated to a host of rope tricks. Susannah watched in amazement, unable to believe what they could do with a simple rope. Her amazement turned to startled surprise when Wes's rope suddenly shot out and sailed over her, neatly pinning her arms as it tightened. Susannah had no option but to come to her feet as Wes tugged her to him. He grinned mischievously as she reached him. Taking off his hat, he bent and planted a firm, warm kiss against her lips.

The whole campground was whistling and laughing and clapping when he released her and Susannah realized that all four of his friends had done the same to the females they had roped. She grinned at Wes as he removed the rope from around her, then taking off her own hat, she reached up and planted a soft kiss against his cheek before she sat down again. Becky and Gloria laughingly teased her.

Wes's rope was exchanged for a guitar, and Susannah watched as he began strumming it as he walked around the campfire, seeking everyone's attention. And then he began to sing.

Susannah's amusement faded to pleasure. The man had a voice, and a charming way of getting everyone to sing along, filling the night with one camp song after another, from *Home on the Range* to *Oh, Susannah* which he seemed to aim at Susannah herself. But it wasn't until Wes began singing his last song that her heart stopped. The song was a country love song: a familiar country love song.

When the Time is Right.

It was Cade's song; a song he had sung often, whether along with the radio or his CDs; whether to her and her brother, or just to himself. Wes's voice faded as Susannah was swept to the past. Even after all this time, she could still hear Cade's rich, deep voice resounding through her as he sang the words.

A melancholy ache spread through Susannah. The song was about the promise of love and she had imagined all those years ago that the song was their song, hers and Cade's; that he sung it for her alone. That it had been his promise to her of *his* love and just for the moment, Susannah let the warm memory of that promise fill her once again…

A sharp nudge brought her back to reality. Everyone around her was coming to their feet. "Come on, Susannah!" Debbie was urging. "Let's go saddle up."

Susannah's eyes flickered to Becky and Gloria to find them eyeing her with amusement. "Kind of got to you, huh?" Becky teased.

Susannah, with a brief smile to the girls, gave herself a mental shake in the attempt to dispel Cade Candlewood from her mind. The man was an arrogant, mean brute and didn't deserve any thinking of. None! She forced her attention instead to Wes, complimenting him on his singing. "You're good," she told him as he helped her mount the pinto once again. "And I really hope you can go somewhere with it."

"Thanks," he said modesty. "I sure am trying."

The ride back to the ranch was just as pleasurable as the ride out had been, though it was quieter, due no doubt to the cloak of darkness now surrounding them. Not that everyone was silent; there was talking and laughing and singing going on but it was more subdued and filled with a feeling of well-being. Wes and the other ranch hands sang soft country and western songs as they rode up and down the line of guests checking on everyone which only added to the good feelings.

"That was wonderful," Debbie stated as the ride came to an end; a sentiment that Susannah echoed.

"I'm glad you enjoyed it," Wes said as he helped both her and Debbie dismount.

Susannah with a contented sigh took off her hat and held it out to Wes.

"Keep it," he told her warmly with a shake of his head. "Consider it a souvenir of tonight."

"I'll do that," Susannah said placing it back on her head. "Thank you for everything, Wes."

"You're more than welcome." He smiled softly, drawing her to him. His lips came down on hers in a gentle kiss. "Come back someday," he murmured releasing her.

"I would love to," she returned. With a wave of her finger she joined Becky and Gloria as they walked leisurely back to the ranch house with Debbie and her two brothers. They said their reluctant good-byes outside on the back patio, then the twins disappeared in one direction with their sister and Becky, Gloria, and Susannah walked in the other toward their room.

Gloria sighed. "Oh, I wish we were all staying longer."

"So do I," Becky agreed with a sigh of her own. "Now we can only hope that they call like they promised." Both Becky and Gloria had exchanged phone numbers and addresses with the guys.

"I'm sure they will," Susannah soothed. "They both looked rather smitten with you."

"Well, I have to say that cowboy seemed awfully smitten with you," Becky said with a knowing eye. "Did you give him *your* phone number?"

"Nope."

"Susannah!" Gloria protested. "You should have!"

Susannah merely laughed and pulled her card key from her pocket. But she didn't use it.

Their door when they reached it was already open, a mere two inches, but open. Their eyes flew to each other.

"I know I shut it!" Becky said, staring at the others. "I checked it! It was shut and locked!"

"It isn't now," Susannah stated. She took a tentative step closer and pushed the door the rest of the way open. No one appeared inside. With nervous caution, they checked the whole room including under the beds and in the bathroom. There was no sign of anyone.

Becky closed and locked the door, bolting it as well as slipping on the security chain. "Let's check our belongings," she advised. The girls had left their purses inside the hotel room when they had left to go riding. They all searched for them now.

They were found exactly where they had hid them away. Not one of them appeared tampered with or rifled through. None of their belongings appeared to have been touched.

"Maybe the maid came through and forgot to check the door when she left," Gloria suggested.

"Maybe," Becky said. Her eyes met Susannah's. "No one else would have a card key."

"And even if they did, the dead bolt is now locked and the security chain's in place."

Feeling safer, the girls made an effort to forget the incident and turned their thoughts to tomorrow's destinations, going over the route they would be taking before they all climbed into bed. It was Becky who climbed back out at the last minute. Susannah and Gloria watched as she checked the door again and made sure it was bolted and secured.

"Just double-checking," she admitted wryly at the others.

Susannah gave her a thumbs up and laid back, letting her mind roam back over the pleasant evening. Wes's smiling face swam in front of her eyes then suddenly faded into Cade's; his smile warm and dimpled, his eyes crinkled with that touch of mischievousness, his whole being oozing with that easy, confident masculinity as he...

With a groan, Susannah pushed the image away and turned over, closing her eyes.

CHAPTER SEVEN

Despite wanting to be up and gone early, all three of them slept in not waking until well after eight. By the time they were all showered and dressed it was after nine. They packed their belongings and loaded them into Becky's car before they headed down to the main lobby. There they settled their bill and headed over to the restaurant for breakfast.

Though both Becky's and Gloria's eyes roamed the room, neither caught sight of the twins. "They did say they were leaving early," Gloria recalled in disappointment.

"Which they probably did," Becky acknowledged. She picked up the menus from the table and handed one to each of them before opening one of her own. Susannah, deciding to indulge herself, ordered eggs benedict, and with only a slight hesitation, both Becky and Gloria followed suit, each of them adding a cup of fruit on the side.

They took their time over breakfast, enjoying not only the food, but their recollections of the night before. Both girls teased Susannah about being lassoed and kissed and Susannah teased them back about their obvious attachment to the two twin brothers. "How do you tell them apart anyway?" she asked.

Becky shrugged. "We just do."

"Must be the way they kiss," Susannah murmured, coming to her feet. Then, "Come on, girls. The ruins and Finch Falls are both waiting for us!"

They went up and paid for breakfast, then skipped out to the parking lot, loading into the car. Heading back to the highway they drove the half hour to the turnoff that took them to the Indian ruins.

All three of them found the Indian ruins both intriguing and interesting. They spent their time walking around, listening as the guide explained the ruins past history and what they were seeing. They visited the small gift shop afterwards, then with their several purchases, returned to their car and headed for the highway once again.

"How far is the turnoff to the falls?" Gloria asked as she turned south onto the highway.

"About forty to fifty minutes," Susannah said pulling her eyes from the book she had purchased. "It's just called Finch Road. There should be a sign."

There was. Gloria turned onto the smaller road to the small town of Finch, and then followed the signs to the falls themselves.

Finch Falls, unlike Bristel Falls, came crashing over the top of its rocky cliff edge to fall thunderously 212 feet to the river pool below where it swirled until it broke free and continued its journey on down the river. There were signs prohibiting swimming at the bottom, due to its rocky depth and fast swirling waters, but several young college students could be seen braving the waters regardless.

Despite the foolish students marring the perfect scene, Susannah, along with Becky and Gloria, stood in awe of the deafening falls, marveling at how straight it seemed to cascade down. They took pictures then took more as the disrupted students climbed out and meandered on down the river.

"Well," Gloria said sighing in contentment. "I have to admit, your waterfalls have the same natural beauty as most gardens."

Susannah dimpled. "Why thank you!"

Gloria pushed her with a laugh. "Come on, let's go find something to eat!"

The girls meandered back down to the car, but before they could head out, Becky's phone sounded. Susannah and Gloria watched her flush rosily as she took the phone call. "It's Ian!" she mouthed to Gloria, her eyes shining.

"Yes!" Gloria whispered excitedly.

Susannah, knowing the phone call most likely would take a while, involving both girls considering the men were brothers, meandered contentedly back to the waterfall. She was glad the man had called knowing how smitten Becky was with him. Becky, like her, had had a hard time with relationships, struggling to find that one special man who would love her as much as she loved him. Maybe Becky's luck was changing; maybe this was the man. For Becky's sake, Susannah hoped so; prayed so.

It was almost a half hour before her two friends, their faces beaming, came and retrieved her. "I'm sorry," Becky said. "I hope you didn't mind?"

"Why would I mind, you idiot?" Susannah admonished. "I'm happy he called." Her eyes went to Gloria. "I take it you got to talk to your man, too?"

"Oh, yes." Gloria giggled happily.

Susannah smiled again. "I'm glad. What do you say we go find someplace to eat?"

They drove into the small town of Finch. There they stopped at a local diner with a fifties motif that had them pausing to take it all in. The floor was a black and white checkered tile. The booths were a gray vinyl with matching gray Formica tables as was the counter and its stools. Pictures of Elvis and Marilyn Monroe dotted the walls along with other stars of the era. Several Route 66 signs could be seen here and there between the pictures. The sounds of both the fifties and sixties were coming from the juke box in the corner.

Even the menus, they found when they were seated, continued the motif. Dishes with names such as *The Juke Box Special, The LP Platter,* and *Hit Parade* were advertised.

"Who would have thought we'd find something like this way out here?" Becky whispered.

"I guess the love of music is universal," Susannah said. She herself loved the music of the fifties and sixties. She looked up and smiled at the waitress that came over to their table. *Hit Parades* – club sandwiches in disguise – and sodas were ordered. The girls then sat back, their eyes again roaming the decorated walls.

Gloria suddenly stilled. "Oh, oh," came her quiet voice. "I think we've got company."

Both Susannah and Becky turned to her.

"Over there by the wall," she whispered.

Susannah glanced over to find herself looking at the man who had not only knocked her and Gloria down, but had forced them off the road. He was just being served his own lunch. Without a glance in any direction, the man began to eat.

"Do you think he knows we're here?" Becky asked quietly, her eyes on the man.

"He doesn't appear to," Susannah replied slowly, "but looks can be deceiving."

"Should we leave?" Gloria asked nervously.

Susannah's head shook. "Let's let him leave first. I don't think I want him behind us."

"I'll second that," Becky agreed.

The girls took their time eating once their orders arrived, all the while keeping their eye on the man. Not once did he look in their direction, but Susannah didn't believe he wasn't aware of their presence. It was almost as if he was purposely avoiding glancing their way.

Was he afraid they would recognize him and press charges? Afraid they'd realize he was following them? Either way, the man seemed to be taking just as long with his lunch as they were with theirs. It was a relief when he finally stood and made his way to the cash register...almost.

Just as he reached the door, he turned and sent them all a malicious, knowing smile before making his way outside.

Gloria shivered. Susannah came to her feet and quietly made her way to the window, watching to be sure the man left without bothering their car.

To her relief, he simply climbed into his own vehicle, a foreign Faber, she ascertained, and without even a backward look left the parking lot. "Did he leave?" Becky asked as she sat down again.

Susannah nodded. "He didn't even look back."

"Maybe it was just a coincidence," Gloria said hopefully.

"Maybe," Susannah said though she wasn't too sure. "But let's not take any chances."

"What do you mean?"

"Well, he seems to be heading down 83, just as we are," Susannah explained, "stopping at some of the same scenic spots. I suggest we flip over to a different route to get to the bison reserve. It most likely will take longer, but maybe that way if he's heading that way at all, he'll have already come and gone before we even arrive."

"Sounds like a plan," Becky said coming to her feet. "Let's go take a look at the map."

They paid for their lunch then headed for the car, pulling their map out immediately. Finch Road, they found, though it changed names, continued straight across the highway. They could take it to Dylan, and then come down Route 25 to Highway 50, staying on that until they reached the reserve.

"Okay, that's our route," Becky stated decisively as she started her car. "You guys keep your eyes out for that creep."

They saw no sign of the man or his car by the time they reached the highway. Becky cruised across it and headed for Dylan without incident. Route 25 was easy to find and they began to relax as they found no sign of the man along the way or following them.

In fact, their thoughts of him almost disappeared when they reached the Variat Bison Reserve. The Reserve was privately owned, large, and amazing. Not only were there easily assessable viewing corrals holding the large animals, but acres upon acres of open grassland where the bison could be seen grazing naturally in large groups. Logically they knew the area was fenced in, but it was hard to tell. Their eyes went to the corrals.

"Wow!" Becky said as they neared them. "I never knew they were such large beasts!"

"The largest terrestrial animals in North America," Susannah told her. "Some of them are as high as six and a half feet at the shoulders and can weigh up to 2400 pounds," she recited the brochure she had read earlier.

"I believe it," Becky said as one of the bison moved closer to the fence. The animal had a large, massive head with short, sharply pointed horns that curved out from it and a huge, solid body covered with a thick, dark brown coat of long, straggly hair in the front and shorter hair toward its end.

"Is that a male?" Gloria asked, eyeing the large beast.

Susannah shook her head. "That's most likely a female. Now *that,*" she said pointing to an even larger bison hosting what looked like a long, black beard in the next corral, "is likely the male."

"You're right about that," came a cheerful male voice from behind them. The man, about thirty–thirty-five, they guessed, sent them a warm smile. "His name is Thunder. He's one of our most famous bulls."

"Famous?"

The man grinned. "He's actually been in several Native American and western movies."

"I see," Susannah commented.

"I always thought only males had horns," Gloria stated, her eyes going from one bison to the other.

"Both male and female bison have horns," he said informatively.

"Why are they called bison instead of buffalo?" she asked.

"Buffalo is the common American name given to them ages ago," he replied easily. "Bison is their scientific classification name. The plains bison of America are actually classified as *Bison Bison Bison*. Come on and I'll show you around."

Susannah thoroughly enjoyed the personal tour. The man pointed out both young and old bison and actually took them out to the prairies to view the animals in their natural habitat. Though she had known how important the buffalo had been to the tribes of the plains, she had not known just how vital they had been to their existence. Not only were the animals used for their meat and hides, but their horns and bones had been used for tools and other implements and even their dried dung was used for fuel.

"Do they mate all year long?" Becky asked as they watched several bulls scuffle with each other.

"They're just coming into their mating season," he said willingly, "Which is usually from July until about September. That's why the males are getting much louder."

"Aren't they almost extinct?" Becky questioned.

The man's head shook. "Their numbers are coming back." There's now over 200,000 bison thanks to the number of protected areas that have been developed."

It was definitely an informative and interesting tour, one which all three of them were happy and pleased they had taken the time for. Tired and content, they drove over to Variat and checked into a nearby motel. It wasn't the motel they had planned staying at, but it would do. It was off the main highway and they felt safe. They spent the rest of the afternoon lazily swimming in the motel's pool then walked down to a nearby restaurant for dinner.

"You know," Gloria suddenly said after having glanced around the restaurant, "I think we actually gave that creep the slip! We haven't seen him all day!"

Susannah giggled. "Maybe observing a buffalo herd just doesn't appeal to him."

"It could have been he just likes visiting waterfalls," Becky suggested in afterthought. "After all, those are the only places we've seen him at outside of that first time at the gas station; near Bristel Falls, and earlier just outside Finch where their falls are."

"You have a point," Susannah said.

"So we just don't go to anymore waterfalls," Gloria stated.

"Actually, we're not visiting any more waterfalls until after the reunion," Becky said.

Gloria grinned. "Then the man's probably history! What a relief."

Both Becky and Susannah echoed her thoughts. They went back to the motel and spent the evening watching television and playing cards before they turned in for the night…

Cade heaved a tired sigh as he lay back in the motel room. It was twelve-thirty in the morning and he was exhausted. He had been searching again since early dawn; going up and down the highway. He was close; he knew he was close. He knew he was on the right track. Susannah and her friends had been to Bristel Falls just yesterday. They had spent the night at the Lone Tree Guest Ranch.

And they had stopped at the Indian ruins and had been in Finch to see the falls just this morning.

But he had no idea where they were now; where they had gone after Finch Falls. They hadn't been to Chalk River or to Basin Rock. He had checked. Nor had they stopped at the Loff Stagecoach Museum or Shady Waters or Cassidy's Monument or the museum, zoo or the gardens here in Gardenville. He had checked them all.

What was left? He could try the Bison Reserve or Teepee Village in the morning. They were just off of the highway as was the Butterfly Haven. Or maybe they had headed down to the Wilderness Reserve. He would try them all.

Tomorrow he would find them. He had to. If he was this close, then that monster who had a whole day's head start might even be closer. Cade shuddered with the thought and sent up a prayer to the Almighty above…

CHAPTER EIGHT

Susannah was up early the next morning. Not wanting to disturb her friends, she quietly dressed and slipped from the room settling outside on the steps to watch the sunrise. Sunrises and sunsets came right behind waterfalls in her pleasures of life and she never hesitated to take advantage of them when she had the chance. She found them awe-inspiring, and this morning's sunrise was no exception.

The sky, already a mixture of faint blues, red oranges, and yellow-white clouds, was picture perfect. The nearby trees were still black shadows against the brightening sky. Off in the distance, the sun, just a half dome of bright yellow was peaking over the horizon. The clouds overhead shimmered in the early light almost in anticipation of the day to come.

The sun seemed to hesitate, then rose silently from the horizon into a round ball of brightness; the sky became lighter and bluer wakening the world surrounding her. She could hear the birds beginning their morning songs and saw three coyotes loping across the wide open land in the distance…and she heard the beginnings of movement from the people around her.

The door behind her opened and Becky stuck her head out. "Susannah?"

"Just watching the sunrise," Susannah said coming to her feet.

Becky's eyes flickered to the sky. "Looks as if it's already risen," she commented.

"Just," Susannah said. "Is Gloria up yet?" Out of the three of them, Gloria was the one who liked to sleep in the most.

"She's in the shower," Becky told her, making way as Susannah entered the motel room.

"I take it she's hungry," Susannah said in return.

Becky laughed. "Yes, but so am I for that matter. You want to shower after her?" she asked noting Susannah, though dressed, was wearing yesterday's clothes.

"Definitely." Grabbing clean clothes from her bag, Susannah took over the bathroom as soon as Gloria was out. Knowing the others were waiting on her, she took only a mere twenty minutes to shower and dress, then an extra ten to brush out her hair and take care of her teeth.

"Anybody else?" she asked as she began packing her belongings away.

"Nope. We're ready to go," Gloria said.

"Okay. Okay," Susannah muttered. "Just give me a sec."

"Second's up," Becky stated then giggled. "Come on, lady! We're hungry!"

Ten minutes later they were ready to go. "It's your turn to double check the motel room," Gloria informed Becky as she carted her suitcase out to the car.

"I'll go take care of the bill," Susannah called out having already shoved her bag into the trunk. She skipped down to the manager's office and walked in, paying for the room and handing in the keys before she headed back to Becky's car. Gloria was pushing Becky into the driver's seat.

"Okay, girls," Susannah reprimanded, "Enough. Let's go eat."

"We need to fill up the gas tank first," Becky returned.

"Okay," Gloria said. "You look for a gas station and I'll look for a place to eat!"

They found both almost together, the gas station on one side of the street, the restaurant on the other. They filled the car up, then went on over to the restaurant directly across from them and ordered breakfast.

"Okay," Becky started, pulling out the map she had brought in. "Today we go see the Gardens in Gardenville, then head over to Betsy for the fossil site."

"Then on to Gingertown for the Gingertown Tea House," Gloria added.

"Of course," Becky agreed grinning at her. "By then I think we'll all be ready for some cool tea."

"As long as we eat breakfast first," Susannah said as the waitress arrived with their meals.

They finished off their breakfasts and headed out, taking the freeway into Gardenville. A half hour later they were at the Gardens following

Gloria around as she went from one flower bed to another in obvious delight. Not that they didn't enjoy walking through the gardens themselves.

Ready to leave at last the girls ambled back to their car. Becky again took the wheel. She had just pulled out into the street and stopped at a light when Gloria sucked her breath in.

"Girls, isn't that that creep's car? There, in that gas station!" she added pointing.

The car was a small and black foreign Faber and did look very much like the creep's Faber. Not that they could be sure for there was no driver in sight, but it was too much of a coincidence. "Let's not take any chances and say it is," Susannah advised slowly.

"Maybe he came down the highway and spent the night in Gardenville," Becky said biting her lower lip.

"Possibly," Susannah returned. "But…"

"Why take the chance?" Becky said turning on her blinker and making a sudden right hand turn. She drove a half block then turned into a parking lot.

"Do you think maybe we should cut our trip short and head for home?" Gloria asked hesitantly.

"And let that creep literally ruin our vacation?" Becky shook her head as she pulled into an out-of-the-way parking space. Shutting off her car, she held out her hand. "Hand me the map."

Susannah complied. All three girls poured over it. "Okay," Becky said at last. "Instead of taking the freeway route to Betsy, let's take this county road here over and down to Betsy. Again, it might be longer, but at least he isn't likely to know which direction we're headed."

"Especially with three other freeways and the highway to choose from," Gloria added.

"And if he *is* trying to follow us, he's most likely to believe we're still heading south and take the highway," Becky said.

"And instead, after the fossil site, we can take this road from Betsy straight to Whitcomb and pick up the freeway there," Susannah stuck in, tracing the road with her finger. It wasn't exactly the highway they were intending on traveling on, but it was close; they could still get to where they were going with it.

"Okay. That's the plan," Becky said decisively. She started the car once again and edged it to the street. With all three of them looking and not seeing any sign of the small, black car or its driver, she headed out and wove her way through town and over to the county road leading out of the city. Though both Susannah and Gloria kept watch, neither spied the man's car following. A sigh of relief escaped them all.

"What a creep trying to ruin our vacation like this," Gloria said with a disgruntled sigh as she sat back at last.

"Well, he's not going to," Becky returned stoutly. "We won't let him! It's most likely we really gave him the slip this time *if* he was following us in the first place," she added. "Besides," she added with a slight grin. "There are no waterfalls anywhere near where we're going."

"That's right," Gloria said with more confidence. "There isn't."

Susannah remained silent, her mind in a quandary. Yes, despite the sightings of the man, it *could* just be a coincidence. It *was* possible that the man, like her, just happened to like waterfalls. It *was* possible that the man just happened to be going in the same general direction they were.

But it was also possible the man was following them!

Susannah shook her head. She didn't like this, any of this. Not one iota. And if his face showed up again, even briefly, they were going to play it safe and head directly to Gloria's parents, vacation or no vacation!

Their minds wandering, they missed their turn off to Betsy and had to back-track a mile when they realized. The county road, to their surprise when they found it, was busier than they expected.

"I can't believe that so many people want to see a dinosaur site," Gloria grumbled.

Apparently they didn't the girls surmised as most of the traffic seemed to turn off on the road heading for Chimeron. As it was, it was mid-afternoon by the time they finally entered the small town of Betsy.

"Let's eat before we head over to the fossil site," Becky said.

"I'll go for that!" Gloria returned, "How about that restaurant with the dinosaur in front?"

"Why not?"

The restaurant indeed had a statue of dinosaur bones in front of it, made of plaster they found out later. It was called the Fossil Café. The girls sat down and ordered iced teas immediately, then after checking over the menus, decided on taco salads for something different.

"So what is it we're supposed to see in this dinosaur site?" Gloria asked.

"It's a working fossil site," Susannah informed her. "We'll get a chance to see some paleontologists actually digging up dinosaur bones; how it's done. And we'll be able to talk to some of them."

"Talk to some of the bones?" Gloria squealed in fake surprise. "What will they tell us?"

"That life was just as hard then as it is now."

Gloria laughed. "I see." Her eyes came up as the waitress arrived with their salads. "In that case, let's eat!"

Susannah glanced around the café before she dug into her salad, noting that Becky had done the same. They were about half way through eating when Becky stilled.

"I don't believe it!" she hissed at the other two girls. "That creep just walked in!"

Susannah's heart jumped as she cast a quick glance in the direction Becky indicated. It was definitely the same man, and considering they had changed directions twice already after realizing he might be following them; considering they were now off the beaten path, it was just too much of a happenstance. She turned to the others.

"Ladies, forget the vacation. I suggest we chuck down this food and get out of here and head immediately to Gloria's parents' home."

"Then he is following us," Gloria said nervously.

"He's definitely following us," Becky stated eyeing the man again. She shivered. "He keeps looking over here."

And it wasn't an uninterested look. It was more of a malicious glare as if he had set his sights on them.

"Then forget the food. I'm for getting out of here now!" Gloria said standing.

The other two followed suit. Susannah dug several bills from her pocket and threw them on the table and the girls hastily made their way to the car together. Becky slipped behind the wheel.

"Okay," she said as she pulled quickly out onto the county road. "Somebody give me directions."

"Turn at that first road there," Susannah told her having picked up the map. "We can take it to Whitcomb then pick up the main freeway there."

"Are we planning to drive straight through then?" Gloria asked from the back seat. She was known to hate night driving.

Becky shook her head. "I think we'll be safer stopping in Whitcomb than being on the road at night." Her eyes went to the rear view mirror. "At least he doesn't appear to be following us at the moment," she added.

Susannah shivered. He hadn't seemed to have followed them the last several times either, yet he had found them.

"I'd like to know what he wants!" Gloria muttered. "Why he's following us."

"Maybe he just wants to scare us," Susannah soothed.

"Well he's doing a darn good job of it!" Gloria snapped.

Becky glanced at Gloria in the rear view mirror then exchanged looks with Susannah. "If he finds us again we'll go straight to the police," she said increasing her speed. "We're not going to fool around with this."

"Agreed." Susannah dug the binoculars out from under her seat and handed them to Gloria. "You take first watch," she told her. "Let us know if you spot him."

"As if I want to know he's after us!" Gloria groused. Yet she had already turned and trained her eyes onto the road behind them. "What if he's changed cars?" she asked after a moment.

Susannah's head shook. "It's not likely. I doubt he'd take the time. He's got to be driving the small black Faber."

No black car was spotted following them despite the hours it took to reach Whitcomb. Feeling much better about stopping, the girls checked into one of the better known motels then headed for one of the local restaurants just down the street. It was after 8:00 pm, and they were all starving, having given up half their lunch earlier.

Susannah and Becky talked and joked; trying to ease the tension that was running through them though Susannah couldn't help but keep an eye on the other customers who entered the restaurant after them. Again she noted that Becky was doing the same.

The man didn't appear. Had they actually left him behind this time? They hoped so though none of them were actually sure. He had shown up too many times for any of them to feel totally safe.

Plans were made. They would take the freeway, driving straight on through to Gloria's family home tomorrow with no more side trips, each taking their turn at driving. Once safely there, they would discuss it with Gloria's father, letting him know what had been happening. Having that decided, they climbed into bed and drifted off to sleep one by one.

Susannah slept fitfully. Nerves, she told herself when she came fully awake in the early dawn. Both Becky and Gloria were awake as well.

"Since we're all awake, why don't we just get up and dressed and head out?" she suggested. "We can stop for breakfast along the way."

"Sounds good by me," Gloria said climbing out of bed. "Becky?"

"Sounds good by me," Becky echoed.

The girls didn't bother showering. Instead they quickly dressed, packed their bags, and then hurriedly threw everything into the trunk of the car. Becky slipped behind the wheel and headed out of town toward the freeway.

"I figure if we all take two hour shifts driving we can be there before dark," she told them.

"As long as we don't stop for long breaks along the way," Susannah said. "We'll stick to fast-food eating with no stop longer than twenty to thirty minutes."

"Agreed," the other two answered in unison.

Though the freeway was only four miles east of the mid-sized town, the girls never made it even halfway to the freeway. Becky's car suddenly sputtered and rolled to a stop.

"What the –?"

The three girls exchanged nervous looks. "Let's go take a look and see if we can find the problem. Now," Susannah said already climbing out of the car. This new development was just too…suspiciously coincidental.

Just how suspiciously coincidental, they found out as they looked under the hood. The transmission line had been sliced.

"Think it could have been a rock?" Gloria asked.

Susannah slowly shook her head. The line had been cut, definitely with a knife. "I think we've been set up," she said quietly. "Where's your phone?"

But Becky already had her phone out and was dialing 911. Both Susannah and Gloria glanced nervously around as they listened to Becky reporting that all three of them were being stalked and now were stranded out on the road leading to the highway.

Before she could even hang up a Whitcomb police car drove up behind them. Two officers stepped out.

"Trouble, girls?" they asked, eyeing both them and the car carefully.

"Big trouble," Gloria managed shakily.

"We think we're being stalked," Becky said quietly.

"And that our car's been purposely immobilized to strand us out here in the middle of nowhere," Susannah added.

Gloria merely shivered again.

The two officers eyed them a moment, then with a short whispered conversation with his partner, the older turned back to them and barked out, "Your names?"

"I'm Rebecca Weaver," Becky told them, "The one who just called in."

The officer nodded and looked to the others.

"Gloria Hazelton," Gloria told them.

"Susannah Brockman."

Both officers' eyebrows shot up. Again they exchanged glances. The younger went immediately back to the patrol car and could be seen talking on his radio. The older turned back to them. "Come on," he said, urging them quickly toward the patrol car. "Let's get you off this road and someplace safe."

The girls hesitated only long enough to grab their luggage and other belongings from their car before willingly following the officers. To their surprise, they were led immediately to the back of the patrol car and ushered in. "We'll take care of your luggage," they assured the girls.

"You had better," Gloria muttered as the door shut. But despite the assurances, both officers left the luggage outside the car and went back over to Becky's vehicle, examining it carefully. Another patrol car pulled up and two more officers joined the first.

"Oh, my car," Becky said on a groan as her eyes ran across it. "Now what are we going to do? We can't just leave my car here!"

"The officers will make sure it's towed in," Susannah assured her.

"They'd better! That creep! How dare he!"

Not one of them doubted that it was the same man who had been following them. Not one of them doubted he had intended in stranding them out here in the middle of nowhere.

For what purpose?

Susannah fingered the cowboy hat in her hands as her eyes followed the officers. They were conversing briefly with the other officers, their glances coming back to them as they talked. Then abruptly, the first two officers returned, shoved the girls' luggage into the trunk of their patrol car and slipped into the front seat themselves. They made a U-turn and drove back toward town.

Susannah eyed them nervously. The officers had not once asked them what had happened. Not once even asked if it was their car or how it had been vandalized or who they thought was stalking them. They had done nothing but ask them their names and ushered them into the back of a patrol car as if they were the criminals.

Why? What was going on?

Susannah felt only slightly better when they drove up to the Whitcomb's police department. Becky must have been wondering the same as she commented, "At least we're at a police station."

The officers escorted the girls into the station, but didn't stop at the front desk. Instead, they led them down one hallway and another before leading them into the jail which was attached to the police building. Six empty cells stared at them.

"Now wait just one minute!" Susannah said as one of the cell doors was opened.

But despite the girls' protests, all three of them found themselves in the cell with the door closed.

"You can't do this!" Susannah cried out.

"I'm afraid we can," the officer returned. "We've been instructed to put all three of you under protective custody. I'm sure someone will be with you in a while to get your statements and explain."

Susannah with a frustrated groan slapped her hat against her thigh.

"Great!" Becky grumbled as the officers disappeared out of the room. "I had to go and state that we were being stalked and that we felt our lives were being threatened!"

Susannah shook her head, her disquiet growing. "They asked no questions, Becky. This isn't right."

"What do you mean?" Gloria asked nervously.

"Just asking who we are isn't grounds to have us put into custody," Susannah voiced, "Protective or otherwise."

"Then –?"

Susannah replaced her hat. A breath came out of her. "I don't know, Gloria. I just don't know…"

Cade impatiently checked the register of the local motel. It was the third motel he had checked in the last hour. Without luck. He knew he had been on the right track. He had found two of the motels that Susannah and her friends had stayed at previously. A multitude of the scenic tourist spots they had been to. But there was no longer any sign of the girls. No sign of Susannah. Not one. His stomach cramped with the thought; his tension increased.

She and her friends were safe he muttered silently refusing to believe anything else. They were together and safe and God was with them.

But where were they?

Apparently no longer heading in the direction they had been heading. Why had they changed directions? What direction were they now headed in? Evidently not in the direction he had guessed. There had been no sign of the girls at any of the motels or tourist spots he had recently checked. Not since yesterday!

And, blast it, there should have been!

His cell phone rang and he impatiently grabbed it up as he exited the motel office. "Candlewood," he stated.

"We've got the girls," a voice said through the phone.

Cade's heart slammed against his ribs. "You've got Susannah?"

"She and her friends were just picked up and put into protective custody about a half hour ago. The transmission line of their car had been cut, leaving them stranded. Luckily they had the sense to call 911. The officers who answered their call recognized your girl's name and immediately took them in."

"Thank God. Is she okay?"

"Appears fine," the officer said. "Just a little frustrated and upset at being detained."

That sounded like Susannah. "Where?" he asked.

"Whitcomb police department off Highway 144."

"Tell them not to release Susannah under any circumstances," Cade ordered jumping into the car. "I'm on my way."

"What about the other two?"

"Have them call the nearest parent to pick them up. Just make sure Susannah stays put until I can get there."

"Will do."

Cade turned off his phone and started Susannah's car then headed toward Whitcomb as fast as he dared, his heart thumping. Susannah was in custody. She was safe. Relief filled him, but his tension didn't diminish. Her safety was only temporary. There was still a man out there after her. And he was close. Too close.

Cade's foot pressed down on the pedal. He had to get to her now, before *he* did.

CHAPTER NINE

"Miss Hazelton? Miss Weaver?"

All three girls looked up. They had been in their cell all morning and through half the afternoon already. Though an officer had come and taken their statements earlier that morning and they had been fed lunch, they had not been released or told why they had been placed under protective custody. They hadn't been told anything. Were they about to be?

Susannah watched as both Gloria and Becky stood. "Yes?" Becky questioned. The officer was unlocking the cell.

"If the two of you will come with me," he stated, holding the cell door open.

Susannah came to her feet. "But…"

Becky stopped in her tracks. "What about Susannah?"

"I was only asked to retrieve the two of you," the young officer replied.

Susannah froze. *Just Gloria and Becky?* Why?

"I'm not going anywhere without Susannah," Becky said adamantly.

"Neither am I," Gloria said, stopping behind Becky. "We either all go together or not at all."

The officer sighed. "Please, ladies. Your friend will be fine. If you'll just come with me?"

Both Becky and Gloria sat down pulling Susannah down beside them. The officer eyed them a moment, then with a heavy sigh, relocked the cell and disappeared.

"Thanks," Susannah murmured her eyes on the disappearing officer. Her tension was high. What was going on now? Why was she being singled out to remain?

"We won't leave without you," Becky told her adamantly. "I don't care what they say!"

Her statement proved false as the door to the room opened again several minutes later and a different officer walked in with another gentleman following. Gloria recognized him immediately. She came to her feet.

"Daddy?"

"Dear God, Glory," her father said darting over to the cell. "Are you all right? Are all you girls all right?"

"We're all fine," Gloria returned giggling in relief. She slipped through the cell door as the officer opened it and threw herself into her father's arms. "But, oh, are we glad to see you!"

Susannah and Becky had stood as well and both made their way to the now open cell door. The officer moved to let Becky through, then barring Susannah's way, quickly pulled the cell door closed once again with a quiet, "You need to stay put."

Stay put?

Disquiet filled Susannah, then fury. Her hat came off her head. "You have no right keeping me here!" she bit out. "Now let me go!"

"In time," the officer returned, leading Mr. Hazelton and the two girls toward the door. But both Becky and Gloria again stopped in their tracks.

"If she doesn't go, we don't go!" Becky said.

"Right!" Gloria added. She turned to her father. "Daddy, *do* something! We can't leave Susannah here!"

"Let's go talk to the sergeant," her father soothed. "We'll get this straightened out."

The girls, with only a slight hesitation followed him from the room. "We'll be back for you," Becky turned and assured Susannah.

Susannah nodded, but her hopes of being rescued along with her friends died when thirty minutes later they hadn't returned. She began pacing her cell, both her anger and worry building. Dinner came and went but she found she could eat nothing.

She had just sat herself on the small uncomfortable cot when two officers came striding into the room, with another man; one she recognized immediately. Her heart jumped into her throat, then crashed at his purposeful stride.

She glared at Cade Candlewood as an officer unlocked her cell. "What are you doing here?"

"Taking you into protective custody," he replied, eyeing her carefully.

Susannah backed away from the door. "I'm not going anywhere with you!"

"I'm afraid you don't have a choice," he returned grimly. He threw a t-shirt at her, "Change."

Susannah threw it on the cell floor. "Where's Brock?"

"Unavailable," Cade returned stepping into the cell and picking up the t-shirt. He thrust it at her. "Put the shirt on, Susannah, or I'll put it on you."

Susannah, knowing the stubbornness of the man, threw down her hat and yanking the t-shirt from him, shoved it on over the t-shirt she was wearing. Cade immediately handed her a small pillow.

"Now stick this under your shirts."

Susannah glared at him. She knew instinctively that Cade, for some reason, was trying to remove her from the police station undetected, but she resented it just the same. "Is this really necessary?"

"Yes!"

With a frustrated sigh she stuck the small pillow beneath her shirts. She then bent and picked up her hat, slapping it back on her head. Cade immediately removed it and held out a baseball cap to her. She stubbornly shook her head.

"I want my hat, Cade!" she demanded.

"Don't argue with me, Susannah," he said. "This situation is too dangerous."

Susannah grabbed the baseball cap he held out, slamming it down onto her head and shoving her hair beneath it. She glared at Cade. The man was a brute, an unfeeling brute!

He turned to the two officers. "Grissom Road, right?" he asked handing one of them Susannah's hat.

Both nodded. Cade turned back to Susannah and held out his hand. "Come on, Susannah. Time to get you out of here."

Susannah ignored the hand but came out of the cell, eyeing the cowboy hat now in the officer's possession. She knew it would do no good to demand it back. The hat would identify her.

"This way," the officer said. Cade took her arm and they followed the two officers out of the jail and down the hall.

The two officers left down another hallway and Cade led her up to the main desk. There he thanked the officer on duty, signed a form, and led Susannah outside and down the steps to the car he had waiting. She stopped.

"This is *my* car!"

"Your car," Cade acknowledged opening the door and pushing her into the front seat. He then climbed in the car and immediately started the engine, driving off down the street. Susannah glanced nervously around but saw no small, black car pull suddenly behind them. But that meant nothing. They themselves had evaded the man more than once and he had found them every time *if* that man was even the problem. She shivered.

"Cade?"

"Let me try and get out of the area before I answer any questions," he told her his attention still on both the road in front of them as well as behind them.

With a sigh, Susannah removed the small pillow from under her shirt and placed it against the window, then leaned against it and closed her eyes.

They opened again as the car slowed and Cade rolled to a stop at the sight of a police barricade a mile or two out of town. Susannah recognized the two officers that they had left earlier. One immediately opened the trunk of the police car.

"So far, so good," the other told Cade. "The closest car behind you is a ways back. And it looks like there might be one or two behind that. "We'll do our best holding each one back a good ten minutes or so."

"Thanks," Cade managed. "You say the crossroads are just up the road?"

"Two hills straight on," the officer corrected, as the other placed Susannah's duffle bag and another bag in the back seat of her car. "Take the second from the left."

Cade saluted them both and drove on. The summer dusk was just settling as they sped over one hill, then the other, but he refused to turn on his car lights. Ten minutes later they came to the crossroads where five roads met at one intersection. Without any hesitation, Cade veered slightly left onto the second road and stepped down on the gas pedal. He wanted to be out of sight before any of the cars behind him made it to the intersection. He wanted the vicious monster chasing Susannah to have no idea which road they had taken if by chance the man was following them.

The crossroads eventually faded from view. Cade slowly relaxed as no car came into sight behind them. Flipping the car lights on, he reached into his pocket and drew out his cell phone. Punching the number he had entered just days before, he waited for it to be picked up at the other end. "This is Candlewood," he said when it finally connected. "How's Brock?"

"Holding his own," he was told.

"Can he talk?"

"Sleeping," came the reply. "Want me to wake him?"

Cade shook his head. "No. Just tell him the minute he wakes that I have Susannah."

Cade hung up the phone and glanced over to find Susannah watching him.

"What do you mean, *how is Brock* she demanded. "What's happened, Cade?"

"The same vicious monster that's now after you did a number on your brother first, after he attempted to blow me to bits."

Susannah's heart stopped. *"What?"*

Cade sighed heavily. "The man has a personal vendetta against all of us, Susannah. Look, I need to know what's been happening. You girls told the officers that he's been stalking you for several days."

"Tell me about Brock," she demanded, ignoring the question.

"Brock's holding his own," he said briefly. "Now give me the facts."

"How bad is he?"

A frustrated sigh came out of Cade. "Bad enough," he told her brutally. "But he'll pull through."

"And just what does *bad enough* mean? Cade, talk to me!" Susannah cried out. This was her brother they were talking about! Didn't the man understand that!?

Cade sighed heavily. "I took off after you before I had a chance to find out how bad Brock was. But I have been keeping in touch," he added as she opened her mouth. "He's cut and bruised, has several broken ribs, a collapsed lung, and both his legs and his left foot have broken bones. They tell me he's going to make it despite all that."

"I want to see him!" Susannah demanded, her heart in her throat.

Cade shook his head. "Not on your life, sweetheart."

"Blast it, Cade! I've got to!"

He shook his head. "What we've *got* to do, is get you safe."

"Cade, *please!*"

Again his head shook. "Brock's in good hands, Susannah. He'll mend as long as he knows you're safe. Now I need to know what's been happening."

But Susannah was having none of it. "You take me to Brock, Cade, then I'll tell you what I know," she told him stubbornly. "Otherwise forget it."

Cade's head shook. "You are one stubborn woman, Susannah."

"Just take me to Brock," Susannah demanded again.

But Cade didn't. He drove half the night before he pulled into a motel in the small town of Shale.

"All we have is two non-smoking rooms left," the manager told them sleepily. "A single queen bed or two doubles. Your choice."

Cade took the room with two doubles to Susannah's relief. He secured the door and checked the windows once they were inside, then barely slipping from his clothes, was out like a light.

Susannah took much longer to fall asleep. Worry for her brother, worry for herself, and anger at Cade's uncaring high-handedness kept her mind running. She slept only fitfully, and even then woke early.

Cade was still sleeping.

Susannah dressed quietly, and then grabbed her purse, tossing the strap over her head. Putting the baseball cap she had worn the night before back on, she unlocked the door and slipped quietly outside. If Cade wouldn't take her to her brother, then by crackers, she would take herself!

Glancing quickly around, she headed for the manager's office, then getting directions, headed down the street toward the local bus station. She didn't care what Cade thought when he found her gone. He had no right to make a prisoner of her!

But she didn't even make it half way to the bus station before her own car screeched to a stop on the street beside her. Susannah had the urge to run as Cade jumped from the car but fought it down. Instead she just kept walking.

He caught up to her in mere seconds. His hand rounded her arm and he pulled her around. His eyes were blazing furiously as he shook her.

"Of all the stupid, idiotic, asinine… I'm going to blister your hide Susannah Brockman!"

"Leave me alone, Cade!"

He shook her again. "Don't you ever – *ever* – take off on me again!" Before she could answer he had pulled a pair of handcuffs from his back pocket and had clamped them around her wrists.

Susannah turned livid. "Cade Candlewood, how *dare* you!"

"Shut up!" he bellowed, shoving her into her car. He slammed the door, rounded the car and slipped behind the wheel.

"I want to see my brother!" Susannah shot at him.

"No way, sweetheart. Not now."

"I'm not your sweetheart!" Susannah stormed.

An angry, self-depreciating laugh escaped him. "At the moment, I wish you weren't."

At the moment he wished she wasn't?

Susannah's heart jumped as she stared at him. Was he implying…?

She shook her head. No! It wasn't possible. There was no way he could have any feelings for her! None! Anger filled her again.

"I want to see Brock!"

"And I want your word you won't disappear on me again!" he countered.

"Then take me to Brock!" Susannah demanded.

"No. It's too risky! This man isn't just whistling Dixie, Susannah," Cade bit out. "He means to get you. He's already destroyed everything you own."

"What do you mean?" Disbelief filled Susannah.

"You're entire house is in shambles. Everything inside it was destroyed. Everything."

Susannah's heart stopped. *"Everything?"*

"Everything," Cade verified. "Just an indication of what he wants to do to you. If he gets his hands on you, Susannah, he has every intention of destroying you in the same way. Of torturing you in every little way he can think of before leaving you for dead. Now I want your word that you won't take off on me again!"

"He really destroyed everything?"

A frustrated sigh came out of Cade. "Clothes, pictures, furniture. Everything," he told her quietly. "Nothing I saw was left untouched except your car."

"But why?" It never even crossed Susannah's mind that Cade could be feeding her a line; that he could be lying. That wasn't Cade. Cade was as honest and forthright as they came. Sometimes brutally so.

A heavier sigh came out of him. "Because you're Brock's sister," he told her. Then at her look. "Apparently Brock and I sent this man's sister to prison where he claims she was repeatedly tortured and raped. He's determined to pay Brock back in like form through you."

"Dear God," she whispered as the truth slammed into her.

Cade's hand slipped around hers. "Relax, Susannah," he told her quietly. "I'm here to see that he doesn't succeed."

Susannah swallowed hard. "Do...do you know who he is?" she asked nervously.

Cade shook his head. "Not as yet. But they're working on it. I promise. It will be a lot easier once we know his identity."

Right. How would knowing who he is help stop him from anything? If he was as determined as Cade implied...

Susannah shuddered and her hand tightened around Cade's. His hand squeezed hers comfortingly as he turned off the small road that had led them out of town onto the highway. Letting go of her hand, he dug out his phone.

Brock was awake. "You've got Susie?" he asked Cade immediately when he was given the phone.

"I've got her," Cade returned. "Though it may be a challenge to hang onto her," he added, casting a side-long glance at Susannah.

"Let me talk to her," Brock demanded.

Cade held the phone out to Susannah. She took it eagerly, if not a little fearfully. "Brock?"

"Thank God you're all right; that you're safe." Relief filled his voice. Yet even through the relief, Susannah could hear the tension and repressed pain in her brother's voice. Her heart skipped painfully as her eyes filled with tears.

"What of you?" she asked tentatively.

"You don't worry about me, Susie," he ordered. "I've been assured I'll pull through. You just keep yourself safe. Stay with Cade. No matter what, stay with Cade."

"I can't come and stay with you?"

"No." His voice was more than adamant. "It isn't safe here. You stay with Cade. Promise me, Susie. I want your word you'll stay with him."

"All right."

"And no giving him any trouble. You do as he says."

"That's asking a lot, Brock."

"This is nothing to fool about," her brother warned adamantly. "That man is dangerous. Now give me your word, Susie."

"You have it." A tear slipped down her cheek. Her brother sounded so serious, and so much in pain. "You sure you're going to be okay?"

"I'm going to be fine. I promise," he said. "Now let me talk to Cade."

Susannah mutely handed the phone back to Cade as another tear slipped down her cheek. She didn't move, but stared unseeingly out at the road ahead.

Dear God, what a mess. Her brother lay beaten and in pain and she couldn't even go to him; could do nothing to help him. Because it wasn't safe. Because someone now wanted to do the same to her.

She took a deep, shuddered breath and stared morosely out the side window. Cade continued to talk quietly into the phone. Eventually he put the phone away, and with another unreadable glance in Susannah's direction, turned his full attention back to his driving.

The small highway he had turned onto was busy, making it impossible to determine if they were being followed or not. Susannah found herself watching for the small black car. But there was no sign of it. The fact didn't relieve her.

What if the man was no longer driving a small black car?

CHAPTER TEN

"Hungry?" Cade asked quietly several hours later.

Susannah shook her head.

"It's best we eat something anyway," he told her. "We've missed breakfast and noon isn't that far away." Without waiting for her reply, he turned off the highway into the small town of Thornwell. He pulled into the parking lot of a well-established restaurant. Susannah sat where she was. Cade rounded the car and opened her door. "Come on," he told her.

She didn't budge. "I'm not moving until you take these handcuffs off me," she said stubbornly.

Cade reached down and taking her arm, pulled her from the car. Digging into his pocket he came up with the key and unlocked one of the cuffs. "You give me your word you'll do as I say; that you won't disappear on me again?"

Susannah mutely turned her head. Not for the world would she promise Cade anything! The fact that she had already given Brock her word didn't come into this. Cade himself would not get such a promise.

"I thought not," Cade muttered clamping the opened handcuff closed around his own wrist. Taking her hand within his, he pulled her with him.

"Cade Candlewood, you can't!" Susannah protested trying to stop him. "You can't expect me to walk into a restaurant handcuffed to you! Cade! Please!"

Cade stopped in his tracks. "Give me your word you won't leave my side; that you'll obey me without question, and I'll remove them."

"Take them off, Cade!" she hissed. "I'm not going into that restaurant handcuffed!"

"Your word then, Susannah."

"Just take them off me!" she half-pleaded, half-ordered.

He looked determinedly down at her. When she refused to give him what he wanted to hear, he turned and pulled her into the restaurant, ignoring her protests.

Susannah's embarrassment was overwhelming as Cade led her inside. Part of her knew it was her own fault. All she had to do is give him her word; the same promise she had already given her brother.

But she was still too angry at Cade to do that.

Though Cade bought her a breakfast of scrambled eggs, hash browns, and ham and forced her to eat it all, Susannah hardly tasted any of it. Despite her anger and embarrassment, she was also nervous and wary not to mention apprehensive as her eyes continually surveyed the room.

"Do you see him?" Cade asked her softly.

Susannah shook her head.

"But you have seen him?"

Susannah glared at Cade. "I'm not telling you anything, Cade Candlewood."

Cade repressed his sigh. "Susannah, I'm doing everything possible to protect you," he said quietly. "Your lack of cooperation is not making it easy." And then catching the gleam of satisfaction in her eye, "Look, I can't protect you efficiently if I have to watch out for you as well as that vicious monster chasing you. I need your cooperation."

Susannah looked away, knowing she was being both stupid and stubborn, not to mention childish. Nor was she being fair to either Cade or her brother. Brock more than likely had sent Cade after her, only because he couldn't come himself. He was counting on Cade to protect her; counting on her to cooperate.

She bit her lip and turned back to Cade but he was already pulling her arrogantly from the booth. Her sudden resolve to cooperate vanished instantly. The man was a brute!

"I've got to use the bathroom," she told him as they passed the restrooms.

"Fine," he told her. "We'll use the one at the gas station across the street. It's more private."

Definitely a brute!

Susannah let him drag her across the street, but protested when he took the key to the restroom and not only ushered her into it, but followed her inside. "Cade! You can't come in here!"

"Try and stop me," he returned evenly. He unlocked the handcuff from his wrist. "Go," he said indicating the stalls in the small restroom. "Take care of your business. I'll be right here waiting."

Susannah, knowing he wasn't about to remove the handcuff from her other wrist, slammed herself into the stall, locking it behind her. "Fine," she muttered under her breath. "See if I hurry."

She heard the outside door to the restroom open and her heart jumped, but it apparently was another woman. She heard Cade tell whoever it was that it would be several more minutes before they would be out. With a heavy sigh Susannah finished and exited the stall. Glancing at Cade, she turned and washed her hands.

He reached over and reattached the handcuff to his own wrist then taking her hand, led her out of the restroom, handing the restroom key to the lady waiting.

He walked Susannah quietly back across the street and down the sidewalk toward their car. A heavy sigh escaped him.

"Susannah, listen. I know…"

He had stopped suddenly. Susannah heard his breath catch, heard a pained hiss come out of him as his whole body seemed to jerk. Something buzzed past her ear.

Cade yanked them down behind a parked car before she could even react. There had been no sound of a gunshot, no sign of a gun, but there was no mistaking that it had been a bullet shot at them. Susannah forgot about her anger; forgot even about the handcuffs in the wake of the new danger now facing them. Cade, she noted, had his own gun pulled.

Though they both looked cautiously around, neither could see who had fired the bullet; where it had come from. Cade's eyes continued darting around them as he assessed the situation.

"On your feet," he said suddenly, coming to his own. Under the protection of the other parked cars on the street, he pulled Susannah quickly into the restaurant's parking lot toward their own car.

Susannah stayed as close to Cade as she could, her heart in her throat. Though they neither heard nor felt anymore bullets flying their way, the left shoulder of Cade's t-shirt was slowly soaking with blood.

"Cade –?"

"Not now," he muttered.

Cade, unlocking the handcuff from his own wrist shoved her into her car. He climbed in behind the wheel, taking off straight away.

Susannah sat helplessly beside him, guilt running wildly through her. Tears began trickling down her face. Dear God, Cade had been shot! And it had been her fault!

"Cade?" she whispered shakily.

"Help me get my shirt off," he ordered quietly. It wasn't easy. Cade had to finally pull off the road in order to untangle himself from his shirt. He pulled back onto the road immediately, then into the turning lane for the highway. "What does it look like, Susannah?"

A dark red line cut across Cade's upper arm, just below the shoulder. It was still bleeding profusely. "It…looks like the bullet just grazed you," she told him shakily.

"Good. Try and find something to stop the bleeding," he said as he turned onto the highway. "Use the t-shirt if you have to."

Susannah looked around, hoping to find her first aid kit but in the end had to settle for the t-shirt. Cutting it into a strip with the knife Cade provided, she wrapped it tightly around his upper arm.

Cade immediately changed hands on the steering wheel and reached for his phone with his good one. Punching in the pre-set number, he glanced at Susannah as he waited impatiently for the phone to be picked up. Tears were trickling down her cheeks as she stared straight ahead. His hand tightened around his phone.

"Chief?" he said into the phone the moment it connected. "It's Candlewood. Look, I've got problems here. That S.O.B is on our tail and closing fast."

"He's tracking you?"

"Definitely," Cade returned. "Not to mention he just took a pot shot at me, whether because he realized it was me or because I've got Susannah, I can't know."

"You all right?"

"Just a graze. You have any idea yet who he is?"

"We think its Rico," his chief said.

"Rico? – *Luis Rico?*"

"That's the man."

"Oh, God." Cade shuddered. Luis Rico had been one mean son of a gun. He and Brock had put him away about four years ago, along with his sister and his two partners, one which they had shot and killed. Cade shook his head. It had not been easy. The man had been pure evil; smart and devious as well as vicious and dangerous.

"When did he get out?"

"He escaped custody two months ago while being transferred and no doubt is now seeking revenge on the two of you. He blames you for his sister's death in prison."

Cade glanced at Susannah and shuddered again. "He's one mean S.O.B.," he informed his chief tightly.

"So noted," Bartlett answered. "Give me your location."

"Heading North on 193. Coming up on Wynal."

"With him trailing you."

"Most likely."

Cade heard a rustle of papers, then a moment later, "Stay on 193. Head directly for the police department in Kerring. Should be about two to three hours from where you are. We'll have a command post set up there. If he's trailing you, we'll have him."

"Chief –"

"Leave him to us, Candlewood," he told him. "You just take care of Brockman's sister."

"Thanks." Cade flipped the phone off and pocketed it, glancing again at Susannah. Tears were still trickling silently down her face and his heart went out to her. None of this was her fault. None.

"Susannah?" he called softly.

"He was driving a small, black car when he first rammed into us," she told him hollowly. "Becky and I thought it was a foreign model, but Gloria thought it had been an old, dark blue Liberty."

"Which was it?"

"A black foreign Faber. He didn't have a front license plate and mud was smeared on his back plate."

"What happened?"

"I don't know. I was driving and suddenly he was right there behind us. Next thing I knew he had rammed us from behind. Not hard, just enough to swerve the car. I...managed to keep the car on the road. He rammed us again then swerved around us and disappeared." She sent a glance in Cade's direction. "Gloria and I were sure it was the same guy who had knocked us down in the gas station earlier."

Cade shot her a look. "Explain."

Susannah sniffed and told him what had happened at the gas station. "We figured that since he blamed us for the run-in that that's why he tried to bump us off the road. We thought that would be the end of it, but...

"Cade, I'm so sorry!" she cried. "I never thought...I mean. Oh, God, he could have killed you!"

"Hey, take it easy," he soothed. "He only grazed me, sweetheart. Look, I know you didn't know what to expect from him, but I did. I just didn't expect him to have been that close behind us."

Susannah bit her lip in an attempt to control her tears. "How do you think he's tracking us?"

"Most likely a tracking device on the car," Cade muttered, wondering where and when the man had had the opportunity. When he had first gone in to pick Susannah up in Whitcomb? It would have been brazen of him with the car parked in front of the police station, but Cade wouldn't put it past the man.

Susannah shuddered. "He must have planted one on Becky's car, too. Every time we thought we had lost him, there he was. We finally decided to drop the vacation and drive directly to Gloria's."

"Smart thinking."

It might have been smart thinking, but it had been too late. He had already... Again Susannah shuddered. She was quiet a moment, then, "What are we going to do, Cade?" she asked nervously.

"They're setting up a command post in Kerring," he told her. "We should be safe there." He shifted uncomfortably.

"You okay?" Susannah asked apprehensively, noting his restless movement.

"I could use an aspirin or two if you've got any," he said. His arm was throbbing more than he cared to admit.

Susannah dug some from her purse and handed him three. "I just don't have anything to wash them down with," she told him hesitantly.

"Unnecessary," he stated tossing the aspirin down his throat and swallowing.

"Did you want me to drive for a while?" she asked.

His head shook. "Not at the moment," he said. "Why don't you sit back and rest a bit. I'll let you know if I need you to drive."

Right.

Susannah sat back with a frustrated huff. She was both nervous and scared and very thankful that Cade had her under his protection though she had no desire to let him know it. It was easier to vent her nervous anger at Cade than admit how scared she actually was...or how much she counted on him.

Which wasn't fair, she admitted. Cade had done nothing but take care of her; protect her, putting his own life on the line... *for her.* True, it was most likely as a favor to Brock, but the man was determined and tenacious about keeping her safe and alive regardless of his own cost.

Why couldn't she just accept it?

Susannah sat back with a heavy sigh, fingering the handcuff still attached to her wrist. She was half-tempted to ask for the key but decided against it. Cade had enough to think about at the moment. With another sigh, she sat back, keeping her eyes trained on the side mirror...watching.

CHAPTER ELEVEN

"Susannah?"

Susannah's eyes popped open. The car was stopped in front of the Kerring police station. Her car door was open and Cade was already leaning over her, unlatching her seatbelt. The handcuff, she noted absently, had already been removed.

Susannah grabbed up her purse and climbed from the car. Cade took her arm and led her up the steps and into the police station. They were greeted immediately by two men in street clothes. The first disappeared outside with the keys Cade had handed him. The other led them down a hallway and into a large room. A handful of other men and two women were inside, apparently in deep discussion. They all looked up as Susannah and Cade entered.

"About time," Cade was greeted, "Any more problems?"

Cade shook his head. "Not since Thornwell, but I wouldn't doubt he's not far behind us."

"We're already in the process of spreading a net out," he was told. "With any luck, we'll have him by tonight or tomorrow." The man, Chief Bartlett he introduced himself to Susannah, turned to her. "Miss Brockman, would you be able to identify the man pursuing you?"

Susannah nodded. "Without a doubt."

He pulled a photograph from his breast pocket. "Is this the man?"

She shuddered as she glanced at the picture. It definitely was the man. "That's him," she muttered, moving closer to Cade. His arm tightened.

"Luis Rico," Bartlett verified taking the photo from her and re-pocketing it. "Now we know for sure.

"So," he went on. "Let's get on to business. Noble, you and an officer take Candlewood over to the health clinic and have that arm looked at."

"What of Susannah?" Cade asked immediately, loathing the thought of letting her out of his sight.

"Miss Brockman will remain here in the capable hands of Schelly until you return," Bartlett replied. "Now go get that arm looked at."

With a squeeze to Susannah's hand and an "I'll be back," Cade disappeared out the door with an agent and two officers. Susannah felt nervous and bereft with his going. It must have showed for the woman agent Cade's chief had called Schelly came over to her.

"Miss Brockman?"

Susannah looked at her questioning.

"He'll be back," she said gently. She smiled. "Why don't you come with me? You look like you could use a shower and change."

"Thank you. I'd like that," Susannah returned with a nervous smile. "But my clothes…"

"I'll see to it that your belongings are brought in."

Susannah followed the female agent out of the room and down a hallway to the officer's locker room. "The women's showers are right through that door," she was told. "There's shampoo, soap, and towels available. Feel free to take as long as you want. I'll leave you to get started while I see about your belongings." With another smile, the woman turned and disappeared back the way they had come.

Susannah, with a deep breath, walked into the shower room and stripped off her watch and clothes. She welcomed the shower; not only had she not had one for two days now, but her head itched and she still had remains of Cade's blood on her hands and clothes. Besides, the spray was forceful and energetic as well as warm and soothing. She took the agent's suggestion and stayed under the water long after she was done washing. With a sigh, she eventually turned it off.

Susannah found towels as well as her bag waiting when she finally climbed out…and a female police officer who was sitting on the bench flipping through a magazine. She smiled briefly at Susannah. "Go ahead and get dressed and I'll take you back to the conference room."

Susannah dried herself off and searched her bag for clean clothes. Finding them, she dressed, then brushed her teeth at one of the sinks available and took care of her hair. Feeling presentable at last she glanced at the officer to find her watching her.

"Ready?" she asked.

Susannah nodded and picking up her purse and belongings, she followed the officer back to the room she had first been led to. Chief Bartlett, Cade, and four or five other agents and police officers were leaning around the table in deep discussion. She thanked the officer, then putting her belongings down in a nearby chair, she quietly went and joined Cade.

He took her hand in his as she sat down beside him, giving it a reassuring squeeze. "You okay?" he asked softly.

"Yes," she said. "Much better now that I'm clean. What about you?" The man now had a wide, clean white bandage secured around his upper arm.

"I'm fine, Susannah," he returned, "Sore, but fine."

Susannah's eyes flickered around the table. "Has anything been decided?" she asked nervously.

Cade's eyes went to his chief.

Bartlett smiled briefly. "Actually, yes," he told her quietly. "Agent Candlewood there, as well as Agents Schelly and Drusky are going to escort you to a safe location and stay with you while we attempt to trap Rico."

"How will you do that?" she asked.

He sat up and laced his fingers on the table. "Two tracking devices were found on your car, Miss Brockman, so we know Rico has been tracking it. It is our intention to leave your car with the tracking devices still in place at an out-of-the-way location and wait with a squad for him to make his move."

"You think he will?"

The man nodded. "The fact that he went ahead and disabled your friend's car to isolate you as well as the fact he took a pot shot at Candlewood there, tells us he's ready and impatient to, shall we say, now claim you."

Susannah shuddered.

"Easy," Cade soothed softly, his hand tightening.

"You should be in no danger, Miss Brockman," Bartlett continued, "not as long as you stay put. Rico will have no idea that you aren't with the car. Chances are he'll wait till he figures you're asleep or alone and make his move. Instead of finding you, he'll find himself facing a squad of agents ready to take him down."

And then this would all be over.

"When are you going to put the plan in motion?" she managed to ask.

"It already is." Bartlett smiled briefly. "Your car is already sitting across town waiting with a squad of agents."

"Well, let's just hope he bites," Cade muttered, "And soon!"

"I have no doubts he'll bite," Bartlett returned. "And then we'll have him."

Cade sent his chief a tight smile. "So when do we slip Susannah to the safe house?"

"Any time you're ready now that the car's in place."

"Then no time like the present," Cade stated coming to his feet. "I'd rather get Susannah settled as quickly as possible."

"Why can't I just stay here?" she asked nervously. Wasn't a police station the safest place?

It was Chief Bartlett who answered. "Because if Rico somehow escapes our trap, he's likely to suspect you're here," he told her, "and we have yet to move you to a more secure location; one we have no intentions in having him following you to." He came to his feet. "You go on with Candlewood and the others now. I guarantee they'll keep you safe."

"Thank you," Susannah said with a weak smile. She took her purse Cade held out to her and let him lead her out the back door and into the back of an unmarked car. Both he and Agent Schelly slipped in the back with her, one on each side, while the other agent slipped behind the wheel.

They took her to a house not too far from the edge of town. It was a small house, just two bedrooms with a bathroom in-between, and a single front room with a fair sized kitchen off of it.

"What about my other belongings?" Susannah asked as she was ushered into the house. All she had with her was her purse. Even her watch, she realized, was still back at the station.

"Someone will likely bring them out later," Cade assured her.

"I see."

"Relax," Agent Schelly ordered softly. "Everything will be taken care of. I promise. I'm Joanne, by the way."

"Susannah," Susannah returned with a deep breath.

"Susannah," the agent repeated with an understanding smile. Her eyes flickered between her and Cade. "Why don't the two of you sit down and rest," she said indicating the sofa. "I'm going to go in and get something started for dinner."

But Agent Drusky – Sam, he informed her – had other things on his mind and urged Cade to go with him. "You need to know the layout of the land," he told him. Cade reluctantly went with him, knowing the man was right. If he had to get Susannah out fast, he wanted to know the safest, most direct way.

Susannah, not wanting to be by herself as Cade left with Sam, joined Joanne in the kitchen. "Anything I can do to help?" she asked the agent lightly.

Joanne sent her a surprised look. "I thought you and Cade were going to rest for a while."

Susannah shrugged. "Sam – Agent Drusky – said he needed to show Cade the lay of the land."

"Wise idea," Joanne said.

Susannah bit her lip as she slipped onto a counter seat. "Are you expecting trouble then?" she asked hesitantly.

"Expecting it, no," the woman replied with a gentle smile. The smile disappeared. "It's just that through past experience we know that even the best laid plans can go awry. Unexpected things happen and we've learned to be ready for anything."

"I see. Have you been an agent long?"

"Ten years now," Joanne replied walking over to the refrigerator and pulling out two eggs and a plate of ham. She returned with both. "Want to cube the ham for us?" she asked handing over the plate with a thick slice of the meat on it.

Susannah took it and the knife offered and began to cut. "Don't you find this line of work dangerous?" she asked. She could not believe it would be a job a woman would choose to do.

Joanne however shrugged as she cracked the eggs into a bowl and began whipping them. "It's dangerous, yes, but it's also rewarding. Protecting people, getting the criminals off the streets, somebody's got to do it. Often times, a woman is a necessary factor in getting the job done. And it's not as if we're totally helpless in the face of danger. The Chief keeps us all up to date on new techniques, technology, weapons, and safety gear. Not to mention, we almost always work in teams, helping as well as protecting each other." She poured the whipped eggs into the dish of potatoes she had already pealed.

"Do you often work with Cade?" Susannah found herself asking.

"When necessary," Joanne said flickering Susannah a glance before adding the meat to the casserole dish. She stirred the dish a moment, covered it with cheese, then turned and slipped the casserole into the oven behind her. "What do you say we go sit down while this cooks?" she suggested smiling at Susannah.

Susannah willingly complied. They wandered into the front room and sat down. A moment later both Cade and Sam came in from the hallway. Cade came and sat down beside her. His eyes were full of concern. "Are you okay?" he asked softly, his arm rounding her shoulders.

"Fine," Susannah answered, "Just tired."

Not to mention, wishing it was over!

Cade drew her against him. "Relax then," he murmured.

Susannah surprised herself by doing just that. She closed her eyes and drifted off before she could stop herself. Cade planted a soft kiss against her temple and closed his own eyes, letting himself relax. Within moments, he too, was asleep.

It was a short sleep, Joanne waking them a mere fifty minutes later for dinner, but it had been what they had both needed. Cade felt rested and alert, and Susannah with the help of dinner, felt much the same.

They took their time over dinner, talking and teasing each other and Susannah could almost forget about the dire situation she was in. She offered to do the dishes when the eating was done, but Joanne refused to leave it to her alone. They cleaned the small kitchen together.

"How 'bout a game of cards?" Sam suggested when they were done.

"Sounds good to me," Susannah said. Not that there was much else to do. The house had no television and it was too early to go on to bed. Besides, she *liked* playing cards!

They decided to play *Alley Cat,* a type of back-alley-bridge. Susannah hadn't played it before but she quickly caught on and came close to winning the first game. She had begun to relax and enjoy herself, for the easy talking and teasing that had gone on during dinner continued as they played cards. She found she really liked both Joanne and Sam. And even Cade wasn't so bad at least until she had retrieved her purse.

"What do you need that for?" Cade demanded teasingly.

"You wouldn't understand," she retorted.

Cade reached over and tried to take the purse from her but Susannah was quicker. She swiftly moved the purse out of his reach and threw the strap over her head, preventing him from dragging it away. Pulling off the ring she wore, she opened her purse and threw it in. She looked up to find Cade eyeing her with a raised eyebrow.

"Well, my finger itched," she retorted rubbing the finger the ring had been on.

"I see," Cade murmured, smothering his laughter.

"Oh, go soak your head!"

Joanne grinned. "How 'bout some popcorn and more soda instead?" she suggested as she shoved the cards toward Sam.

"I'll go for that," Sam said eagerly, "As long as there's plenty of butter on that popcorn!"

Joanne merely laughed and walked into the kitchen. The laughter stopped abruptly. They heard the sound of the back kitchen door banging open and Joanne's single cry of, "*Rico!*"

The next few moments were swift and total bedlam, but to Susannah they seemed to advance in slow motion. She heard a gun go off in the kitchen; heard the thump of a body falling…saw both Sam and Cade surge immediately to their feet, their own guns drawn…heard Sam's frantic "*Joanne?*" Then his harsh "*Go!*" to Cade and Susannah as he tipped the table, sending everything flying.

Cade didn't hesitate even a half-second. Grabbing Susannah by the arm, he pulled her from the chair and across the room, then down the hallway past the bedrooms. They heard another several gunshots as they ran toward the door at the end. But the sounds faded as Cade shoved her through the end door.

It was the door to the garage. Cade pulled Susannah around the car parked inside and through the small side door on the other side. It shut silently behind them. They found themselves in a narrow area between fence and the side of the house. There was no gate that Susannah could see. The only way out was to head down the side of the house to the backyard.

But Cade wasn't doing that. Instead he was pushing against the side of the fence. To Susannah's surprise, a small section swung open without a sound and Cade immediately shoved her through closing and latching it behind them. Taking her hand, he ran her across the small field into the grove of trees beyond. Though he didn't stop there, he did slow, weaving them in and around the trees. He stopped suddenly.

"Blast it!" she heard him mutter as his eyes searched the area around them, "Where is – there it is!"

And they were off again. Susannah, concentrating solely on keeping up with Cade, didn't even see the car at first, not until they had almost reached it. And then she saw not only the car but a large form come out from around it. A man's form, and there was no mistaking the gun in his hand.

Susannah's breath sucked in, but the man merely opened the back car door for them.

Cade shoved her into the back of the car and climbed in after her. Relief filled her as she recognized the other man as he slipped behind the wheel. He was one of the agents she had met earlier at the police station; the one who had taken Cade to the medical center. Cade exchanged a host of hurried words with the man then settled back. The car then took off at a high rate of speed. Susannah was hardly aware of it. She gulped then gulped again, trying desperately to control her panic. She was shaking uncontrollably. The man Rico had found her again; had again shot at those protecting her. Joanne could be dead because of her! Sam killed!

"Dear God, Cade!" she muttered burying herself against him.

"Hush," he soothed wrapping her in his arms as he tried to calm his own racing heart. "Hush, Susie. I have you, sweetheart. I have you. I won't let him touch you. I promise."

She shuddered against him, glad he had such a hold on her; glad of his protection; hoping against hope that he would be able to keep his promise. Because if he couldn't...

"Dear God," she whispered again.

Cade's arms tightened in both compassion and agony. Blast it! he cried silently. Why hadn't it worked? Rico should have followed the car to the trap. Instead...Cade shook his head. The man couldn't have seen them leave the station! Couldn't have! They *hadn't* been followed. Rico had to be tracking them – but how? They didn't even have...

His eyes landed on Susannah's purse still wrapped around her neck.

Dear Heaven! Without a word he let her go, then reached over and removed the purse from her.

Susannah's heart jumped. "Cade?"

"Give me a second," he muttered digging into the purse. It took him several minutes after he started emptying the contents to find the tracking device. Rico must have slipped it into her purse when he had bumped her that first time at the gas station.

"What is it?" Susannah asked shakily as he studied the small object.

"A tracking device," he said.

"A tracking device?" Her stomach seemed to fall out from under her.

Cade nodded. "Apparently he planted one on you for good measure."

"Cade, get rid of it!" she cried out. *When was this all going to end?*

Cade rolled down the window, but suddenly hesitated in throwing the device out.

"Cade?" Susannah questioned nervously.

She watched as he dug into the purse again and pulled out her wallet. Opening it, he checked it thoroughly. Susannah flushed as he did so, knowing he would find the picture of him that she still carried despite the fact that it was buried behind her brother's picture. He was too thorough not to see it.

Cade didn't comment however. Instead he pocketed the wallet and flashed her a look. "Is there anything else in here that can't be replaced?" he asked briskly indicating the purse still in his hands.

"You're going to throw my entire purse out?"

"It has to go, Susannah," he answered with a touch of compassion. "There's no way of knowing if he slipped more than one tracking device into your purse."

"Well, can't you just look and see?" she wailed, not wanting to give up her purse.

"And what if I miss one?" he demanded gently with a shake of his head. "No. The purse has to go, Susannah. It's the only way I can guarantee our safety."

Susannah swallowed hard, knowing Cade was right. If the man had hidden one tracking device in her purse, he easily could have hidden more than one. After all, he had put more than one on the car. He was that desperate. Another shudder shook her.

"Susannah?"

"Is it safe if I keep a few things?" she asked shakily.

"It's safe," Cade assured her handing her the purse, "As long as we check them thoroughly. I suggest however, you only remove those things that you absolutely need."

In the end, outside of the wallet Cade had already taken out, Susannah removed only the ring she had thrown in earlier, her comb, her keys, and the small phone book she kept with her. She pocketed the keys after they checked them over, and then handed the purse back to Cade.

"Nothing else of importance is in here?" he asked, looking through it one last time.

Everything in her purse held importance to her, but Susannah didn't say so. She couldn't afford to say so. "No," she whispered.

Satisfied, Cade tossed the tracking device back in and zipped the purse closed. He stared out the window as he contemplated just where to throw it.

Susannah watching couldn't understand his hesitation. "Just toss it," she urged desperately.

Cade seemed to consider it then shook his head. "I've got a better idea!" He leaned forward and Susannah heard him talking in low tones to Noble. The other agent nodded. Almost immediately the car changed direction. Susannah sent a nervous, questioning look at Cade.

"There's a rail yard just east of here," he said. "We'll dispose of it there in a passing train."

Susannah wanted to protest. The thought of stopping at all made her uneasy; extremely uneasy. Luis Rico could be gaining on them right now and to stop and make any kind of detour would let him get that much closer. She shuddered with the thought.

But the stop at the rail yards to her relief was short and there was no sign of Rico. Cade stayed in the car with her while Agent Noble took the purse and disappeared. He was back within minutes without it. "A freight heading to New York was just pulling out," he informed them as he slipped behind the wheel and with a quick turn, headed the car back around and up the highway once again. His hand went to his phone and Susannah had no doubts he was calling in to his and Cade's boss.

With a nervous, thankful sigh, she sat back, even closer to Cade than before. It was an unconscious move, one she wasn't even aware of making. Cade however, was very aware of it. His arm rounded her shoulders and he pulled her gently against him. "You okay?" he asked quietly.

"I'm fine," she lied shakily.

"Just hang in there, sweetheart," he soothed, planting a light kiss against her temple. His eyes went to the rear view mirror and locked with Noble's as the man continued to talk in low tones into the phone. The phone was eventually set down.

"The chief is meeting us at the airport. Schelly and Drusky were just picked up, but Rico got away," he informed them.

"Are Joanne and Sam okay?" Susannah asked nervously, her heart in her throat.

"Very alive," Noble confirmed, "but as I said, Rico is still out there."

Susannah shuddered, his last statement over-shadowing the relief she felt over Joanne and Sam's lives. Rico was still out there; still after her, still determined to get her at no cost. "Oh, Cade!"

"Easy," he said. "He won't find us."

"But –!"

"Hush. The airport should be just up the road. We'll be out of here in no time."

"Are we flying to Denton then?" Susannah managed to ask shakily.

"It's too dangerous," Cade told her gently.

A tear slipped down her cheek.

"Honey, I know you want to see Brock; to be with him. So do I for that matter, but it really is too dangerous. It's likely one of the first places Rico will look once he realizes he's lost track of us."

Another tear slipped down. "Then where are we going?"

"To a very safe place where we can hide out until Rico is caught," he told her soothingly, wrapping his arms tighter around her. "Now, relax," he ordered gently.

Susannah honestly tried to despite her nervous fear. She closed her eyes and buried herself into Cade, so thankful she had him to cling to. But relax? She was too uneasy and scared to relax. Suppose Rico was already tailing their car, despite the fact that they had thrown out her purse? Despite the fact that there were no longer any tracking devices?

"Relax," Cade whispered again.

CHAPTER TWELVE

"There's the Chief," Agent Noel Noble said with a touch of relief to his voice.

They were sitting in the airport lounge, having a drink while they waited tensely for him to arrive. Not that Susannah could tell either man was tense. To her they looked perfectly calm and in control.

Not like her. She was so tense and scared and apprehensive that Rico would walk in on them any moment not caring who he gunned down while he grabbed her, which was probably why Cade had suggested the drinks while they waited. He *knew* how out-of-control she felt.

Both Noble and Cade stood as their chief and another agent strode over to their table. Though Susannah didn't recognize the other man, she did recognize the bags he carried; one which was hers, the other, Cade's. She managed to send him a thankful smile as he put them down beside her. Chief Bartlett confiscated two chairs from a nearby table. "Let's sit down. We have some quick decisions to make."

Noble and Cade reseated as Bartlett and the other agent, Agent Askin, lowered themselves in chairs. Bartlett's eyes flickered to Susannah then returned to his men.

"Alright," he said. "Luis Rico slipped out of our hands. It is imperative that we get him back under custody or eliminate him as quickly as possible for Miss Brockman's sake as well as for the obvious reasons." His eyes flickered to Cade and then to Susannah again before turning back to the table at large. "Unfortunately," he went on, "our man-power for this has just been dramatically reduced. Our superiors have just pulled the majority of our agents off this case for a more pressing security matter, not to mention I still need a handful for the situation in Arizona." He took a deep breath and again glanced up at Cade, "Which leaves you, Candlewood, to yourself to ensure that Miss Brockman remains safe."

"She'll remain safe," Cade vowed stolidly.

"I know she will," the chief returned quietly. Again he glanced around the table. "Because of our man-power situation, I believe the safest thing at the moment is to put Miss Brockman in seclusion, away from all searching eyes, at least until the situation in Arizona is cleared up and I can put more men on this."

Cade visibly relaxed. He had been so afraid that his chief would have wanted to set another trap for Rico, using Susannah herself as bait this time, something he would have objected to adamantly.

"How long do you think it's going to take to clear up the Arizona situation?" Noble asked quietly.

"It could be as long as three months," came their chief's answer.

Susannah swallowed. "You mean I'd have to be in hiding for three months?"

"Or at least until Rico is caught," Bartlett said. "You won't be safe otherwise, Miss Brockman. Luis Rico's a mean, ruthless piece of trash who now has a personal vendetta he's tenaciously determined to settle. He's not going to let it go."

Susannah shivered at the man's description of Rico for she knew every word of it was true. Her hand slipped into Cade's.

"My plan for the moment," Bartlett went on, "is to just wait. There's already an APB out for Rico both through the civil governments and the FBI as well as more than one warrant. Maybe we'll be lucky enough to have one of them pick him up for us happenchance. If not, then as soon as the Arizona situation is over, we'll double our efforts and get him off the streets ourselves."

"So where do I keep her safe?" Cade asked.

"The most secure place would be the underground bunker under the center, but…"

Cade's head shook adamantly. "Susannah would go bonkers being that confined underground for that long. What about my grandfather's cabin up in Oregon?" he countered. "We've used it before. It's out-of-the-way, secure, and I know the town, the sheriff, and surrounding area well."

"That was my second choice," Bartlett said with a slight smile. "I'll see to your tickets to Oregon and have an agent meet you there with a vehicle. After that, it's solely up to you, Candlewood."

"Understood." His voice held both determination and confidence to which Susannah was thankful for. Right now she needed him to have both, for she had little of her own. Rico had pursued her too long and too successfully for her to have any hope that he wouldn't find her yet again. He could already have his sights on her. She shivered again with the thought only to feel Cade's hand tighten securely around hers in a comforting squeeze. His attention, however, was still with his chief.

"We'll need food and supplies for the cabin."

"Not a problem," Bartlett said. "I'll have them ready and waiting. Why don't you and Miss Brockman start on a list while I go see to your tickets?"

It wasn't just a suggestion. Bartlett pulled a small tablet from his pocket and handed it over then stood and made his way out of the lounge. Cade picked up the tablet and pulled a pen from his pocket, then turned to Susannah. "Okay. You heard the man. Let's get a list made."

They spent the next twenty minutes writing a list of the foods, drinks, and supplies they would likely need for at least the first month's stay. "There's a nearby town we can visit if we find ourselves short or forget anything," he assured her.

"What about cooking utensils?" she asked.

"The cabin's well stocked with utensils as well as dishes," he said. "Now, what about personal items?"

By the time Bartlett returned they had a sizable list for him. He took it and quietly placed it in his pocket after only a quick glance and a nod. He held one of two envelopes out to Cade. "Your tickets. The airlines were very accommodating. You'll be traveling first class, under the name Michaels; Mr. and Mrs. Mr. Noble, here," he added handing the other envelope to the man, "will be accompanying you to see you settled and secured."

Both Cade's and Noble's eyebrows shot up.

"It's just temporary," their chief clarified. "I want to be sure you and your girl are secure. Once that's accomplished, I'll be needing him down in Arizona."

Cade nodded. "Understood."

Susannah swallowed hard. "You mean it will just be Cade protecting me?" *Alone, in some faraway cabin?*

"You'll be quite protected, Susannah," Cade said. "I promise. Not only will I be there with you, but we'll have the added protection of both the sheriff and his deputies. They'll be looking out for us as well."

"And we, ourselves, will be in close contact," Bartlett added. "We'll be there if either you or Candlewood are in need. Now relax. Candlewood's quite capable. He'll keep you safe."

"I know," Susannah whispered. At least she prayed he would. "Thank you."

"Not a problem," he returned with a slight smile. His eyes went back to Cade. "A security officer will meet all of you at the Blue Skies desk in about forty minutes and take you directly to the plane. You'll be allowed to keep your firearms with you, but they ask that they be emptied and kept completely out of sight while on the plane. They don't want any panics on board."

"Understood," Cade said, unperturbed. After all, the chances of needing to use their firearms while on board the airplane were less than minimal. Susannah however, wasn't so understanding.

"What if Rico follows us onto the plane?" she asked nervously. How were they to protect her if their guns were useless?

Cade opened his mouth but it was his chief who answered. "He won't," he assured Susannah. "Right now, there's no reason to believe Rico even knows you're here at the airport."

"But…"

He sent her another brief smile. "I'll tell you what, Miss Brockman, just to ease your mind, Agent Askin and I will be watching at the gate while they're loading the airline to be sure."

"Thank you," she managed to say, knowing she was causing them more time and effort than she was probably worth.

He pushed her thanks aside. "What's everyone drinking?" he asked glancing around the table.

"Our usuals," Cade answered lightly, meeting his chief's eyes. Cade didn't drink, not when on an assignment. A fact his chief was well aware of. Bartlett's eyes flickered to Susannah's glass.

"And the lady?"

"Spiced rum on the rocks."

Bartlett nodded. "I'll go order another round of drinks while we wait."

Cade slipped his hand around Susannah's. "You okay?"

Susannah nodded then let out a breath. "It's just...I've got to use the restroom," she ended nervously. She didn't want to leave Cade; leave the security and protection of the men with him. She felt safe with them around her. And she didn't want to leave that safety. Not for a moment.

"Come on, then," Cade urged pulling her gently to her feet. "There's a restroom right back here."

Susannah's hand tightened. "You'll come with me?"

"I'll wait right outside the door," he promised.

Susannah would have preferred him inside the restroom with her, but she settled with him just outside the door. At least the restroom was empty. At least... She shoved the thought away and quickly took care of her business. Cade, to her relief was waiting just outside as he had promised. He wrapped his arm around her and walked her back to the table. Bartlett was just sitting down with a tray of drinks.

"Relax," he ordered gently, handing Susannah a fresh glass.

"I'm trying to," she said shakily. She took a long gulp of the drink and set it down, nursing it between her hands. Her eyes went to the clock on the wall, wishing they were already safely on the plane.

Thirty minutes later they were.

Chief Bartlett led them down to the service desk, leaving them in the hands of a security guard that led them through a door, then down a hallway and up a set of stairs. They came out again at the terminal itself where they were led directly onto the plane. They were introduced to the personnel on the plane before being seated at the back of first class. Noble was given a tour of the plane itself. Susannah knew it was for safety reasons, but she didn't comment. She simply settled back and closed her eyes.

Eventually the other passengers were let on the plane. Eventually the doors closed and then Noble came and settled in his seat beside Cade. "Everything's secure," he stated quietly as he buckled himself in. But it wasn't until the plane actually lifted off that a sigh of relief came out of Susannah.

She was safe, at least momentarily.

The stewardess gave the normal airline safety speech then several others stewardesses came around offering drinks, snacks, and even decks of cards. Susannah willingly took a bottle of water, and then in afterthought, the deck of cards that were offered. She set up the tray in front of her and opened the cards in order to start a game of solitaire, but found herself sitting back several minutes later absently sipping water. She was oblivious to the troubled look Cade sent her way. His hand touched hers.

"Susannah?"

"Have you heard any more about how Joanne and Sam faired?" she asked looking up at him.

"They're fine, Sweetheart," he said quietly, "Just a sprained ankle and a slight concussion."

Susannah sent him a startled look. "They weren't shot?"

"Shot at," he corrected lightly, "Their security vests prevented any bullets from penetrating."

"Bullet proof vests?"

"Top-of-the-line bullet proof vests," he corrected with a slight smile. "We all wear them for protective measures."

"You have one on?" she asked in surprise.

"I do," he said knowing she was thinking about when he had been shot. "Unfortunately, they only protect the torso."

"So you were wearing one before?" she asked.

"I was, but like I said, the security vests only protect our torso."

"And he hit you in the arm."

"With no real harm done."

But it could have been worse; much worse. "I'm sorry," she whispered.

"Don't be," he returned quietly wrapping his hand around hers. "The fault was all mine, on all counts. I should have known how worried and upset you were about Brock and handled things differently. I'm sorry I didn't."

"How is Brock?" she asked after a moment. "Have you heard?"

"He's getting better," he assured her, his hand tightening. "The doctors have told him he's likely to have a full recovery. It's just going to take a little time."

"Is he safe?"

"Safe and protected, sweetheart," Cade returned. "You have no need to worry about that. Why don't you go ahead and try to sleep?"

"I don't think I can," she said shakily. It was already close to eleven-thirty but there was no way she was going to be able to shut her mind off.

"Then how 'bout a game of cards to pass the time?"

"Sounds fine." A game of cards would help take her mind off everything, which, she knew, was why Cade had suggested it.

Agent Noble joined them and they played cards until the plane began coming in for its final approach. Susannah buckled herself in and prepared for landing, her heart back in her throat. She knew logically Rico could have no idea where they were; knew logically he wouldn't be there waiting as they disembarked, but again, her logic wasn't in control; her fear and emotions were.

Cade, noting it, slipped her hand in his as they exited the plane. It was dark, near 12:40. The small airport was quiet with just a small handful of people milling around. "Let's go see who's meeting us," Cade urged.

They were met by Agent Willows, a man in his late thirties. He greeted both Cade and Noble then turned to Susannah. "Your brother, Miss Brockman, asked me to give you this," he said handing her an envelope.

Susannah, letting go of Cade's hand, eagerly took the envelope, ripping it open. Brock's letter was short.

> *Susie - I'm safe, and I'm mending, so don't worry about me. Just take care of yourself. Please! Rico's no one to fool with. He's mean and violent and revengeful. And he's determined to get his hands on you. Stay with Cade, Susie. He'll protect you, keep you safe. I'd give anything to have you here, to protect you myself, but as you know, that's impossible not to mention dangerous. So stay with Cade. No matter what, stay with Cade. And listen to him; do what he says. Remember, you did give me your word. I love you, sis. Always, Brock*

Susannah read it, and then read it again, her eyes tearing. She missed Brock; wanted to see him, be with him; worried about him despite the fact that he was mending.

And he was just as worried about her.

"Susannah?" Cade was suddenly beside her, his arm rounding her shoulder. "Come on, sweetheart," he urged gently. "Let's get you safe."

Cade led Susannah over to a sturdy, compact SUV. The vehicle looked heavy duty in the dark she noted absently, most likely an all-terrain vehicle with four wheel drive. One full of supplies she observed as Cade helped her in. She watched as Cade exchanged a few words and gave a thankful shake to the agent who had meet them, then climbed behind the wheel and switching on SUV's headlights, started it up.

Her heart jumped. "What about Noble?" Wasn't the man supposed to see them safe and settled?

"He's in the SUV right behind us," Cade soothed. He shot her a look. "He's not going to be staying at the cabin with us, Susannah," he reminded her.

"Not even tonight to ensure we're safe?"

Cade's head shook. "He and Willows will be staying in the nearby town of Kirtley for tonight. They'll likely stay through tomorrow, then leave on Monday if there's no sign of trouble."

"You mean if there's no sign of Rico."

"Yes. Rico." A breath escaped him. "Rico would have to come through the town in order to get to us, Susannah. Both Noble and Willows will be watching out for him. If they spot him at all, they'll put a call into us immediately, giving us fair warning. Then they'll either take him in or take him down. Now, relax. They won't leave without making sure we're secure."

"But what if he shows up after they leave?"

"By then the sheriff and his deputies will be on watch," Cade soothed. "I promise you." He pulled the small SUV out into the dark, quiet street. Noble and the other agent pulled out right behind him.

A nervous breath escaped Susannah as she watched them following through the side mirror, wishing they were coming all the way to the cabin with them…Wishing they were staying…

Susannah bit her lip. "Cade?"

"What sweetheart?"

"Do you think Rico will show up?" she asked hesitantly.

Cade's head shook. "No," he said gently. "To be honest, I don't think he has a clue as to where we are and absolutely no way now in which to trace us. We're just prepared in case he somehow does."

"The typical boy scouts."

"Yes," Cade said and laughed softly, his hand rounding her neck. "Now, relax," he ordered, his fingers urging her to do the same.

"I'm trying to, Cade," she said.

"I know. What did Brock say?" he asked to change the direction of the conversation.

Susannah took in a deep breath. "That he's safe and he's mending and I'm not to worry about him. That I'm to stay with you."

"And will you stay with me?"

"Yes," she whispered.

"I have your word?"

"Yes," she whispered again. She wasn't going to be stupid with Rico out there looking. Despite her feelings for Cade, she needed him; needed his protection. Because she wasn't near as confident as he that Rico wouldn't find her.

"You won't regret it, sweetheart," he said, hiding his relief. "I'll take very good care of you. I promise."

"I know." She took another deep breath. "How long is it until we reach the cabin?"

"About two, two and a half hours," he answered. "Why don't you try and get some sleep?"

Try was the word. She had a hard time shutting off her mind; shutting out the questions and fears and worries that still plagued her. But eventually she must have succeeded for Cade had suddenly pulled up to a sizable, rustic cabin and woke her. To her surprise, Willows and Noble were pulling the other SUV up beside theirs.

"I thought you said they weren't coming to the cabin with us?" she questioned.

"They're just seeing us settled," Cade returned climbing out of the vehicle. "Not to mention they have half of our supplies," he added.

Susannah climbed out of the SUV and looked up at the cabin that was to be her home for the next several months, not that she could see much in the dark. There was a railed porch, with a decent sized window looking out onto it. Another window off to the side of the porch, and above the porch roof, three taller windows looked out. The cabin itself seemed to be constructed out of stone. With a heavy sigh Susannah turned and joined Cade and the agents Noble and Willows who were already unloading the back of both SUVs. Taking her own bag as well as Cade's, she followed them up the steps and into the cabin.

The inside of the cabin surprised her. For some reason she had expected it to be two story. Due to the three large windows she had seen above? It wasn't. Though the cabin appeared roomy, it was basically a large one-room dwelling. It did have a fair-sized bathroom with a large storage closet beside it, but the rest of the cabin was simply one large open area. There were two large sofa chairs and a rocking chair on one side near a fireplace, and what looked like a queen-sized bed and a nightstand further down. The kitchen appeared to be across from the bedroom area.

If she had been wider awake, she'd have likely called it quaint. As it was, she merely placed the bags on the bed and went to help bring in everything else. The food they put away immediately, but the rest of the supplies they simply dumped in the large room to be put away later.

It took them a mere twenty minutes. Five minutes later they were saying good bye to both Noble and Willows. "We'll contact you in the morning," Noble assured Cade, "And then again before we leave."

Susannah sighed heavily as the two men drove off and the cabin door shut. Cade turned to her immediately. "Go change and crawl into bed," he told her lightly. "Get some sleep."

Susannah hesitated. "Where will you sleep?"

"In bed with you," he said quietly, "Alright?"

"Yes," she said and swallowed. She knew she should object to Cade climbing into the same bed as her, but she couldn't. Not at the moment. At the moment she wanted him as close as she could have him; holding her, comforting her. Protecting her.

"The bathroom's just around the corner," he said indicating the door around the side of the large bookcase that came out from the wall behind the front door.

Susannah, with a brief smile, retrieved her bag and headed for the bathroom. She took little time changing into her night shirt and brushing her teeth. Even so, all the lights save the one by the bed were now off and Cade was already in bed, his hands laced behind his head as he stared up at the ceiling.

Susannah rounded the bed and crawled in. Flipping off the bedside lamp, she laid down. "Cade?"

"Yes?"

"What if Rico comes while we're sleeping?"

"He won't, Susannah," Cade answered patiently. "Even if he did know where we were heading, there's no way he could get here before tomorrow afternoon."

"You sure?"

"Yes, Susannah, I'm sure."

Susannah was quiet a moment. Then hesitantly, "Cade?"

"Yes?" It was almost a tired sigh.

"Would you…hold me?" she begged shakily.

"Willingly," he returned turning and gathered her against him. His lips found hers in a gentle kiss. "Go to sleep, sweetheart," he murmured, his arms tightening. "I'll keep you safe."

Susannah, with a tired sigh of her own, did exactly that.

CHAPTER THIRTEEN

Susannah didn't know what it was that woke her. A noise? What? Her heart was pounding. The cabin appeared quiet; Cade sleeping soundly beside her. The light of the full moon filtered in through the windows. Yet something wasn't right. She rolled over and her heart stopped. There, in the center of the bedroom window was Rico, a large branch in his hands.

"Cade!" she screamed as Rico's arm raised and the window shattered in a single stroke. "Cade!" she screamed again. Cade didn't move: didn't respond in any way. She watched in horror as Rico forced himself inside, his hands reaching out...

"No!" she screamed. "NO!"

"Susannah!"

She woke with a start, her heart still pounding. Hands still held her; real hands. She struggled in terror. A sharp, desperate shake met her struggles.

"Susie!"

Her heart stopped as her eyes focused wildly on Cade's concerned face.

"Relax," he soothed, his own heart thumping. "It was just a nightmare, Susie. Just a nightmare."

"Nightmare?" She gulped, still breathing hard.

"Just a nightmare," he repeated gently.

"Nightmare." Susannah took a deep, shuddering breath, then burying herself into Cade, she burst into tears.

Cade's arms tightened protectively around her. "Shh. You're safe, sweetheart," he soothed. "I've got you. I'm right here." He rocked her until she calmed and eventually drifted back to sleep. Only then, with a deep, relieved breath of his own did he close his own eyes.

The second nightmare came just after dawn. Cade, already awake, recognized the signs in her restless movement and woke her before it could fully develop. "It's okay, Susannah," he soothed as she gave a start, "You're dreaming again. Relax, now. Go back to sleep. I'll keep you safe."

With a deep sigh at the reassuring words, Susannah drifted off again almost immediately. It was hours later before she woke.

Cade was not in bed with her. She glanced around and found him in the kitchen, apparently reading. Ever aware of her movements, he glanced up, his eyes meeting hers across the open expanse between the kitchen and the bed. He smiled gently. "Good morning."

"Good morning," she returned quietly.

"The coffee's still hot, would you like some?"

"Thanks," she said managing to smile. "That sounds good."

With another smile, Cade got up and walked over to the counter. Susannah slipped from the bed and walked into the kitchen, not caring for the moment that she was dressed in only her night shirt. It was a heavy nightshirt; heavy t-shirt material and hung down almost to her knees. She glanced around.

The kitchen was cheerful. Its walls were a pleasant yellow, the tile on the floor a burnt orange-brown. The curtain in the window was bright yellow gingham as was the curtain above the kitchen door. Counters were across two of the walls hosting all the modern conveniences; a sink, stove, refrigerator, coffee pot...even a microwave. Susannah tentatively sat down at the wooden table in the middle of the decent-sized kitchen.

Cade handed her a mug of hot coffee, then refilling his own mug, sat down himself.

"What time is it?" she asked, stifling a yawn.

"About 10:45," he answered lightly.

"That late?" she asked in surprise.

He smiled briefly. "It's been a rough 48 hours. You needed your sleep."

Susannah couldn't fault that. "How long have you been up?" she asked.

"About an hour and a half," he said. His eyes met hers. "Would you like some breakfast or would you rather wait for lunch?"

"I'll wait for lunch," she said with a shake of her head. The coffee for the moment was enough. She wasn't hungry. Her eyes flickered nervously to the windows and kitchen door before she forced them back to Cade.

"Did you get everything put away?" she asked to change the direction of her thoughts.

"I thought we could do it together," he said. "That way you'd know where everything was."

"I see."

"I'm sure you do." A soft laugh accompanied the words.

A smile flitted across her face as she picked up her mug. "Was everything brought in last night or is there still more in the SUV?"

"Everything's in," Cade answered. "Now it's just a matter of putting it all away."

Susannah sipped at her coffee. "Cade?"

"Yes?"

"What's going to happen to my car?" She hadn't seen hide-nor-hair of it since they had arrived at the police station in Kerring. "Will I get it back?"

"You'll get it back," he assured her quietly. "Bartlett is having it driven to Denton as soon as he's sure it's clean." He took a deep breath, not sure however, how she would take the following news. "Susie, he's also having a team going through your house to salvage anything that might be able to be salvaged. Then he's having them clean it all out. He strongly suggests you give up your lease on it and move elsewhere."

"I see." A sigh came out of her. She played with her mug a moment then looked up to find Cade's eyes on her, a look of concern in them. "Do you think they'll be able to salvage anything?" she asked hesitantly.

"They might," he said with a slight shrug, and then added honestly, "Just don't expect very much."

She fought back her sudden tears at the thought of losing most everything she had owned. "At least all my important papers are safely at the bank," she said shakily. At Brock's urging, she had leased a Security Box several years ago to safeguard her important papers. She had diligently kept it up to date.

Cade smiled softly. "Always knew you were smart. Why don't you go dress then we can start putting everything away."

"Alright," Susannah said. She managed a smile as she came to her feet. "Just give me time to shower. Do you need any help changing your bandage first?"

"Already changed," he said. "But thank you."

Taking the last sip of her coffee she set the mug on the table and made her way to the bathroom. There she took a quick shower and dressed, taking time to brush both her teeth and hair. Feeling presentable at last, she picked up her bag and joined Cade in the front room area of the cabin. He was sitting in one of the chairs staring at the mound of supplies still on the floor.

"Okay," she said on a deep breath as she dropped her bag on top, "Where do we begin?"

"Let's start with the clothes," he replied coming to his feet. "Grab your bag."

Susannah picked up the duffle bag she had just dropped, watching as Cade picked up his own bag as well as two others. He handed her one. "Come on," he urged, leading her to the storage closet beside the bathroom. He opened its door and flipped on the light.

The size of the closet surprised Susannah, for it was almost as big as the bathroom itself. One side of the long closet was shelf after long shelf from ceiling to floor. The other side had definitely been designed for clothes. There were two rows of dresser drawers built in along the floor, one row on top of the other. Above those, was a rod and hangers. And above that, closet shelves.

"Why don't you take those four drawers," Cade suggested lightly indicating the four closest to the door. "I'll take these."

In actual fact, Susannah only used two of the drawers, as well as a handful of the hangers until she opened the other bag Cade had handed her. There she found more clothes for herself, everything from underwear to jeans. There was even a new pair of tailored white jeans that she couldn't see wearing while living in a cabin.

"Cade, these clothes…"

"Thought you could use a few extra items considering the amount of time we may be here," he explained.

"Thanks." Her head shook as she wondered how he had managed her size as she put away the new clothes. Deciding it didn't matter, she closed the dresser drawers and stood, her hand going to her wrist. She hadn't found her watch in her belongings. Her camera, yes, but not watch.

"I'm sorry, sweetheart," Cade said when she told him. "They must have missed it when they went through everything." He gently pulled her to her feet. "Come on; let's get the rest put away."

Susannah followed Cade back out to the front room area and for the next half hour, the two of them put away the rest of the items. Most went into the storage closet, onto the shelves built on the opposite side from their clothes.

"Who designed this?" she asked of the closet.

"My grandfather," Cade said leading her out of the closet. "He was tired of living in the city and dealing with its hassles and wanted to go back to the kind of quiet life he had grown up to. So he bought the land, designed the cabin and had it built. It was his and my grandmother's home from then on. My father never cared being up here but I loved it. I spent most of my vacations up here with my grandparents."

"It's a nice cabin," she commented, glancing around again. Her eyes landed on the upper windows. "Why didn't he build a loft?"

"I think he always meant to, but he just never got around to adding it."

"Is the electricity run by a generator?"

"Actually it's hooked up to the town's service," he informed her as he led her into the kitchen, "As is the plumbing."

"You're hooked up to the city's electrical and sewer system?"

"Yup."

"Way out here?" she asked in surprise.

"Way out here." He grinned. "Actually, if the cabin had been built even 500 yards further out, it wouldn't have been. It's right on the town's border as it is."

"I suppose your grandfather planned it that way."

Cade chuckled. "I suppose he did. How 'bout we have some lunch?"

"Sounds fine. Why don't you make it while I make the bed?" she suggested.

"Fair enough."

Susannah willingly made the bed while Cade started fixing a lunch of sandwiches and chips. She joined him as soon as the bed was made. "Anything I can do?"

"You can get us drinks from the refrigerator," he said. Susannah complied.

They took their time over lunch, eating at the wooden kitchen table.

The quiet surrounding them had Susannah's mind worrying yet again. "Have you heard from Noble or Willows?" she asked hesitantly.

"Earlier this morning," Cade said. "They're both settled in town and keeping their eyes open, Susannah," he assured her. "And they've already put the sheriff and his deputies on alert. Rico's not likely to get by any of them."

"But what if Rico does manage to?" she asked, unable to quell her biggest fear.

"Relax," he ordered. "If he somehow does, we'll be ready for him."

"How?"

"Through precautions. The first being making you aware of your surroundings," he told her. "Finish eating and we'll take care of that as soon as you're done."

Susannah managed to finish. Cade took her hand the moment she was done, pulling her gently to her feet.

"The cabin," he began as if she was seeing it for the first time, "has two doors; the back door in the kitchen and the front door in the main room. Both are solid doors and equipped with dead bolts. The cabin also has, as you can see, a multitude of windows, all with security glass. Unfortunately, the windows open, so we need to make sure they are all locked any time we go out and every night before bed."

He led her over to the closet next, then inside. "If it becomes necessary, you can always lock yourself in here. The door's solid and has a deadbolt on the inside," he added, pointing it out. "But considering our opponent, I suggest you use this only as your last resort."

"Why is that?"

"Because the man wants you, Susannah," he told her bluntly. "And putting yourself in here traps you. He'll either wait you out or find a way in."

"So what do I do?" she asked, desperately trying to hide her shudder.

"You get out of the cabin by either door. Get to the Bearcat, if at all possible."

"The Bearcat?"

"The SUV," he clarified, taking her hand. "Come on," he said leading her out the front door and around to the side where the sport-sized SUV was parked. "It's a Liberty Bearcat," he told her pulling a set of keys from his pocket and unlocking the driver's door with its fob, "Specialized for us by the Liberty Company. Climb up," he ordered. "Get yourself familiar with it."

Susannah tentatively climbed up behind the wheel. To her surprise, Cade rounded the vehicle and climbed into the passenger's seat. "The lever to move the seat forward is right at the side of the seat," he told her.

Susannah reached down and moved the seat slightly forward and then sat back. It was surprisingly comfortable and easy to see out of. "This is nice," she commented in pleasure, eyeing the controls around her.

"Yes," Cade said watching her. "It's my favorite of all the vehicles the Corps uses. Now I want you to pay attention," he went on. "As I said, the Bearcat is specialized. All the corps vehicles are hooked up to a satellite safety security system. Every vehicle is tracked twenty-four seven. This button here," he told her pointing to a small button on the steering wheel hosting a lightly engraved S, is our security button. It instantly alerts the Corps security center that there's trouble and they immediately pull up the tracking on the vehicle. Press it once, and it's a silent alarm; twice and they'll connect with you over the speakers."

"They'll talk personally?"

"Yes," he said. "There's a similar alarm button on the passenger side, Susannah, right here, but it's strictly silent, giving the center the added information that you're not in control."

"I see…What about this switch?" she questioned pointing to a switch on the side.

"That's the drive switch; it changes it from two to four wheel drive." He handed her the key. "Go ahead and start her."

Susannah took the key and started the engine. To her surprise it came to life quickly and idled even more quietly and smoothly than her own car. "Definitely nice," she commented again.

"Yes," he said and grinned. The grin disappeared. "Pull out and turn right. You need to know the way to town."

Susannah followed Cade's directions to the small town a mere six minutes away. Though she saw what she thought was Noble and William's SUV parked in the motel parking lot when they passed it, they saw no sign of the two agents themselves. Susannah turned her attention to the town.

It definitely was a small town she noted, for Kirtley appeared to be one long street with a cross street in the middle; Main Street and Center Street, aptly named considering they were the entire central commerce area of the town. Main Street was wide and long, with a motel, and a scattering of restaurants, businesses and stores lining both sides of the street. There was one gas station at the end of one side and a small bus station across from it.

Center Street on the right, hosted the sheriff's office just off of Main Street and the Post Office just across the street from it as well as other city offices. On the other side of the intersection, on the left side of Center Street were the town's medical center and several doctors' offices. Further down was a church and the town's only school.

Cade had Susannah drive down both streets. Though it was definitely small, she found Kirtley charming and restful, and quiet. Only a few people could be seen strolling the streets. Most, she assumed, were in church as the church parking lot when they passed it, was full. The man beside her however, wasn't admiring the town.

"If you have to take flight, Susannah, I want you to drive directly to the sheriff's office here," Cade told her, pointing it out. "They've been informed of the situation. They'll keep you safe until I can come and get you."

Her heart jumped. "You won't be with me?"

"If at all possible, yes. I'll be with you. But if it's not, if I tell you to go, you go. No hesitation. You high-tail it here as fast as you can drive. Understand?"

"Yes." Not that she was happy about it! "What about you?" she asked.

"You don't worry about me," he ordered. "I can take care of myself. You just get here where you're safe."

"I will," she promised shakily.

"Good girl," he said with a smile. "Now turn us around and see if you can get back to the cabin by yourself."

Again Susannah did as she was told. She had no problems finding the cabin again. She pulled up to the gravel drive, and then backed the small SUV in, parking it as she had found it. She turned off the engine and held out the keys to Cade. His head shook.

"Those are your keys," he told her, "to both the cabin and the Bearcat. I have my own set. Make sure you have them on you at all times."

"Alright." She bit her lip. "Cade, what if I can't get in the SUV fast enough?"

"Then you run," he told her. "But try for the SUV first. If you can get in it and lock the doors, you're safe. The windows are bullet and shatter proof and the doors are lined with the same material our security vests are made of. Just get the key in the ignition and drive.

"Now," he added as her mouth opened, "If like you say, getting into the Bearcat becomes an impossibility, then you run, as fast as you can, in any direction you can, though I highly suggest you head either into the trees across the road, or to the trees in the back. They'll give you some added protection. Across the road will lead you to town. Again, get to the sheriff's office."

"And the trees in back?"

"About a half mile through them, you'll run into a large creek. You can't miss it. Follow it downstream and it will take you to civilization. Find the nearest sheriff's office there and have them call the sheriff in Kirtley to let us know where you are. We'll come and get you."

"Thank you," she whispered.

"You're more than welcome." His hand came up and caressed her cheek. "Relax," he soothed, "This is all just precautionary, Susannah. Rico's not likely to find us unless someone directs him here and no one's going to do that. Okay?"

"Okay," she managed to say on a deep breath.

Cade sent her a warm smile. "That's my girl. Now, how would you like to hike down to the creek and take a look?"

"Sounds like a plan."

CHAPTER FOURTEEN

Armed with a bottle of water each, Cade secured the cabin and led Susannah across the clearing in the back and into the trees beyond. The trees were cool and thick and pleasant to walk through. Bees hummed and birds could be heard chirping and singing. Susannah found herself beginning to relax. "What kind of wildlife is around here?" she asked curiously as she heard rustling off to their left.

"The normal. Deer, bear, cougar, bobcat, wolf--"

"*Wolf?*" Susannah cried out in surprise. "I thought there weren't any wolves left in the United States."

"The government's been reintroducing them into certain locations. These mountains just happen to be one of the locations."

"I see. Are they thriving?"

"From all indications." Cade smiled as he reached out and took her hand. "Come on. The creek's just over here."

The creek was nestled in trees and underbrush and strewn with a multitude of rocks which gave it its name: Rocky Creek. It looked more river than creek, about six to eight yards across, she guessed. It didn't appear deep, in fact in places it looked as if a person could walk across it.

"It is deep in spots," Cade warned when she commented. "Just make sure you look before you step."

"Are there fish in it?"

Cade's head shook. "Maybe a few. Most of the creek is too shallow and rocky, though there are fish further down where it joins the Merriam River."

"How far down is that?"

"About a mile," he told her. "Maybe we can go fish it sometime. Come on," he said tugging on her hand. "There's something I have to show you."

With her hand in his, he turned and began walking upstream along the creek. Susannah loved the walk. The birds were more visible around the creek as were the smaller animals. Squirrels, chipmunks, and even skunk were spotted. But the most enjoyable was the creek itself as it moved quietly in and around and over the multitude of rocks.

The quiet eventually faded into the sound of rushing water and the next moment Susannah found herself looking up the creek in awe. A flow of rocks filled the creek as it came down the hillside in an easy slope. The creek water, swelling over the top, tumbled over and around the moss-covered rocks causing a cascade of miniature waterfalls all the way down the rocky slope. Some falls fell no more than a few inches, others close to a foot; some were narrow, others spreading out like Niagara. All rushing from tumbling falls to tumbling falls down to the bottom where they drifted on down the creek.

"Oh, Cade," she breathed as she took it all in. The cascade of miniature falls framed by the lush green of the brush and trees edging them was picture perfect, and just as beautiful and awe-inspiring as the other waterfalls she had seen.

"Some have named it the Lilliput Cascades," he said softly.

"Lilliput Cascades," she murmured, liking the name. She let go of Cade's hand and wandered closer, taking in all she could see. Cade stood by indulgently waiting as she explored, glad he had brought her. The pleased smile on her face was warm and true and for the moment had brushed away the nervous fear and concerns that he knew plagued her. For the moment, thoughts of Rico and his pursuit did not exist.

Susannah took her time simply enjoying the cascades. Eventually she turned to find Cade sitting on a large boulder lazily watching her. "We're going to have to come back," she told him. "I want pictures of this!"

"I thought you might," he said with a grin, "Ready to go?"

"I suppose." She sighed as she looked back at the falls.

Warm laughter came out of Cade as he stood and held out his hand. "Don't worry. We'll come again."

"Well, I should hope so!" she said taking the hand offered. They walked leisurely back up to the cabin, Cade subtlety pointing out landmarks along the way. He wanted Susannah just as familiar with the country as he was, just in case.

The pleasure of the outing slowly faded for Susannah as they reached the back clearing of the cabin, her nervous fear swelling once again. Cade was carefully searching around for any signs of Rico, though he was trying hard not to make it apparent. But she knew. Her hand slipped back into his.

"Relax," he soothed, unlocking the door and ushering her into the kitchen. "Want something to drink?"

"That sounds fine," Susannah said.

"Soda, tea, or water?"

"Tea?"

"No problem," he said with a smile. "Why don't you go make yourself comfortable in the front room area. I'll bring it in."

Susannah, with a half-smile, did as he suggested, dropping herself in one of the sofa chairs. Cade came in a moment later and handed her a glass of iced tea then settled in the other chair with a glass of his own. "You can put some music on if you want," he told her lightly indicating the CD player on the bookshelf.

Susannah's head shook. "Not at the moment," she said preferring the quiet. She didn't want anything to prevent Cade from hearing anything out of the ordinary creeping up on the cabin, not that she would tell him so.

They sat quietly for a time, just drinking the tea. Cade eventually pulled her to her feet. "Why don't you go lay down awhile," he told her. "You look tired."

"I guess I am," Susannah admitted. She bit her lip. "Cade?"

"Yes?"

She flushed and shook her head. "Nothing," she told him afraid to admit she wanted him lying down with her.

"I'm not going anywhere," he said gently. "I'll be right here. You go get some sleep."

With a brief smile, Susannah did as he suggested. To her surprise she drifted off almost immediately. Cade put the glasses in the sink then retrieved the deck of cards from one of the kitchen drawers. Sitting at the table, he played several games of solitaire before his own tiredness had him crawling carefully onto the bed beside Susannah and closing his eyes. With a sigh, he too, was asleep.

Susannah was the first to wake. She was surprised to find Cade sleeping beside her. She turned on her side just watching him sleep, and wanting desperately to just crawl into his arms. But she knew if she did he would wake and he needed his sleep just as much as she had. With a muted sigh she carefully climbed from the bed freezing momentarily as he stirred. But Cade seemed to settle again and Susannah quietly made her way into the kitchen where she poured herself another glass of tea then found herself checking the doors to be sure they were locked, and just wandering around the cabin. She looked through the CD's that were on the shelf. There were a few show tunes, some from the late fifties and sixties, but most were Country and Western.

Susannah next looked through the host of books that filled the bookshelf. She was surprised with the variety: Science fiction, western, war, history, adventure, nature books, and even some of the classics. Though several spiked her interest, she was too restless to read.

She walked back toward the kitchen but froze with the sudden pounding on the front door. Her heart in her throat, her eyes flew to Cade. To his credit, he was off the bed and halfway through the cabin with his gun drawn before the three sharp knocks had come to an end.

Motioning Susannah back, Cade glanced cautiously through the peephole. He relaxed as he found the Kirtley sheriff standing on the front porch. "It's okay, Susannah," he said sliding his gun back in its holster. He opened the door.

"Hello, John," he welcomed the officer, holding out his hand.

"Hello, Cade," the sheriff said taking it. "Good to see you again. I'm just sorry it's under these circumstances."

"So am I, believe me," Cade answered opening the door wider. "Come on in." His eyes went to Susannah as the sheriff stepped in. "Any tea left?" he asked lightly.

Susannah, with a glance at the man who had entered, answered. "I'll go check."

Both Cade and the sheriff followed her into the kitchen and settled at the table as she poured them each a glass of tea then refilled her own glass before she joined them. Cade sent her a warm smile.

"Susannah, this is Sheriff Ogden – John Ogden. And this, John, is Susannah Brockman."

"How do you do, Miss Brockman," the sheriff acknowledged, holding out his hand.

"I'm surviving," Susannah answered with a brief smile as she shook hands. The sheriff was both fit and athletic and looked about the same age as Cade. Her hand left his and slipped into Cade's. The sheriff turned to Cade.

"Your chief e-mailed me the details of your situation and I've talked to both Agents Noble and Willows. But I thought I'd swing by and meet your girl myself; let her know we're on top of this as much as you are."

"Thanks, John," Cade said, thankful for the sheriff's efforts. It could only relieve some of Susannah's tension to know that they weren't alone.

"It's the least I can do." The sheriff sent a brief smile in Susannah's direction. "Be assured," he went on to tell them both, "Luis Rico's picture has been posted and all my men will be on a constant look-out for him. They already have orders to run a patrol by your cabin every few hours. If, by chance, the man does show up, we're likely to have him before he knows what hit him." His eyes went back to Susannah. "Miss Brockman…"

"Susannah, please," she interrupted.

"Susannah." Another brief smile came out of him. "I understand we're looking for a small, black foreign Faber?"

"At least that's what he was driving the last time we saw him," Susannah said with a nod. "One with mud smeared across the back license plate and no license in the front. Of course, by now…"

"He could be driving something else," the sheriff finished. "That goes without saying. Just be assured we'll be watching for the man not the car though it does help to know what he might be driving."

"Thank you." Susannah's hand squeezed against Cade's. It was a relief to know Cade wouldn't be on watch by himself; that there would be more eyes out there watching. But at the same time it made her nervous, too. It almost appeared as if everyone expected Rico to come after her; to show up *here*!

"Relax," Cade soothed when she voiced her fears after the sheriff had left. "It's just precautionary," he told her again.

"*Relax!*" Susannah snapped. "Relax! That's easy for you to say, Cade! Rico's not after you!"

"Actually he is," Cade said quietly.

That stopped Susannah cold. Because it was true. Luis Rico wanted Cade dead as much as he wanted to get his hands on her. "Dear God, Cade!" she cried bursting into tears.

Cade dragged her into his arms and held her to him, his heart going out to her. Blast it! He knew how scared she was; how hard this was on her. It was hard on him, too. But there wasn't one darn thing he could do about it except try and sooth away her fear, and keep her safe. Something he was bound and determined to do even if it meant laying down his own life in order to do just that.

"Easy, Susannah," he murmured, drawing her closer. "Easy. I'm going to keep you safe. I promise you. Rico's not going to win this one. Just trust me, sweetheart."

"I'm trying to," Susannah wailed through her tears. "It's just he's always found me before. No matter what we did, he's always found me!"

"That was when he could track you, sweetheart," Cade said soothingly. "He can't do that anymore, Susannah. He's lost that ability. He has no way to track you now. No way."

"I know." She gulped, trying hard to believe it, "Oh, Cade! I'm sorry," she wailed. "It's just I'm so scared!"

"I know you are," he soothed drawing her back against him. "I know."

How long he stood and just held her, Susannah didn't know. But he eventually eased her away and planted a warm, tender kiss on her lips.

"Hungry?" he asked lightly, brushing back the hair from her face.

A surprised giggle rose at the common question in the midst of all the tension. She wiped her eyes. "Yes," she said on a deep breath. "I believe I am."

"Then what do you say you go in and wash those tears from that beautiful face of yours and I'll go get something started?"

"Alright," she said, an actual smile breaking through.

"That's my girl." With a kiss to her forehead he let her go and turned her toward the bathroom. "Scat!"

Susannah scat. She washed her face and then hesitantly joined Cade in the kitchen. He was already busy preparing two steaks. "Here," he said tossing two ears of corn at her. "Make yourself useful."

Susannah caught the two ears. "You sure you've got a pan big enough for these?" The ears of corn were larger than normal.

"Nope. Don't need one."

"You're going to bake them?"

"Barbeque them," he corrected with a grin.

"You're going to barbeque corn-on-the-cob?"

"Yup."

"This I've got to see!" She had never heard of barbequing corn-on-the- cob. But why not? They barbequed other vegetables, didn't they? She shucked the corn then watched as Cade put the two ears as well as the steak on the barbeque that he had apparently already started outside on the back patio.

"This shouldn't take too long," he told her closing the lid to the barbeque. "Why don't you go ahead and set the table."

Realizing she really was hungry now that her nerves were beginning to settle, Susannah willingly did as he suggested. She set the table, got out the bread, butter, and two glasses for milk.

"Anything else?" she asked.

"I'm good if you are," he said. "Just give me another twenty minutes and we can eat."

Twenty minutes later they were sitting down to a filling meal. Cade did his best to keep Susannah entertained once they sat down to eat. He teased her and challenged her to a duel of jokes and riddles. The conversation eventually drifted to other things when Susannah asked him about Becky and Gloria.

"Did they both get home alright?"

Cade nodded. "Gloria's father took both the girls home and saw to the car. Rico won't go after them," he assured her, seeing the hesitation on her face. "He knows you're not with them."

That was true but she shivered with the thought of the danger she had put her best friends in regardless.

"They friends from college?" Cade asked lightly to veer her thoughts away.

Susannah nodded. "The three of us had several classes together."

"So what do they do now?"

"Gloria's a secretary for a local school and Becky works for a health spa."

"I'm surprised you don't all work at the same place."

"We tried," she began then caught her breath. "Cade, what do I do about my job?" She'd have to notify them that she wouldn't be back right away, maybe not for a good three months which would more than likely get her fired. There was no way they would hold her job open for that amount of time!

"I hadn't thought that far ahead," Cade admitted.

"I'll have to call them."

"No," Cade stated immediately. "No phone calls…and no letters," he added before she could bring it up.

"Then how do I notify them? I can't just not show up!"

"I know," he acknowledged. He thought a moment. "Look, I'll let the Chief know. He'll handle it for you."

"I'm likely to get fired."

"Not fired, Susannah. Laid off, maybe."

"Same thing."

"Hey. Don't be so negative. Maybe considering all the circumstances, your boss would take you back without a problem."

"Right," Susannah muttered, but she didn't believe it. Her boss was too much by the book. If she felt that she couldn't hold the job open for that long, she wouldn't, whether it was Susannah's fault or not. She looked up at Cade. "I'm beginning to hate that man Rico more and more," she told him.

"Believe me, I'm beyond hate," Cade told her. "He comes anywhere near us and he'll find himself in a body bag."

"Sounds good to me." Susannah stood and picked up her dishes. She picked up Cade's as well and took them over to the sink before clearing off the rest of the table. With a nervous glance out the window, she started the dishes as well as wiped down the table and counters. Cade, to her relief, sat in the kitchen and watched her.

"Thank you," he said when she finally put the dish towel up.

"Thank you for keeping me company," she returned quietly. She bit her lip. "Would it be alright if I went in and took a bath?" she asked hesitantly.

"That would be fine, Susie."

"Would you double check the bathroom window for me?"

"Of course," he said coming to his feet.

She followed him into the bathroom watching as he checked the window for her, then turned on the bath water while she went and retrieved her nightshirt and clean underwear. Cade was sitting in a chair in the main room when she came out of the closet.

"Cade?"

He looked up.

"Is it okay if I leave the bathroom door open?"

"I'm not going anywhere, Susannah."

"I know. It's just I'd feel better if I did."

"Then leave it open."

Susannah left the bathroom door half open. She stripped and slipped into the tub, settling into the warm, steamy water. It felt heavenly and she could feel her muscles as well as her tension slowly relax. Soft music was suddenly coming from the front room.

A degree of contentment filled Susannah as she simply sat and soaked and listened to the music. Thoughts of Rico she pushed to the back of her mind. Cade was out there watching over her. He would protect her.

Cade.

He hadn't changed much in the last few years she mused as her thoughts drifted to him. He was still as smart and intelligent and competent as he had always been. He was still stolid as well as strong and agile; still stubborn and commanding. Not that Susannah minded at the moment. She was glad he was here; glad he was watching over her despite the fact that she still thought him a brute.

A brute that was still devastatingly good-looking and had been nothing but gentle and understanding and patient with her.

With a restless sigh, Susannah climbed out of the tub and dried off, then redressed for bed. She wiped down the tub, and picked up her clothes, putting them into the small hamper that was against the wall. Only then did she join Cade in the front room. He looked up from the book he had been reading as he listened to his music.

"Ready for bed?" he asked lightly.

"If you are."

"You go crawl in," he said setting down his book. "I'm going to go take a quick shower first and change my bandage."

"Cade…"

"I'll be quick, I promise."

"Will you leave the door open?" she asked nervously.

"Yes."

He was true to his word. Not only did he leave the bathroom door open, but he was out again in a mere twelve minutes. Susannah had sat at the edge of one of the chairs, nervously waiting.

"Come on, Susannah. Let's go on to bed."

Susannah willingly went with him as he turned out the lights. The moment they were in bed, she crawled into his arms. "Hold me," she ordered snuggling deeper into him. His solid, firm arms rounded her protectively. She stirred almost instantly.

"Cade, did you check the doors and windows?"

"While you were taking your bath," he assured her. He gently raised her lips to his, kissing her warmly. "Go to sleep now, sweetheart," he whispered.

Cade waited until Susannah was sound asleep in his arms before he closed his own eyes. Not because he was worried about Rico sneaking up on them, not even to alleviate Susannah's fears, but simply because it was pure bliss holding her...

CHAPTER FIFTEEN

Susannah woke with the rising sun to find she was still snuggled into Cade, his arms still secure around her. A contented sigh escaped her. She felt warm and comfortable, and safe.

"Susannah?" Her name was just a breath.

Her head rose.

"Good morning," Cade said softly, fighting back the urge to meld his lips against hers.

"Good morning. What time is it?"

"About 6:30," he answered. "You get back to sleep alright?" She had woke with another nightmare during the night; one that had her clinging desperately to him.

"Yes," she murmured, snuggling back into him. "I actually did."

"I'm glad." His hand came up and began running gently through her hair. "Do you want to get up?"

"Do we have to?" Susannah didn't want to move. She was too warm and comfortable to move.

"No," Cade said with a smile. "We'll get up when you're ready, Susannah."

"Thank you," she whispered, closing her eyes with a yawn.

They stayed in bed another full hour before Susannah woke enough to become restless. They both got up and dressed, Cade going on to start the coffee, as well as breakfast. Susannah made the bed before joining him.

"Anything I can do?"

Cade shook his head. "It's just about ready. You can pour us both a cup of coffee though if you want."

By the time Susannah had poured the two cups and sat down, Cade was dishing up two plates of breakfast. He set a plate down in front of her and then sat down himself. They took their time over breakfast, Susannah automatically cleaning up the kitchen when they were done. Again Cade stayed in the kitchen with her, finishing off another cup of coffee. It wasn't until she dried her hands and put away the hand towel that he came to his feet.

"Want to come keep me company?" he asked lightly.

"Of course." She wasn't about to let him leave her alone. "What are you planning to do?"

"Just split some wood," he said. "It's supposed to be cool later this week. I want to be prepared."

Susannah understood once Cade led her outside. There was a pile of logs at the side of the cabin, neatly stacked under a lean-to. But they were large logs, too large to burn in the fireplace inside. She watched as Cade dragged them one at a time out into the clearing in the back and split them into four smaller pieces of wood using no more than an axe, and when necessary, the help of a wedge-shaped splitter. The man was definitely well put-together, she realized as she watched his muscles ripple as he split log after log; definitely physically fit. She doubted there was an ounce of fat anywhere on him.

He looked up suddenly and grinned at her. "Want to start stacking them against the cabin?"

Susannah, embarrassed to be caught ogling the man she was supposed to hate, eagerly took the smaller pieces and stacked them on the patio next to the cabin door where Cade had indicated.

An hour later, Cade called it quits. "That should be enough wood to last us for a while," he stated. He sank down on the side bench set out on the back patio and took off his t-shirt, drying himself off with it.

"Tired?" Susannah asked, a teasing light in her eyes.

"Well, it is a work-out," he admitted with a grin.

"That doesn't hurt your arm?" She was eyeing the white bandage still around it.

Cade shook his head. "Doesn't seem to."

Susannah merely shook her head. "Want something to drink?"

"I'd love something to drink, Susannah."

"Let me go get those last two pieces and then I'll go find us both something to drink." Susannah retrieved the last two pieces of wood and added them to the stack by the cabin door then went inside and poured them both large glasses of water. Cade downed his almost immediately.

"Thanks, sweetheart. That hit the spot."

"Want to finish mine?" she asked, having drunk only half of hers.

He took the glass she offered without a word and downed it as well. Susannah took both glasses into the cabin and set them in the sink.

Cade followed her inside. Throwing his shirt into the laundry basket in the bathroom, he put on another and opened the front windows before he settled down in his chair. Susannah was right there, poised on the edge of her own chair. She watched him pick up the book he had been reading the night before and begin reading. It lasted two minutes.

"Why don't you go and find something to read?" he suggested lightly, looking up at her.

Susannah shrugged. She didn't feel like reading; was unsure if she could even concentrate on a book in the situation she was in. She bit her lip. "Cade?"

An eyebrow rose.

"Do you think Noble and Willows have left already?"

Cade shook his head. "They'll notify us before they leave, Susannah. Until then, they'll be on watch."

"I wish they weren't going," she admitted.

"I know."

"How many deputies does the sheriff have?"

"Three," Cade said, "Which is more than enough for this small community."

"Have you lived here long, in Kirtley, I mean?"

"Most every summer while my grandfather was alive," he told her. "Once he died, my grandmother moved down into the valley. She kept the cabin for a general retreat."

"And now it's yours."

"Yes. How would you like to play a game?" he asked putting his book down. "We've got cards, dice, even a board game or two."

"I've never played dice," she admitted on a deep breath.

"Then let me teach you," he said warmly coming to his feet. Leading her into the kitchen, he settled her at the table and then turned and dug several dice from the kitchen drawer. Settling at the kitchen table himself, he began teaching her the rules to several dice games. Susannah found she enjoyed them. All three of the games he taught her were fun and challenging, though she found she liked *Wipe-Out* best. She seemed to have a lucky knack of knowing when to stop and when to keep rolling.

"Beginner's luck," Cade muttered with a shake of his head as she won the third game in a row. He set the dice down between them. "It's past lunch time. You hungry?"

Susannah, surprised they had played so long, nodded. "Actually I am."

"Sandwiches do?"

"Nicely," she said. "Do you need any help?"

"No," he replied coming to his feet. "I can handle it, Susannah."

With a shrug, Susannah picked up the dice and rolled them on the table, absently playing a solitary game of *Soldier* as she waited. It wasn't a long wait. Cade was suddenly placing a plate of sandwiches on the table along with a jar of pickles and a bag of chips. Susannah put the dice aside and taking the paper plate he offered her, reached for a sandwich and a handful of chips. They ate quietly for a while, Susannah's mind wandering, mulling over bits and pieces.

"Cade?"

He looked up.

"What's going to happen to Brock, I mean once he's back on his feet? Will they let him stay in the Corps?"

Cade's head shook. "I doubt he'll want to stay in, Susannah."

"Why is that?" she asked in surprise. As far as she knew, both Brock and Cade loved working for the government's specialized security corps.

"Well," Cade admitted, sending her a wry grin, "The truth is your brother and I have been contemplating leaving the Corps."

Her stomach jumped. "You have?"

"Don't get me wrong, Susannah," he said. "Both Brock and I have been very satisfied working for the Corps; our way of serving our country considering we didn't go into the military. And I admit, it's been exciting; a true rush working for the Corps, but one can't live on a rush forever. We're both ready to settle down to something less…adventuresome."

"What will you do?" came her bewildered voice.

"Well," Cade answered, watching her carefully, "Your brother and I have been offered a good price on a fair-sized ranch out in Wyoming."

"A ranch?"

"Cattle ranch to be exact."

"You're going to raise cattle?"

"As well as horses."

"Oh," Susannah said in surprise.

"It will be a good, solid life for us, Susannah," he told her softly, "A safer life for all of us."

Susannah couldn't believe it. "Brock's really ready to give all this up?" she asked sweeping her arm.

"More now than ever before," Cade told her quietly.

"And you?"

"I'm ready, Susannah," he said. "Putting your life on the line has only solidified the decision."

A sense of relief spread through Susannah. Though she had been secretly proud of both Cade and her brother working for the special government corps, she had never been happy about it; had always worried about them both for she knew how dangerous a job it really was; more so today than ever before. She looked up at Cade.

"Just don't quit before Rico's been taken care of, okay?"

"You have no need to worry, Susannah. I'll see him put away before I take my leave. That I promise you."

"Thank you," she whispered.

"You're more than welcome." Cade smiled and came to his feet. He carried his glass and plate to the counter and rinsed out the glass.

"I'll take care of the clean-up," Susannah offered. "After all, you made our lunch."

"Sounds like a deal," he said coming back over to the table. He lifted her chin and planted a soft kiss on her lips before disappearing out into the main room.

Susannah's heart jerked with the kiss, but she couldn't put any stock in it. It was simply a comforting gesture as his others had been. She knew that was all it was. With an unconscious sigh, she stood and picked up the rest of the table, then the rest of the kitchen. Cade was sitting in his chair reading his book when she finally joined him.

"Why don't you put some music on?" he suggested lightly.

"Anything in particular?" she asked wandering over to the book case where the CD player was.

"Whatever you choose will be fine."

Susannah put on some music from the sixties and roaming the books on the shelf, finally pulled out a science fiction book that took place back in the age of the dinosaurs. Settling in the chair opposite from Cade, she began to read.

An hour and a half later Cade looked up to find her asleep, the book slipping from her fingers. Putting his own book aside, he gathered her up and carried her over to the bed. He meant only to lay her down but found himself settling on the bed with her where he, too, drifted off.

He was restless when he woke an hour later. Slipping off the bed he went in and fixed himself an iced tea then quietly slipped out the front door and leaving it open, settled himself on the front step. Susannah joined him a short while later.

"Isn't it a little dangerous being out here?" she asked him, her eyes glancing nervously around.

"Nope," he said, flickering her a glance. "We're fine, Susannah."

"If you say so," she muttered not feeling fine in the least. She had pulled herself awake from another nightmare and at the moment was feeling far from secure.

Cade reached up and pulled her down beside him. "You have a nice nap?" he asked lightly.

"Until the nightmare invaded it."

"I see," he said, his arm rounding her shoulders. "How would you like to walk into town?" he asked her.

"Walk into town?"

"Walk," he told her standing and pulling her to her feet. "Come on, the exercise will do us good."

They didn't walk down the roads, but instead Cade led her into the trees across the road then eventually around to the small path that meandered down into town. Cade then steered her in the direction of the sheriff's office. He didn't stop there, but walked her around the corner and down the street to the small town's motel where they found both Noble and Willows sitting in chairs out in front of their motel room. Neither looked like agents of any sort. They were wearing t-shirts and jeans as well as an unbuttoned long-sleeved shirt. They looked exactly like two tourists enjoying a vacation in the mountains.

They stood and greeted Cade, then Susannah. "What are the two of you doing in these parts?" Willows questioned.

"Just restless," Cade said with a shrug. "Not to mention I wanted to show Susannah the way to the sheriff's if she needed to go that route."

"Wise," Noble said. "We were just deciding to go on over to the Kirtley Diner for dinner. Want to join us?"

Cade raised an eyebrow in Susannah's direction.

"I'd love to," she said honestly.

The Kirtley Diner was larger than Susannah expected. There were plenty of tables, a small bar area, and even a fair-sized dance floor; yet it was still rustic, and cozy. They found seats around one of the larger tables and ordered. Susannah, though she wanted to ask Noble when he and Willows were leaving, found she couldn't. She didn't want to know, did she? Instead she sat back and enjoyed the light bantering that went on among the men as they ate. It was Noble himself who eventually let them know.

"Willows and I are leaving first thing in the morning," he told Cade quietly over coffee. "Considering there's been no sign of Rico these last two days, I doubt he has any clue as to where to find you."

"My sentiments, exactly," Cade said with a nod. "Where are you heading?"

"The Chief's sending us straight down to Arizona."

"Is he down there?"

Noble shook his head. "He's handling things from the Center. Says he has too many men out in too many locations to do otherwise."

"Thanks," Cade returned with a brief smile.

"No problem." Noble's eyes went to Susannah. "Hey," he said softly gaining her attention. "What do you say we try out the dance floor?" There were already two couples out on the floor dancing to a rather fast-beat country song. Susannah glanced at Cade but the man was adding sugar to his second cup of coffee and didn't even look up.

Didn't seem to care one way or another.

Susannah turned back to Noble and smiled. "I'd love to."

Noble helped her to her feet and led her out to the small dance floor. Susannah enjoyed herself. Both she and Noble giggled and laughed at their attempts to mimic the dance steps of the other two couples. She was grinning when they finally made it back to the table.

"Have fun?" Cade asked in amusement, having watched her from the moment she had left the table.

"Actually, I did," she said happily.

Willows came to his feet. "Then how about enjoying another with me?" he said taking her hand and leading her back out onto the floor before she could protest. His actual name, he told her, was Taite, though most of his friends called him Will, "Which you, dear lady, have permission to call me as well."

"Why, thank you!" Susannah laughed as they began dancing. This time it was a song from the sixties, one Susannah had no trouble dancing to.

"I have this feeling you enjoy dancing," Cade mused when Willows escorted her back to the table.

"Yes," Susannah said with a saucy grin. "I actually do."

"Then I can't disappoint you," he said coming to his feet and taking her hand, "My turn."

Like Willows, Cade led her onto the dance floor before she could protest. The song however, was a slow, country love song; his love song; *When The Time Is Right.* With a rueful shrug and a warm smile, Cade drew her into his arms.

Susannah's heart jumped. Part of her knew she should refuse the dance. After all, the man *was* a brute. But Susannah found she couldn't; found herself instead willingly settling against him. Her arms came up and rested around his shoulders as they slowly began to dance. They didn't talk, just swayed easily to the music. Contentment filled her as she rested her cheek against his chest. She could hear his steady heartbeat under her cheek; feel his firm arms wrapped secure around her. Feel herself floating...

Susannah was unaware of the unconscious sigh that escaped her as the dance came to a close. Cade's heart swelled as he caught it, his hope rising that she was beginning to forgive him for the hurt he had caused her in the past. He raised her chin.

"You dance extremely well," he complimented her with a soft smile.

"Thank you," she said. "Like I said earlier, I like to dance."

The music was starting up again, this time to a faster beat. Cade bit back his disappointment. He didn't feel like fast dancing. He would much rather be holding Susannah in his arms. "Want to go see if the guys want to go play some cards?" he suggested instead.

"Why not?" she agreed hiding her own disappointment.

Cade's co-agents were more than willing to drive them back to the cabin for some cards. They paid for their meal, walked back to the motel and loaded into the SUV Noble and Willows were using. Fifteen minutes later they were settling around the kitchen table in Cade's cabin as they dealt out the cards.

They played several games of Hearts then went on to play Pinochle, Susannah teaming up with Noble against Willows and Cade. Each team won a game, then despite the time, determinedly played a tie-breaker for an over-all winner. It was a close game but in the end it was Willows and Cade who actually won.

"But not by much," Noble said. "We'll get them next time."

Not that there would actually be a next time. Noble and Willows bid their farewells with a last assurance that the sheriff was aware of their impending departure in the morning and would be doubling his efforts to see they remained safe. Not that they expected to see Rico they added for Susannah's benefit. Susannah hugged them both.

Cade closed and locked the door as the two agents drove off. He turned to Susannah. "You ready for bed or would you like to stay up awhile yet?"

"What time is it?"

"Late."

Susannah shrugged. "I'd kind of like to clean up the kitchen," she admitted. But if he wasn't staying up…

"Then let's clean it up," he willingly said.

They worked quietly together straightening the kitchen. So quietly that Susannah jumped with the sound of a lone wolf's howl not too far off in the distance.

"Relax," Cade soothed. "It's not that close. Besides, despite stories to the contrary, wolves rarely attack mankind."

"You sure about that?"

"Absolutely," Cade returned. "There's never been a documented case of a wild, healthy wolf attacking anyone. Now what do you say we hit the sack? I'm done in."

Susannah, tired as well, willingly agreed. She changed and climbed into bed as Cade checked both windows and doors then did the same. Without a qualm, she crawled into his arms and settled against him. She was asleep within minutes.

CHAPTER SIXTEEN

Susannah jerked awake as something brushed against her ear, then her nose. She opened her eyes to find Cade sitting beside her, already fully dressed. He was bending over her, trying hard to suppress his grin as he tickled her again with a strand of her own hair.

"Cade!" she groaned.

The brute merely continued.

"Cade!" she said again trying to slap his hand away, "Stop!"

He let go of her hair and with a soft grin, planted a gentle kiss on her lips. "Come on, sleeping beauty. Time you were up. Breakfast was hours ago."

Susannah looked up at him. "Hours ago? What time is it?"

"About 10:35."

"10:35? Oh, my."

"Oh, my," Cade echoed, a smile playing at the corner of his mouth. "Tell you what. You get up and dressed and I'll go make lunch. Then when you're ready we'll hike down to the cascades and have a picnic."

"Honest?"

"Honest. So get moving, woman!" he said standing and stripping the covers from her.

"Cade!" But she was up and gathering her clothes before he finished his rumble of laughter. By the time she had finished showering and dressing Cade was almost done preparing the lunch.

Susannah quickly made the bed and found her camera that had been in her duffle bag as she waited for Cade to finish. He shoved the lunch he had made into his backpack along with several bottles of water.

"Got your camera this time?" he asked turning to her.

Susannah held it up.

"Then let's go."

Cade let Susannah lead the way down to the creek. They took their time, enjoying their walk with Susannah snapping pictures of everything that caught her eye, including Cade himself.

She took even more pictures once they reached the creek, but her best pictures were at the cascades themselves. Cade indulged her, even taking the camera from her and taking pictures of her as well.

"Just to prove you were actually here," he teased.

Handing the camera back to her, he sat himself down and watched her indulgently as she snapped more pictures as she explored. Eventually her hunger had her rejoining him. They had a leisurely lunch by the creek, Susannah enjoying every minute of it. Cade had packed more than enough food.

For a while, they simply sat and enjoyed the creek after they ate. The air, Susannah noted, was suddenly slightly cooler than it had been as a light breeze came up. She glanced up at the sky to find the pure blue now dotted with scattered clouds.

Cade's eyes, too, were on the sky and the incoming clouds. "Looks like it may rain before nightfall," he commented.

"Are we going back to the cabin then?" she asked, her eyes going back to him.

His head shook. "We'll go when you're ready to go," he told her.

"Then I might as well enjoy it while I can," she said not ready yet to leave her small piece of paradise. She climbed the nearby rocks to the top of the waterfall just to see where it began. What she found was more of the same: a calm, sleepy creek that meandered from further up the mountain. Knowing she needed to stay in sight of Cade, she didn't walk any farther, but stood looking back down the cascades from the top, taking more pictures.

She glanced again at the clouds rolling in; light gray clouds now mixing with the white. With a sigh, she headed back down to Cade. To her surprise, he was in the middle of doing sit-ups there in the grass. Unable to interrupt him, she stood and waited until he finished, snapping several pictures as she did so. Eventually he laid back and looked up at her to find her smothering a grin.

"Hey, I've got to keep myself in shape somehow!" he countered with a grin of his own.

"I see you're not wearing your bandage," Susannah commented.

"My arm is fine, Susannah. It's already healed over."

"It better be," Susannah muttered, but on closer look, she could see that it was.

With a short intake of breath, Cade rolled back up and onto his feet in one smooth movement. "You ready to go or are you still exploring?"

"I think I'm ready to go," she admitted. "Not that I haven't enjoyed myself."

"I'm glad," Cade said warmly. He reached over and picked up the few pieces of trash still lying around and shoved them into his backpack before fitting it on his back and gesturing to her to lead the way.

Susannah surprised herself by getting them back to the cabin without any help from Cade. She helped him clean out his backpack then they both settled in the front room area of the cabin, Cade opening up the windows.

"Is there any blank paper around?" she asked as Cade picked up his book.

"Try the shelf in the closet."

Susannah willingly checked out the closet shelf, finding several reams of copy paper. She took a half dozen sheets as well as a few pencils and the clip board that was also on the shelf then plopped herself in the chair across from Cade. He glanced her way, but returned to his book.

Susannah thought a moment before she wrote *Merry Christmas* at the top of the page. Becky had told her last Christmas that it was possible to make over three hundred words, counting common names, one-letter words, and plurals, from the letters therein. She was determined to make as many as she could as long as she had the time.

The first thirty were rather easy, though after that she had to hunt just a little harder. Cade interrupted her awhile later.

"Susannah? Mind if I go lay down?" he asked when she looked up.

"Go ahead," she said quietly.

"You can shut and lock the windows if it makes you feel safer."

"Thank you." She smiled absently, her mind still on her word-finding.

Cade, with a half-smile, put down his book and ambled to the bed and lay down. Susannah returned to her word-making search. She and Becky had loved making words from names and phrases, challenging each other to see who could come up with the most words. Becky had found at least three hundred words in *Merry Christmas*. Susannah was determined to find more.

Forty minutes later, she finally put her work aside and came to her feet. She needed a break. She glanced over at Cade to find him sleeping soundly as she made her way to the kitchen. Grabbing a bottle of water out of the refrigerator, she quietly opened the back kitchen door and slipped outside. Leaving the door open, she settled herself on the patio bench that looked out over the clearing and to the trees beyond.

Her eyes went to the sky above. Cade was right. There was indeed a storm blowing in. The sky that had been such a summer blue just this morning was now overcast and filled with clouds; white and gray clouds, and darker blue-gray clouds.

The light breeze had turned both stronger and cooler, causing the trees they had walked through earlier to dance and sway. She could hear birds twittering as they flitted from branch to branch, waiting for the approaching storm. There was a faint smell of rain though there was no rain in sight.

Her eyes went back to the sky above. Though there were no bright sparks of lightening, deep, low rumbles of thunder could be heard in the distance.

A gust of cold air blew through and Susannah shivered. And then the first drop fell; a large raindrop the size of a half dollar. And then another and another. Within minutes a shower of them were spattering the ground, dancing in the dirt of the clearing. The birds twittering ceased. A flash of lighting suddenly split the sky. Thunder cracked and rumbled.

And then the skies opened up into a steady stream of rain.

"Impressive, isn't it?" came Cade's soft voice as he slipped onto the bench beside her.

"You can say that again," Susannah said her eyes flickering to him then back to the storm around them. It was indeed impressive. Though the raindrops were no longer as large as they had been, they were coming down with a force that had them bouncing. The winds had picked up and she shivered. Cade's arm immediately came around her, pulling her to him. "Do you get a lot of summer storms like this?" she asked after a moment.

He nodded. "A fair amount. They usually don't last."

"Do you think this one will?" It seemed to be getting darker and colder, not blowing over.

"It's hard to say, Susannah," he said glancing again at the sky. "This one might actually last through the evening."

They stayed outside only a short time longer, the colder air driving Susannah inside.

"Want some hot chocolate or coffee to warm you back up?" Cade asked, concerned with her shivering.

"Actually, hot chocolate sounds wonderful," Susannah said, wrapping her arms around her.

"Why don't you go close the front windows and find yourself a sweatshirt while I get it started."

Susannah willingly did as he suggested. Shutting the windows and finding herself a sweatshirt, she headed back to the kitchen. Cade was not only heating water for the chocolate, but had begun dinner as well. "Chili and cornbread," he told her when she asked. "The water should be ready in a few minutes."

Susannah sat down at the table with her clipboard, going back to her word searching as she waited. It wasn't long before Cade set a mug of hot chocolate down in front of her and sat down at the table himself.

"*Merry Christmas*, huh?" he commented, watching her work.

"Of course." She dimpled. "Becky claims she's made over three hundred words out of the letters. I intend to beat her at her own game."

"And I'm sure you can do it," Cade said with a grin. He knew how good Susannah was at making words out of other words. She had been doing it for as long as he had known her. "What about the word *each*?"

"Already got it," she told him.

"Okay...*mirth*?"

"Got it." She giggled.

"Okay," Cade breathed, studying the words a little longer this time. "What about *shimmer*?"

Her grin widened. "Now, that one I can use!" she said writing it down. "Thanks."

"Not a problem." He sat and helped her find three more words, then came to his feet and returned to his dinner preparations.

The dinner was wonderful, just perfect for such a cool evening. Cade had placed a slice of cornbread in bowls piled with chili and a sprinkling of jack cheese on top.

"You are one good cook," she said as she enjoyed it.

"Thank you. I happen to enjoy cooking."

"Who taught you to cook?"

"My grandparents, actually. I think it gave them something to do with me when I spent the summers with them." He shrugged. "Not that I minded."

"Liked to eat, huh?" she teased.

"You could say that," he said warmly.

She dimpled. "So what's for dessert?"

"Ice Cream, brownies, or pudding. Your choice."

"Brownies?" Susannah suggested hopefully.

"Good enough," he said. "I'll start them as soon as you finish the dishes."

"Fair enough." They finished their meal, cleaned up the kitchen, and then while Cade's brownies were baking in the oven, they started a game of dice. One game led into another and they spent the rest of the evening playing games and eating brownies. Susannah went to bed content, drifting to sleep within minutes.

It was several hours later that she came instantly awake; her every nerve screaming silent warnings. She didn't know what it was that had woke her. She lay without moving in the darkness of the cabin, her ears straining.

The cabin was silent. She could hear nothing save the pounding of her own heart and Cade's quiet intake of breath.

And then they both heard it again; the soft tread of feet on the patio; the quiet turn of the back door's handle. Her heart jumped. Rico?

It couldn't be! But she knew it could.

"Cade?" Her voice was just a terrified breath.

Cade was already slipping from the bed. "Get in the closet and lock the door," he told her quietly; urgently. Already he was slipping into his jeans, his gun in his hand. Susannah climbed out of bed as well, her entire body shaking with nerves.

"Cade?"

He took her hand and pulled her quickly to the closet. "Stay in here," he said. He thrust his cell phone at her. "If I'm not back in fifteen minutes, call the sheriff. Now lock the door."

With that he was gone.

Susannah stared after him a moment, then almost in afterthought, she shut the closet door and turned the deadbolt. She leaned apprehensively against the door, straining to hear. There was nothing; no sound. Just silence.

"*Dear God,*" she prayed.

Cade stole silently from the front porch after relocking the front door he had slipped through, and just as quietly, cautiously rounded the cabin, his gun drawn. He stopped as he reached the back corner, then darted a careful look.

Two forms could be seen at the back door of the cabin. One was testing the window while the other was trying to pick the lock. Cade, with a steady breath, rounded the corner and aimed his gun.

"Stop right where you are," he ordered.

The two – youths he realized – scrambled a moment then without even a glance in his direction, tore from the patio and off into the trees beyond.

Relief filled Cade as he watched them go. Youths. Just young thieves. That's all it had been. With another relieved breath, he unlocked the back cabin door and stepped back inside, relocking it behind him. He flipped on a light then quietly made his way to the closet door.

"Susannah," he called, knocking on the door. "It's okay, sweetheart. Come on out."

Susannah, who had been leaning in panicked apprehension against it as she had waited in agony, closed her eyes in relief as her legs almost gave out under her.

"Susannah?"

She fumbled with the deadbolt and opened the door. Cade; a strong, healthy, all-in-one-piece Cade stood there. "Oh, Cade!" she cried throwing herself against him. His arms closed around her.

"It's all right, Susannah," he soothed. "It wasn't Rico."

"You sure?"

"I'm sure. It was just a couple of youths trying to break in." He held her a moment, giving her the assurance she needed. Then lightly, "Got my cell-phone? I need to call this in."

Susannah roused herself, and with a deep, shaky breath, handed him the phone.

He took it with a brief smile and punched in the sheriff's number. Steering Susannah over to the front room chairs, he sat her down as he waited for John Ogdon to answer. He didn't have to wait long. With the sheriff on the line, he relayed the events. "There's really no need to come over tonight," Cade told him. "I'm afraid they took off in a scrambled hurry even with a gun pointing at them…Right…See you in the morning then."

Cade closed his phone and looked to Susannah. She was sitting on the edge of her chair, still visibly shaking. He stood and reached out a hand to her. "Come on, sweetheart. Let's go back to bed and get some needed sleep."

Susannah willingly took the hand offered and went with Cade, again crawling into his arms the moment they were in bed. Secure against him, she slowly relaxed and drifted off to sleep.

CHAPTER SEVENTEEN

A snap brought Susannah awake to bright sunlight. The smell of burning wood hit her almost instantly. Sitting up, she found that Cade was already up and had started a fire in the fireplace.

"It was rather chilly in here," he said when he realized she was awake. "You get back to sleep okay?" he asked lightly.

"Yes," she said.

"Any nightmares?"

"Not that I'm aware of."

"Good. Want coffee?"

"I'd love some," Susannah returned, then yawned. She climbed out of bed and realized immediately that Cade was right. The cabin was cold, especially the floor. Deciding she needed more warmth, she headed to the closet for clothes then disappeared into the bathroom to dress. Feeling warmer, she joined Cade in the front room area.

"Thank you," she said taking the cup of coffee he offered. "How come it's so cold this morning?"

"Remnants of yesterday's storm. There's still a cool wind outside."

"Has Sheriff Ogdon been by yet?" she asked hesitantly.

Cade shook his head. "Not yet, but soon, I imagine. How about some scrambled eggs, Canadian bacon, and toast for breakfast?"

"Sounds wonderful."

"You can stay here by the fire or join me in the kitchen," he told her lightly, noting she still looked a little rattled from the night's events. "Your choice."

Susannah joined him in the kitchen. It was colder in there but at least she wasn't on her own. "Your grandfather never put in a heater?" she asked.

"Actually there is one," he told her adding a dribble of water to the bowl of eggs before he began beating them. "But it's unnecessary during the summer. It'll warm back up, Susannah."

"I'm sure it will," she said sipping at her coffee. She jumped however as a knock sounded at the back kitchen door. Coffee splattered across the table. "Darn it!" she muttered.

"Relax, Susannah," Cade soothed, putting down his utensils. "It's John. Let him in, will you?"

Susannah came to her feet and opened the back kitchen door to the sheriff and let him inside, then retrieved a paper towel and cleaned up the coffee that she had spilled on the table.

"Thought you'd likely be here having breakfast about now," John said and grinned, removing his hat.

"I take it you'd like some?" Cade returned with a raised eyebrow.

"Of course," the sheriff admitted. "I haven't had a good breakfast for days. Maree and Justin are down in Ashland visiting her mother."

"When will they be back?" Cade asked, glancing at him.

John shrugged with a sigh. "A week from Saturday." It was evident he missed his wife and son.

"Well, you're welcome here any time," Cade told him. "So have a seat. It's almost ready." He turned to Susannah, "Mind pouring us more coffee?"

Susannah willingly refilled both hers and Cade's mugs then found a mug for the sheriff. Cade dished up the food, dividing it onto three plates. A minute later they were all eating.

"So tell me about last night," Sheriff Ogdon demanded as he ate.

Cade took a long sip of his coffee and set it down. "About three a.m. we were woke with the sound of someone trying to get in through the back door," Cade said. "I shoved Susannah into the closet and then slipped out the front door and around to the back. There were two youths, I figure somewhere between sixteen and twenty, one older than the other, at the back door trying to break in. One was checking out the door's window, the other trying to pick the lock."

"Did you get a good look at them?"

Cade shook his head. "One looked to be about five foot six, the other about five ten. Both were wearing sweatshirts with hoods, jeans, boots, as well as leather-like gloves. Unfortunately, they split faster than jack rabbits when I told them to freeze; didn't even look in my direction before they were off into the trees."

John Ogdon shook his head as he spooned more eggs into his mouth. "Too bad you couldn't have caught them. We've been having a rash of cabin and home break-ins. But this is the first time in this area, and, the first time it's been reported that they tried to break in with tenants in the home. Their M.O. has been to hit morning or afternoon when the owners were gone.

"What area have they been targeting?" Cade asked quietly.

"The other end of town, closer to the highway. Usually in the outside areas where the houses aren't so close together."

"Making it harder to be seen by neighbors," Susannah inserted.

"Unfortunately," he said with a heavy sigh, "Now it looks as if they're spreading out."

"And getting bolder," Cade added.

"Which I don't like in the least. I just hope we can get them before they actually hurt someone."

"I'll keep my eyes open, John," Cade promised. "If I can help you catch them, I will."

"That, Cade, would be a definite plus. Thanks, and thanks for breakfast," he added.

"You're more than welcome," Cade said, "More coffee?"

The sheriff shook his head and stood. "I'd best get back to my office and log this in." His eyes went to Susannah.

"Miss Susannah?"

Susannah's stomach jumped. "Yes?"

He sent her a smile. "I just want to assure you that though we've got problems of our own in catching these two punks, we're still on full alert with regards to Luis Rico. We'll be on a constant watch for him."

"Thank you," Susannah said sending him a smile, touched that he would go so far as to reassure her. He hardly knew her. Both she and Cade walked him to the door and watched him drive away.

"He's a nice man," Susannah commented as they shut the door.

"Yes he is," Cade agreed, ushering her back toward the kitchen. "Not to mention he's very good at his job. Come on," he said deciding it prudent to change the subject, "Let's get the kitchen cleaned up and go sit by the fire where it's warmer."

Susannah willingly washed and dried the dishes as Cade cleaned off the table and counters. He then led her back into the front room area where they both settled; Cade to his book and Susannah to her word searching. Cade fed the fire for another hour then let it slowly die out.

Susannah tired at last with making words, turned to the book she had started the day before. She still had trouble getting involved in it. The love life of two dinosaurs just didn't appeal to her. Deciding it was hopeless, she replaced the book back in the bookcase and looked for something else. She finally settled on a copy of *First to the Waterhole.* To her surprise it was a western comedy and easy to get into.

But not so easy that she wasn't aware of Cade putting his book down awhile later and disappearing toward the kitchen. Susannah put down her own book and followed.

"Hungry?" he asked when he realized she had followed him.

"I could eat or not," she said with a shrug.

"You okay?" He was eyeing her with concern.

"I'm fine," she said managing a smile. "Just trying to get my equilibrium back after last night," she admitted.

"I'm sorry you were scared," he told her softly.

"Try petrified," she said wryly. "I thought it was Rico."

"I know, but at least it wasn't."

Susannah bit her lip. "Cade…"

"I would have had him if it had been him," Cade soothed. "That's what I'm trained for. Now relax. You're in good hands."

"I know," Susannah said on a deep breath. She sat down at the table and folded her hands. "Are you going to miss this kind of work?" she asked looking up at him.

Cade's head shook. "I doubt it, Susannah. I may miss parts of it, but on the whole, no. I'm ready to give it up."

"Does your Chief know you're quitting?"

"I think he suspects," Cade answered opening the refrigerator. "Nothing much gets by him."

"When are you going to let him know?"

"As soon as Rico's been taken care of," he said with a smile. "Want soup and sandwiches?"

"Just soup and maybe some chips." Cade turned back to the cupboard, pulling out a can of soup. She watched him open it, then pour it into a pan and place it on the stove. He then pulled both a bag of potato chips and a bag of corn chips down and brought them over to the table.

"Milk, tea, soda, or water?" he asked.

"Milk."

"Soup should be ready in a minute," he told her before heading back to the refrigerator. He poured two glasses of milk and set them onto the table, then checking on the soup, dished out two bowls.

"Thank you," she said quietly as he placed one down in front of her.

"Not a problem." They ate quietly for a time, each mulling over their own thoughts. Susannah finally looked up at Cade.

"Have you heard anything from Brock?" she asked timidly.

"Nothing new," he admitted lightly. "But he's safe and recovering, sweetheart."

Susannah picked up a chip and munched on it absently. "Cade, do you think we could call Brock?"

Cade immediately shook his head. "It's not safe, Susannah."

"But…"

"Honey, he's under secure protection right now, just as you are. It's not safe for either one of you to breach that just to talk."

Susannah let out a frustrated sigh. She knew he was right, but still… "Could we go on down to the creek after we eat then?"

"Let's give the ground time to dry out first," he said. "It got pretty soaked yesterday. I'll take you down tomorrow. I promise. Okay?"

A heavy sigh came out of her.

"How 'bout a board game or cards for now?" he suggested lightly.

"I'll go for that," she said knowing he was trying to be accommodating despite everything.

They played board games for several hours before Cade returned to his book. Susannah with nothing better to do went to lie down. Though she tossed and turned for a while, she finally drifted to sleep, sleeping until Cade's rumblings in the kitchen woke her. She was surprised to realize that it was already 6:00 in the evening. Climbing from the bed, she joined him in the kitchen.

"Have a nice nap?" he asked lightly.

A yawn escaped her. "Actually I did. Is there anything I can do to help?"

"Keep me company?"

She eyed him a moment as she sat down. "You know," she said solemnly, "I *can* cook, and rather well at that."

"I know," he returned just as solemnly. "I don't mind doing the cooking."

"So long as you don't have to do the cleanup," she added shrewdly.

"Well, there is that." He laughed softly, his eyes sparkling.

"I see."

"I'll tell you what," he said compromisingly. "I'll do the cooking this month and you can do it next month. Deal?"

"Deal as long as you do the cleanup next month," she said, adding her own stipulation.

"Fair enough," he said.

"So what are we having for dinner?"

"Leftover chili so no complaints."

"I'm not complaining," she said trying to hide her smile.

"Better not," he growled, happy to see a smile back on her face. He dished up the cornbread and chili and set them down on the table along with two glasses of milk.

Dinner was light and relaxed. Cade teased her constantly throughout the meal, Susannah giving as much as she was getting. It was both enjoyable and comfortable, the contentment of it staying with Susannah as she later cleaned the kitchen.

Too restless to sit and read, she grabbed a sweatshirt from the closet. "Is it alright if I go sit outside?" she questioned deciding it was best if she had Cade's approval.

"That's fine, Susannah," he said, then suddenly, "Want company?"

"Only if you want to come out," she replied. "Otherwise I'll just leave the door open."

"Just let me finish this chapter and I'll be out," he promised.

Susannah, not minding in the least, meandered outside and settled on the patio bench. It was quiet outside. The winds had died, leaving nothing more than a light, gentle breeze that was hardly noticeable. The sky above was still blue though the sun was heading for its final decent. The air smelled fresh and clean. She could hear the birds in the trees beyond the clearing but their twittering did not seem to disrupt the surrounding quiet; they were more a part of it Susannah decided.

She took a deep, content breath, enjoying the quiet as she took in the view before her. The back clearing was the size of a small backyard, and just that; a clearing. The brush and trees and grasses had been cleared away, leaving only an area of dirt. No doubt to protect the cabin from fire, Susannah guessed. Her eyes continued to wander.

The clearing was edged with long, thick green grass and the deeper lush green trees just beyond; trees that were tall and full and majestic with smaller trees that were just starting to gain their stature.

There were several large boulders of different sizes gathered together in the left far corner of the clearing, the largest standing a good ten to twelve feet up from the ground. Susannah took pleasure in the natural arrangement of the boulders, for they seemed to add a sense of symmetry to the property. Her eyes swung back around the area and suddenly stopped. Two dark, golden eyes were staring intently at her from across the clearing; two dark golden eyes of an animal.

The animal was standing in the grass at the far edge of the clearing on three legs, the forth was poised; raised as if it had been about to take another step. Susannah's first thought was that it was a large dog, but the longer she watched it, the more certain she was that it was not a dog.

It was a big and lean, with long legs and a thick, almost bushy tail. Its fur was a grizzled color; a mixture of brown and black and gray, with a white lower chest and under-belly. Its head hosted a long, white muzzle with a wide, rich brown stripe down its center and a large, coal black nose.

Susannah's stomach jumped as realization took hold. She was looking at a wolf; a wild timber wolf. Her immediate inherent reaction was to get up and dart inside the cabin, but the urge became weaker and weaker as she continued to gaze at the animal. Despite the close distance of the wolf, something inside Susannah was telling her that it was no threat.

Awed pleasure bubbled through her as she continued to watch the beast. *She was looking at an actual timber wolf…in the wild!*

"Oh, my," she whispered. She wanted to call for Cade, to share the experience with him but was too afraid that any sound from her would frighten the wolf back into the trees.

There was no doubt that the wolf was alert. His head was raised, his ears straight up. His eyes were ever-watchful. Yet Susannah had the distinct impression that all was not well with the animal though she could not reason why. But then the wolf took two limping steps bringing it to the very edge of the clearing where it sat on its haunches. His right front paw again came up as if it was causing him pain. He licked it once, then his head rose once again as he continued to stare steadily at her. His round, dark golden eyes appeared almost human and Susannah couldn't help but feel he was reaching out to her. There seemed an almost cautious hopefulness to his intent look.

"Oh, you poor thing," she whispered, her heart going out to the animal. "You're injured." It meant the animal couldn't hunt; couldn't eat or protect himself. Was that why it had come to her?

But wild animals didn't normally approach people, she knew, not even sick or injured wild animals. Not unless it had known man somewhere in its past. Had this wolf been raised by humans? Maybe it was a hybrid; half wolf, half dog? No, Susannah's head shook as she studied it. It was a wolf; pure wolf. She could not imagine it being anything else.

Susannah's heart went out to it as she sat and watched the lone timber wolf. She wanted to do something for it; anything for it, but she couldn't think of what. The alertness about the animal told her it was unlikely he would let her approach him in any way, let alone examine its foot. It was too cautious, too watchful. Not that she would make such an attempt. She knew better. It wasn't safe to approach any wild animal, and definitely not an injured one.

But she could feed it, couldn't she?

Susannah slowly, carefully, came to her feet. The wolf's head rose up fractionally, his intent golden eyes vigilantly fixed on her. Her eyes still on the wolf, Susannah backed herself toward the door of the cabin, one slow step at a time. She had just reached the door when two large hands came down on her shoulders.

The unexpected action startled Susannah and she let out a yelp. The wolf, ever alert, came immediately on its feet. Cade backed Susannah quietly into the cabin.

"Cade!" she hissed, wrenching herself from his grasp. "You scared it!" The wolf was gone.

"Your yelp scared it," he corrected without a qualm.

"Well, if you hadn't grabbed me –!"

"You were backing into me," he said reasonably.

"Well, you could have stepped back out of the way," she retorted. She turned and walked over to the refrigerator. Opening it, she pulled out one of the large, thick steaks.

"What do you think you're going to do with that?" Cade demanded.

"I'm going to feed it to that wolf," Susannah said defiantly.

"The hell you are."

"Cade, it's injured! A wolf can't hunt like that. It will starve if we don't help it! And I'm not about to let that happen!"

Cade's head shook. "Susannah, that timber wolf's already gone."

"It'll be back," she said stubbornly. It would! And she wasn't about to ignore its plea for help. She set the steak down on the table and began tearing open its packaging.

"Honey," Cade tried again, "It isn't safe to try and feed it. It's an injured animal."

"I don't care Cade! I'm doing it anyway!"

Cade eyed Susannah, taking in her stubborn, determined actions. He knew without a doubt that she wasn't going to back down. She'd try and feed that beast one way or another the minute his back was turned if he tried to stop her now whether she caught sight of it again or not. It was a foolish, unsafe thing to do, but an unsafe thing he knew he wasn't going to be able to talk her out of.

"Alright," he agreed against his better judgment. "But we do it my way, okay?"

Susannah stared suspiciously over at him.

"First," he said, "We decide just where we're going to feed him before we take out the meat."

"Why not leave it right where we saw him?" Susannah said reasonably.

Cade's head shook. "Too dangerous, Susannah. He could be just inside the trees and depending on how hungry and sick he is, he could easily force an attack. We'll set out the meat about twenty feet to the left. It's far enough away from where he disappeared and a fair distance from the path."

"Are you sure he'll find it?"

"Unless his sense of smell is damaged, he'll find it," Cade returned. *If* he was still around to look for it, he added silently. "Now, I want your word that you'll just put the meat down and leave. No stopping. No calling out to him. You just put the meat down and come immediately back to the cabin."

"I will," she agreed, anxious to get out there. If she waited too long, the wolf was likely to disappear for good.

"And you don't go out there alone," Cade added stolidly. "I go with you."

"Okay! Can we go now?"

"Okay. We can go." But a moment later he stopped her with a sudden thought. "Let me go get something first. I'll be right back."

Susannah with a frustrated sigh, watched as Cade dashed out of the kitchen. He was back a moment later, a medication bottle in his hand. "Give me the meat," he demanded.

Susannah handed him the meat, then watched as he set it down on the table, and grabbing a knife from the drawer, cut a slit in it.

"What are you doing?"

Cade held up the medication bottle. "Antibiotics. Maybe it will help him recover." Shaking out a pill from the bottle he had brought in, he shoved it into the slit. His eyes again went to Susannah. "There's no guarantee he'll eat it, but it's worth a try."

"Definitely worth a try," she said. Maybe with antibiotics in its system, the wolf would have a chance to fight off any infection that had set in.

"Then let's go give it a try," he said on a deep breath. He handed her the meat and followed her outside. Stopping her at the edge of the patio, he pointed out exactly where he wanted her to place the meat. "Slow and easy, Susannah," he warned. "Then leave immediately, just as slowly."

"I will," she assured him. Her glance at him however had her stopping. His gun was drawn. "Cade."

"Just for protection, Susannah," he stated, not about to let her go near that injured wolf with meat in her hands without the gun. Healthy wolves didn't attack; sick, hungry, injured wolves did. "If he attacks, I shoot. Otherwise I'll leave him be. Now go."

Susannah's heart was pounding in both nerves and excitement as she walked slowly toward the spot Cade had pointed out. Cade, she knew, was just several yards behind her. There was no sign of the timber wolf, but that didn't mean he wasn't there. Susannah hoped he was. If he had left, wandered into some other cabin's backyard, it was likely he could be shot, not fed and she didn't want that.

There was a small indentation at the edge of the clearing where she was to leave the meat, and Susannah, with just a moment's hesitation, placed the thick steak into. Then, as she had promised, she backed away and turning, walked back to Cade.

Cade's arm came around her as she met up with him and they quietly walked to the cabin together. He led her inside under her protest. Susannah relaxed as she came to understand his reasoning. The timber wolf was not likely to come out and eat with them in sight. Susannah had to agree.

"Do you think I could watch out the window?" she asked.

"If you remain still," Cade conceded, "Though I doubt he'll come for it before dark."

"True," Susannah said, but she watched out the window for a while regardless. As predicted, there was no sign of the wolf. Eventually she wandered into the front of the cabin and sat.

"Cade?"

He looked up from his book with a raised eyebrow.

"Do you think he'll be alright?"

"I don't know, Susannah," he said. He sighed, closing his book. "I don't know how sick or injured he is, and that may not be his only problem."

"What do you mean?" she asked looking up at him.

Cade took an unconsciousness breath, trying to decide how to say it. He didn't want Susannah to look at this through rose-colored glasses. He wanted her facing the truth. "It's evident this wolf has been around humans," he said, "Most likely a hybrid or a wolf that was taken in as a pet when it was young. In any case, he's now out in the wild, most likely dropped off by some owner who no longer wanted him. And it's more than likely he has no real concept in how to fend for himself. Wolves are taught at an early age how to hunt and how to protect themselves by the older members of their pack. This wolf may not have gotten that training. So even if it does heal, he may not be able to hunt well enough to stave off starvation. He may continue to seek out man for his needs and consequently may seek out the wrong man and get himself shot for his efforts."

"I know, Cade. But he didn't appear under-nourished," she said, "Just injured."

Cade willingly conceded the point. The timber wolf hadn't looked under-nourished. But that didn't mean it could hunt. There was no telling when the animal had been let loose, or had escaped its captivity. It could have been as recently as yesterday.

Susannah sat back and mulled that over. She knew Cade was probably right, but she didn't want to accept it. She couldn't stand the thought. And besides, even if the wolf had been released into the wild without any life skills, it deserved a chance, didn't it? She again looked up at Cade.

"Well, if it comes back, I'm going to keep feeding it," she told him belligerently.

"For how long?"

"Until it's well again," she said.

"And then what?" Cade demanded quietly.

"Then it will be up to him," Susannah said evenly. Then at his look. "That wolf deserves a chance, Cade. It's not his fault he was taken out of the wild. And who knows, given the chance, he might actually succeed."

If he lasted that long, Cade thought though he didn't voice it. "Okay, Susie. You can feed your wolf under the same guidelines as today, but only for a month. If he's not well by then it means he isn't going to be. And if he is well, then it's time for him to learn to find his own food."

Susannah's heart jumped. "You'll give me a month to feed him, a whole entire month?"

"I'll give you one entire month."

A brilliant smile came out of her, one that lit through Cade like warm sunshine. The next thing he knew she was in his lap, hugging him. Cade took advantage of the situation and found her lips with his own. It wasn't a long kiss, but it was warm and heady and satisfying.

"Thank you, Cade!" she said when he let her go.

For the kiss, or for the opportunity to feed the beast? Unfortunately he figured he knew her answer to that one.

"You're welcome…I think," he returned with a rueful grin. "Just remember, you don't go off that patio when the wolf's in sight without me there. In fact, you don't go off the patio without me period."

Susannah was too happy to refute the order. "I won't. I promise."

CHAPTER EIGHTEEN

Susannah was awake early the next morning. She found herself snuggled into Cade who appeared still sound asleep. She slipped carefully from his arms and off the bed and then made her way to the bathroom where she showered and dressed. To her surprise Cade was at the bathroom door waiting when she exited.

"Start the coffee, will you?" he half-asked, half-ordered as he slipped into the bathroom with his own clothes.

Susannah, anxious to see if the wolf had returned, stared out the back door's window. There was no sign of the timber wolf, nor could she tell if the wolf had taken the meat. She let out a heavy, disappointed breath and begrudgingly started the coffee pot, then with a resigned sigh, started breakfast as well. It wasn't likely Cade would let her outside until they had both eaten anyway.

If the man was surprised that she had started breakfast, he didn't show it. He merely kissed her on the cheek, poured himself a mug of coffee, and sat down at the table with a newspaper.

"Where did the newspaper come from?" she asked, surprised to see it.

"I ordered a subscription the other morning," he said, flickering a glance her way. "I figured it wouldn't hurt since we'll be here awhile. It'll keep us up to date with the national news as well as the local."

"I see," Susannah murmured turning back to the stove. She tested the temperature of the frying pan and added butter. Once it had melted, she dipped a slice of bread in her egg batter and stuck it in the pan. It wasn't long before she had a stack of warm French toast. She served them to Cade along with a bowl of bananas.

"Milk or orange juice?" she asked opening the refrigerator.

"Milk is fine," he said setting his paper aside. "It looks good," he added as she set everything on the table. "Thank you, sweetheart."

Susannah ignored the endearment having come to realize that it was no more than a common greeting to him. She wouldn't have put it past the man to call all the girls he knew *sweetheart*. Not that Susannah was thinking about that at the moment. Her thoughts were on the wolf outside.

"Do you think Timbers came back and ate the meat?" she asked as they began eating.

His eyebrow rose. "Timbers, huh?"

She shrugged to hide her flush. "Well, I just thought he deserved a name. And since he is a timber wolf…He is, isn't he, a timber wolf?"

"Yes, he's a timber wolf," Cade laughed softly, "Though scientifically he's considered a gray wolf."

"A gray wolf?"

Cade nodded. "There are really only two species of wolf in the world; the gray wolf and the red wolf, though the gray wolf is also widely known as the timber wolf."

"What about the arctic wolf?"

Cade smiled indulgently. "Also a gray wolf though some are now beginning to think of it and the European gray wolf as a sub-species of the gray wolf, as is the Mexican gray wolf."

Susannah shook her head. It was all scientific hogwash as far as she was concerned. An arctic wolf was an arctic wolf, a red wolf was a red wolf, and a timber wolf was a timber wolf! "Well, he's still a timber wolf in my books," she said to Cade.

"Mine, too," Cade acknowledged with a warm smile.

"And speaking of timber wolves, can we go out and see if Timbers has taken the meat?"

"As soon as I finish my coffee," he returned, cradling his mug in his hand.

Deflated, Susannah blew her bangs from her face with a frustrated breath.

Cade laughed setting his mug down and coming to his feet. "Okay. Let's go see if your wolf took the meat."

Timbers was nowhere in sight when they walked outside, neither was the meat when they looked. Not that they were sure that it had been the wolf who had taken it. Susannah was elated regardless. She was sure it had been Timbers who had taken the meat. Now she only hoped the wolf would return.

She and Cade walked back to the cabin where Cade insisted in cleaning the kitchen since she had cooked breakfast. Susannah, leaving him to it, made the bed, cleaned the bathroom and dusted the cabin in return. She had just sat down for a break when Cade came in and pulled her to her feet.

"Come on, woman. You're driving us to town."

"I am?" she asked in surprise.

"You are," he said, ushering her out the door and locking it. "And if you beat me into the Bearcat, I'll buy you a present."

"A present, huh?"

"Yup!"

"Deal!" Susannah said and was off.

Despite the fact that she had a head start, and the fact that Cade had to round the SUV in order to get in, Susannah didn't win. Cade's door closed several seconds before hers.

"Drat!" she muttered. "You can't be that fast!"

"Training," he murmured, hiding his amusement.

"Still going to buy me that present?" she asked brightly.

"Nope."

Susannah deflated. "So what are we going to town for then?" she asked as she started the Bearcat.

"Well, considering you're determined to feed that timber wolf, we're going in to buy it some meat. I'm not about to let you feed him the rest of the steaks still in the refrigerator," he added casting a look at her. "That was an expensive, high quality steak you fed him last night."

"I know," she admitted. "I'm sorry about that but I had to feed him something."

"You're forgiven this time," he said gruffly, "So as long as it doesn't happen again."

Cade himself was quite determined that it wouldn't happen again. He bought over thirty pounds of fresh beef, pork, and venison. "I'd buy more," he told her, "but it wouldn't fit into the refrigerator. We'll come back when this runs out."

Sticking the meat in the ice chest along with a bag of ice and a few other groceries that he had picked up, he ushered Susannah down the street to the small drugstore that was more a country department store than a drugstore. There he picked up a shallow washtub, an outside hose, and several other items.

"Did you buy me a present?" she asked.

"Nope."

"Brute!" she muttered.

Cade only laughed and ushered her out the door, then led her back to the SUV where he opened the door for her and helped her in. Placing his purchases into the back, he climbed into the vehicle and seat-belted himself in. "To the cabin," he ordered.

They unloaded the Bearcat together when they returned. "What's the washtub for?" she asked when he brought it through the cabin and placed it out on the patio along with the water hose.

"Water," he explained to her. "Wolves need a lot of water, especially after they eat. Fresh, clean water, Susannah. So you're going to have to change it daily."

"I will," she readily promised. She was surprised he had thought of it. She hadn't. "How come you know so much about wolves?" she asked curiously.

"My grandfather." Cade glanced up and smiled. "He taught me a lot about nature and life in general."

Apparently not how to let down girls came unbidden to Susannah's mind. She shook the thought away. Cade was already heading back into the cabin.

Great, she groaned silently, following him. "You're not going to put the water out now?" she asked in disappointment. If he put out the water now, maybe it would entice Timbers into coming in for a drink.

"Got to find the handle for the faucet," he mumbled as he dug through a kitchen drawer. He came up with the handle and moving Susannah out of the way, walked back outside. Picking up the washtub, he headed for the water faucet. He attached the hose he had bought, then the handle.

"Susannah, turn on the water when I tell you." Without waiting for her acknowledgment, he walked cautiously across the clearing with the washtub and hose. She watched as he placed it firmly down just a foot or two from where she had placed the meat the night before. His hand came up and she turned on the water, watching for him to signal when to turn it off again. The signal came just several minutes later.

Susannah turned off the water, removing the handle as she did so. She then stood and waited as Cade walked back to the patio. She handed him the handle immediately.

"Why do you remove the handle?"

He shrugged. "Habit, I guess. My grandmother was always afraid that someone would come in and waste her water during the times she wasn't living here."

"I see."

"Come on," he said taking her hand. "Let's go inside. It's doubtful your wolf will show up before evening."

Susannah however hoped Cade was wrong and gathering her clipboard and pencils, she settled herself on the patio where she continued working on finding and making words.

But Cade had been right. The wolf did not make any appearance, at least not by the time lunch was ready. With an unconscious sigh, Susannah went in and joined Cade at the table. It was a leisurely lunch. Cade asked if she had seen her wolf but they didn't dwell on the subject. Instead they talked of other things. Susannah eventually asked what he had planned for the afternoon.

Cade shrugged. "Well, I had planned on hiking down to the creek with you, but if you'd rather stay in hopes of your wolf showing up, I can always start the new book I bought."

"You don't think he'll show up," she said watching him.

"Wolves are generally active during dusk, or dawn," he told her. "If he does show up, it most likely won't be until then if he's still around."

"He's still around," Susannah said more hopefully than adamantly. "But if what you say is true, that Timbers most likely won't come back until dusk, then we might as well go on down to the creek."

Cade was surprised with her easy acquiesce, though he was careful not to let her see it. "Okay," he said coming to his feet. "Let's get this kitchen clean and go on down to the creek."

It took them barely fifteen minutes to clean up the kitchen. Cade, picking up two bottles of water, locked the door to the cabin and led Susannah across the clearing to the trees beyond. Both were watching intently for any sign of the wolf; Susannah hopefully, Cade much more cautiously. No sign of the wild animal however, was seen. They continued leisurely down to the creek then walked along it to the cascades. There, Susannah played in the creek while Cade sat and watched. Eventually Susannah came back to him.

"Can we follow the creek further upstream?" she asked.

Cade's eyes quickly swept the surrounding area. "I don't see why not," he said, coming to his feet.

They climbed up the cascades' bank and over the top then walked quietly along the meandering creek.

"How far does it go up?" Susannah asked out of curiosity.

"About a mile before we hit the creek's headwaters. You don't want to go that far, do you?" He didn't sound at all enthusiastic.

"Why not?" Susannah said hiding her grin and feeling decidedly pleased. If he didn't want to go, then she definitely did! And he had no choice but to come with her!

Cade ushered her forward with his hand, hiding his own grin. He had counted on Susannah's reaction. After all, he had no objections in walking the extra mile with her despite what he had led her to believe. He wanted to be with her, and he definitely welcomed the exercise. Sitting around doing nothing was just not his style.

It took a solid twenty minutes to reach the beginning of Rocky Creek. Susannah stared at the small pool of calm water. "This is the creek's headwaters?" she asked in surprise.

"Yup. Not what you expected?" he asked lightly.

"Not exactly," Susannah admitted. "With the term *headwaters* I was expecting something more grandeur or exciting."

"Headwaters, is just a term referring to the beginning of a stream or river," Cade explained. "Disappointed?"

"Not at all," Susannah assured him, her eyes again going back to the small, calm pool of water. Moss grew lush green along its banks, bordered by grass, brush and trees that added to the quiet peace that seemed to surround the area. Sunbeams danced on the clear water as it cascaded gently over the pool's edge and down its shallow, rocky path into the deeper creek bed below. "It's such a beautiful, peaceful spot," she said softly.

A soft smile filtered through Cade at her obvious pleasure. "It's actually fed by an underground spring," he informed her quietly. "The water seems to seep up from the bottom of the pool and trickle over. Many great rivers start in a pool of water in just the same way," he added.

"It's so beautiful," she said again, then added on a sigh, "And I would have to leave my camera back at the cabin this time." She hadn't thought to bring her camera. After all, she hadn't expected to go beyond the cascades, and she already had enough pictures of them. Darn it! She should have known better.

Cade grinned as he sat down on a nearby rock. "Don't worry about it, sweetheart. I've got mine," he said reaching in his pocket for it. "Why don't you go over there and I'll snap a few pictures of you at the headwaters."

Susannah with an unsure glance at the man did as she was told. But Cade merely snapped several pictures of her from different angles then held the camera out to her.

Susannah took it from him with a grin. She took pictures of the pool and the surrounding area from several different points and then snapped several of Cade as he settled back on his rock.

"Enough of the pictures," he ordered gruffly, holding out his hand. "Come sit down and just enjoy the beauty of this place," he said as he motioned her to sit down on the rock beside him.

Susannah handed him back the camera and willingly did as he suggested, sitting down beside him. A contented sigh came out of her. So comfortable and at peace in this beautiful little haven, she was hardly aware when Cade's arms slipped around her and he brought her gently against him; was hardly aware of the kiss that was planted on the top of her head. She simply sat and soaked up the tranquility of it all.

It was a nearby snap of a branch that brought them both instantly up onto their feet. Susannah's first thought was the wolf; Cade's was Rico. They both cautiously looked around but could see nothing out of the ordinary. No wolf. No Rico. And no other sound. Susannah looked to Cade to find his hand on his gun as he continued to assess the situation. Eventually he turned back to her.

"Relax," he ordered softly. "It was most likely just an animal."

"Do you think it could have been Timbers?"

"I doubt it," Cade answered. He reached out and took her hand in his. "Come on. I think it's time we head back to the cabin," he said lightly.

He didn't hurry as he led her back down the creek. He appeared calm and relaxed for Susannah's sake, but he was as alert as ever; his eyes continually surveying their surroundings as they walked.

Susannah's eyes, too, continued to watch carefully around them, though not for Rico. Her mind was on the wolf. Could it have been Timbers? Had he come down to the creek for water and happened to see them? Was he, by chance, following them? She saw no sign of him.

Nor was the wolf anywhere around the cabin when they reached it. With a disappointed sigh she followed Cade inside.

CHAPTER NINETEEN

"Cade, is it alright if I go put out some meat?"

Dinner was over and the evening was settling in. Susannah was impatient to put the meat out, in hopes of enticing the wolf back. So far there had been no sign of the animal.

"Let's wait and see if he's still around first," Cade suggested instead.

Susannah deflated. "Do we really have to?"

"It's the wise thing to do," Cade returned.

"I know." After all, she didn't want to draw in and feed any other wild animal, or waste the meat. A sigh came out of her.

"Come on," Cade said taking her hand. "Let's go sit and see if he shows up."

Though Cade really did not expect the timber wolf to show up again, he sat on the patio bench with Susannah regardless.

"Cade?" came her soft voice.

He raised an eyebrow.

"Would you let me put out the meat for Timbers even if he doesn't show up?"

Cade tempered his sigh. "Alright, Susannah," came his quiet reply. "If we don't see him by nightfall, I'll let you put out the meat regardless but just for tonight. After tonight, if we don't see him, we don't feed him."

Relief spread through Susannah. "You know, Cade Candlewood," she said leaning against him, "There are times you're not such a bad guy after all."

"Why, thank you, kind lady," he said solemnly as his arm wrapped lightly around her. "You're not so bad yourself. Now hush. You don't want to scare your wolf off."

So much for compliments, Susannah thought sourly. But Cade was right. Again. The timber wolf wasn't likely to come out into the open if they were talking. Would Timbers come out at all?

Twenty minutes later, he did. They didn't see him approach. He was just suddenly there, watching them from the very same spot he had occupied the day before at the edge of the clearing. Like the day before, the wolf stood silently on three legs, his right front paw raised from the ground, his golden eyes vigilant. He watched them a long moment, as still as a statue, then suddenly sat on his haunches. His steady gaze did not waver from them. Susannah's heart jumped.

"Cade, he's back."

"I know," came his whispered reply. The wolf had surprised Cade; he hadn't expected that it would come back. He took a closer look at the beast. Susannah was right. Though Timbers was lean and slightly scruffy, he was still big and sturdy, giving the distinct impression of being healthy...except for the right paw. It was evident the wolf was still in pain over it. He was again holding it off the ground.

"Can I feed him?" Susannah whispered her eyes still on the animal.

"Alright, Susannah," Cade said, "But no sudden moves. Let's not scare him any more than we have to."

They came to their feet slowly. Timbers, ever alert, came to his feet as well, though he didn't disappear. His eyes remained constant on them. Cade, his eyes on the wolf, eased Susannah backwards to the cabin's door, then inside.

"Cade! He's still there!" Susannah beamed.

"I know," Cade said with a grim smile, "You go retrieve the bottle of antibiotics from the bathroom and I'll pull out the meat."

Susannah dashed to the bathroom and with the medication bottle in her hand returned to the kitchen. Cade had already unwrapped several steaks and was in the process of slitting the meat with a knife when she walked back in.

"Shake one out for me," he requested with a quick glance at her.

Susannah shook out one of the antibiotic tablets, noting for the first time that they had been meant for Cade himself.

"Aren't these yours?" she asked, handing the tablet to him.

"Yup," he said absently as he shoved the tablet into the slit he had created in the steak. "They were given to me for the gunshot wound."

"But why aren't you taking them?"

Cade looked up. "Relax, honey. I was given two bottles. I just finished the first bottle this morning. The second bottle there was given just in case I had any lingering infection which I don't. And, considering your wolf does…" Cade stopped and shrugged ruefully. He knew the animal could possibly die from the medication. After all, the medication was for man, not beast. But the wolf would likely die from his injury if he didn't give it to him. So why not give it a try?

With another rueful smile he handed the meat over to Susannah then followed her outside.

Timbers seemed to stiffen with alertness as they came back out, then with a last look, turned and limped back into the trees.

Susannah looked to Cade.

"Go ahead," he said, relieved the animal had moved back. "He'll come for it, Susannah."

Susannah, with a brief smile, stepped off the patio. As before, Cade stayed several yards behind her as she walked out with the meat, his eyes scanning; his gun in his hand, ready to protect her should the need arise.

There was no need. Susannah put down the meat, briefly checked the water, and then joined Cade who walked her back to the cabin.

Susannah, eager to see if the wolf would come back immediately for the meat, planted herself at the window. For the first five minutes she waited in vain, but then suddenly, she caught sight of the wolf.

His head lowered, his ears up and alert, Timbers cautiously limped out from the trees and straight to the meat. With a last look toward the cabin, he picked the meat up and carried it off.

"Cade! He took it!"

"So I see," Cade said from right behind her. "Let's just hope he eats the antibiotic with it."

"He will," Susannah said confidently, her eyes still searching out the window for the timber wolf. She wasn't sure how long it would take him to eat the meat, but she was sure he would be back for the water.

Cade shook his head in amusement and left her to it. Susannah was hardly aware of him leaving. A short half hour later, Timbers was back, drinking the water left out for him. She watched until he finally disappeared again.

With a happy sigh, Susannah went and joined Cade in the front room area. He glanced up at her but returned to his book with only a brief smile.

Susannah let out a breath. She was too wound up to just sit and read or work on words. "Cade, want to play cards or dice or something?"

"I'll go for that," he said readily, closing his book. "Why don't you go make us some popcorn while I lock up the front windows?"

They spent the rest of the evening munching on popcorn and playing both dice and cards. Susannah drifted contentedly off to sleep that night wrapped in Cade's arms.

To her surprise, Cade was already up and gone when she woke the next morning. *Gone?*

Her heart jumped as she slipped out of bed. It jumped again as she heard a thud from outside, then another. It took her a minute to realize someone was chopping wood.

Most likely Cade, she reasoned though she checked out the window just to be sure. Her nerves eased with the verification. Cade was once again splitting wood out in the back clearing. Susannah turned back and made the bed before heading for the bathroom where she showered and dressed. She then stepped out onto the back patio. Cade was still splitting wood despite the large pile that was already stacked up against the side of the cabin.

"You sure we need that much wood?"

"Nope," he answered as he picked up another log. "I'm sure I need the exercise." Another log split.

Susannah watched him another minute. "Want something to drink?"

"I'd love something to drink," he said before picking up another log. Susannah watched him split it in half then turned and walked back into the kitchen. She fixed herself a mug of coffee then fixed Cade a tall glass of iced tea. She took it out to him carrying her own mug of coffee as well. Handing him his, she sat down. Cade downed the whole glass of tea then returned to his activity. He split wood for another twenty minutes before he called it quits and joined her. "Good morning," he greeted her, kissing her lightly; warmly, on the lips.

"Good morning." Susannah flushed in return, surprised with the kiss.

Cade's eyes danced. "Want breakfast?"

"If you're cooking."

"I'm cooking," he said and smiled in assurance. "Are you going to come keep me company?" Already he was pulling her to her feet.

"I guess I am," she said surrendering to his insistence. She let him drag her into the kitchen and sat at the table while he cooked. This morning it was bacon and eggs, hash browns and toast. Susannah had another mug of coffee with it while Cade had a large glass of orange juice.

"Cade, when do you think I should change Timber's water?" she asked eventually.

"Already done," he said.

"You did it?"

"Yup." He cast a cautious glance at her. "Thought I might as well as I was already out there."

"Thanks." She sighed unconsciously, wishing she had been up to do it herself. "Did he drink much of it?"

"Most of it."

Pleasure filled her. "I'm glad."

"So am I. Look," he added, coming to his feet. "I'm going to go sweep off the porch while you clean the kitchen." With another smile, he locked the back kitchen door and went whistling through the cabin. Susannah heard the front door open though she didn't hear it close. With a sigh, she turned and picked up the table, then cleaned the kitchen.

She glanced out the window often, looking for any sign of Timbers, but the wolf didn't come in sight. She knew it wouldn't do any good sitting outside waiting for him. As Cade had said, it wasn't likely she would see the timber wolf before dusk.

Feeling bored and restless, she meandered out to the front porch to find Cade. He was sitting in one of the porch chairs, staring out toward the road. He looked up however the moment she appeared in the doorway.

"Come sit down and relax," he said.

Susannah walked over and sat down. "The porch looks nice," she commented.

"Thanks. You okay?"

"Just bored," she admitted on a sigh. "There's really not a lot to do around here."

"I'm sorry about that, sweetheart. Want to go down to the creek?"

Susannah shook her head. "I really don't want to do anything except maybe get on with my life."

"Just hang in there, Susie. This won't last forever. I promise you."

"I know. I just wish Rico would make some stupid mistake and get caught now."

"You and me both."

They spent another half hour on the patio before Cade ushered her into the Bearcat. He took the wheel this time and they spent the rest of the morning just driving around the back roads. Cade reminisced while he drove, telling Susannah about past incidents and giving her tidbits of what his grandfather had taught him. He stopped several times as they went along to show her what he considered points of interest, one which was a waterfall.

Susannah's boredom faded in the light of the new activity. She enjoyed traveling around the back roads; enjoyed listening to Cade reminiscing about his boyhood adventures. But her restlessness came back in full force once they returned to the cabin and had lunch. She cleaned the kitchen then tried to get involved in the book she had picked out earlier. When that failed, she gave in and took a nap, unaware of Cade's concerned glance as she slept.

Cade was still reading in the front when she woke late in the afternoon. "About time you resurfaced," he said with a teasing growl.

"Go soak your head!" she retorted, though there was no heat in the command.

"Go change," he countered. "I'm taking you out to dinner."

That surprised Susannah. "Really?" she asked.

"Really," he said. "So go get ready!"

It took Susannah just over twenty minutes to change, brush out her hair, and to add just a touch of lipstick. Cade was just slipping into a clean shirt of his own.

"Ready?"

"Ready," she said, wondering exactly where he was taking her. She stopped suddenly. "What about feeding Timbers?"

"We'll be back before dusk," he assured her, escorting her outside and locking the front door of the cabin. "He's not likely to show up until then anyway."

"If you're sure."

"Positive. Come on."

CHAPTER TWENTY

Cade took her to the Kirtley Diner in town. They had just settled at their table when the sheriff walked in. Cade invited him to join them.

"Don't mind if I do," he said with a grin and taking off his hat, slipped into a chair. "How are you doing, Miss Susannah?"

"Surviving," she said with a smile. "What's happening on your end?"

"Too much," he told them. He glanced up as a menu was handed to them all. Browsing through them, they ordered and handed the menus back.

"Still having trouble with those young thieves?" Cade asked him lightly.

Sheriff Ogdon nodded with a heavy sigh. "They're escalating to home invasions now," he told them, "Going in with young mothers home alone, babysitters watching young children, even while a family was sleeping."

"I'm sorry, John."

"If they weren't so consistently inconsistent maybe we'd have a chance. But they're invading homes and cabins morning, noon, and night as well as north, south, east, and west."

"Has anyone been hurt?" Susannah asked.

The sheriff shook his head. "So far they have done nothing more than tie up the residents or lock them in a closet, but it could get worse if they continue to escalate."

"I'm sorry."

"So am I." John sent them a wry smile. "Look, I didn't mean to ruin your dinners."

"You haven't ruined it," Cade assured him, then proceeded to change the subject. By the time their dinners arrived, they were all talking like old friends. Susannah, though she added her own comments, was more content to just sit back and listen to the two men. Eventually her eyes wandered over to the dance floor where several customers were already dancing. Cade coming to his feet brought her eyes back around.

"Are we leaving?" she asked in surprise.

"Dancing," he corrected. "If you're willing?" he said with a raised eyebrow and an enticing smile.

"I would love to," she returned with a warm smile of her own. They said good-bye to the sheriff who was also coming to his feet and Cade led her out onto the dance floor.

The dance was a slow dance and Susannah easily slipped into Cade's arms enjoying every minute of it. The second dance was a faster one that Susannah demanded Cade dance with her.

"Susannah, I don't *do* fast dancing!"

"It's not that fast," she retorted. "Besides, it's fun!"

"Maybe to you," he grumbled. He gave in however, and danced this last dance with Susannah simply because it was Susannah. Not that he didn't take her hand the moment the dance was over and practically drag her back to their table.

"Come on. I think it's time we head back to the cabin," he told her picking up the tab.

Susannah, stifling her giggles, followed him out and back to the SUV. The man was actually self-conscious about fast dancing! So much so he'd rather leave than subject himself to it again. Not that she had any objections in going. It was almost dusk and she wanted to be home when Timbers showed up.

To their surprise, Timbers was already out when they arrived back at the cabin. He was lying where he normally sat, though his head was up and he was watching the cabin intently; waiting.

"Cade! He's there!" Susannah said looking out the window in the kitchen door.

"Then let's feed him," Cade said heading directly to the refrigerator. Susannah got the antibiotics while Cade got out the steak and slit it, inserting a tablet the moment he was ready. He handed the meat over and followed Susannah out the cabin's back kitchen door.

Timbers sat up immediately the moment they cautiously came out of the cabin. By the time they stepped off the patio, he was on his feet. He didn't move however until they were almost a third way across the clearing. Only then did he turn and retreat into the trees.

Susannah went and put down the meat, briefly checked that he had water then joined Cade as they turned and walked back. "Do you think it would hurt if I sit out here awhile?" she asked as they reached the patio.

"I doubt it, though don't be surprised if Timbers waits until we go in to come out to eat."

Timbers, however, waited only a brief five minutes after they sat down on the bench before he walked out from the trees and picked up the meat. As before he turned and disappeared into the trees to eat.

Susannah was more than pleased. "I think he's walking better," she commented softly.

"I think you're right," Cade agreed. "He must be eating the antibiotics after all."

They continued to sit quietly outside for a while longer. Timbers returned a good twenty minutes later and drank from the tub, then to their surprise, settled back into his original spot, watching them as vigilantly as they were watching him until they finally went in as dusk settled.

"Want to play some cards or a board game?" Cade asked her.

Susannah shook her head. "If you don't mind, I think I'll go in and take a long, warm bath."

"You go right ahead," he said. "I've got plenty to do to keep me busy." It would give him the opportunity to check in with the Chief, something he hadn't wanted to do in front of Susannah. Her nervous fear had begun to dissipate and he didn't want it coming back in full force with thoughts of Rico still searching for her.

Susannah, unaware of such thoughts, went in and took her bath while Cade made his call. He was writing at the kitchen table when she finally came out. He offered her a mug of hot chocolate. A half hour later, they turned off the lights and crawled into bed.

Cade was again out of bed when she woke the next morning. Looking over, she found him in the kitchen drinking coffee while he sat reading the newspaper. Glancing up, he smiled. "Good morning."

"Good morning," she returned fighting back a yawn. "Any coffee left?"

He laughed softly. "Lots. Want me to get you a mug?"

"That would be heaven," she said, sitting up. She fought down another yawn. Though she had had every intention in getting up, Cade walked over and handed her a hot mug of coffee before she could do so. With a happy shrug, she stayed where she was and enjoyed it. After all, how often did she get such pampered treatment?

"Are you going to stay there in bed all morning?" Cade eventually asked.

"Hey, you're the one who served me coffee in bed," she countered.

"A good half hour ago," he retorted.

"Well, I was enjoying it."

"I'm sure you were," Cade said, stifling his laugh, "Now up and at it, woman. The morning's half over."

Susannah stuck her tongue out at him, but crawled out of bed. She handed him her mug and darted to the closet for clothes, then to the bathroom. Cade was just dishing up breakfast when she came out.

"Want milk or orange juice?" he asked immediately.

"Orange juice," she said slipping into her chair. "Have you already changed Timbers water?"

"Nope," he stated, serving up breakfast. "I thought I'd leave that for you today."

"Thanks." She had felt cheated out of it yesterday and was looking forward to the opportunity now. With that settled her mind switched gears. "Cade, what about laundry? We're both running low on clothes and the sheets need changing."

"Want to take care of that today?" he asked willingly.

"Why not? It needs to be done."

"Okay, we'll go as soon as you change Timber's water."

It meant after the kitchen was cleaned as well. They finished eating, Susannah cleaned the kitchen, changed Timbers water under Cade's supervision, and then gathering the dirty laundry they headed back down into the small community town of Kirtley.

Cade directed her to the Laundromat located next to the drugstore. There they spent the next couple hours washing and drying their clothes. Susannah was actually surprised that Cade remained with her, helping as if it was an everyday thing with him. They headed back to the cabin when they were finished. Susannah made the bed with the clean sheets and then joined Cade in putting up their clothes.

"I think I'll go sit out on the back patio and work on my word findings," she told him when everything was put away.

"I think I'll join you," Cade said.

Susannah gathered her clipboard and pencils and Cade his book and they both headed outside. To their surprise Timbers was already there, though not in his usual spot. Instead the timber wolf had settled himself on the uppermost rock in the corner of the clearing. Susannah was elated. She slipped back inside the cabin for her camera, hoping against hope that Timbers hadn't moved while she was gone.

He hadn't. He was still on the rocks. In fact, he had lain down, with his head still high as he surveyed his surroundings. Susannah took a host of pictures of the timber wolf before finally putting the camera aside. She spent the rest of the morning with half an eye on Timbers while she worked on making words. Cade, she noted, was avidly reading his book though his eyes, too, flickered to Timbers every so often.

Timbers looked to be sleeping when they finally went in for lunch. He was still up on the rocks hours later when evening came and Susannah and Cade went out to feed him. To Cade's surprise, the wolf didn't move off the rocks as they set out to feed him. His nerves went on immediate alert and pulling his gun, he kept a sharp eye on the animal as Susannah set out the meat.

Timbers however, didn't move, not until they both had returned to the patio and settled on the bench. Only then did he nimbly jump down from the rocks and head to the meat. Pulling it out from the indentation, Timbers settled a mere two feet away and ate. He drank when he finished, then skipped up the rocks to settle once more.

Sunday was much the same. Timbers was stationed on the rocks when Susannah woke in the morning and didn't move when she went outside to enjoy her mug of coffee. "Can you believe he's still there?" she asked Cade when he called her in for breakfast.

"It's unusual," Cade said. He looked thoughtfully at Susannah. "I just don't want him any closer, Susannah. And I want your promise. If he ventures into the clearing, you'll high-tail it into the cabin."

"Cade..."

"He's still a wild animal, sweetheart, and unpredictable at that. I don't want to see either one of us, or him, hurt because he got too close. Okay?"

Susannah nodded, fighting down her resentment. Cade was right. She knew he was right, but that didn't mean she had to like it.

"What do you say we change and go into town for church?" Cade suggested lightly.

"Sounds like a deal," she said mustering a smile.

Church was a relaxing change for Susannah. There was a feeling of normalcy about it. The people were both friendly and welcoming. The songs were familiar and the sermon was touching. She felt relaxed and content as she headed back to the cabin once she and Cade said their good-byes to those they met.

The rest of the day was lazy and quiet, as were the next several days. Susannah enjoyed her morning coffee out on the back patio with Timbers, then after breakfast, spent the rest of the morning out there as well. Most of the time Cade joined her, whether it was because he enjoyed the mornings outside or whether it was to keep an eye on Timbers who had made the rocks his roost, Susannah couldn't tell.

Not that Timbers left his rocks. Often he sat on them as if he owned everything he could see. At times he lay, or slept. Yet he was always alert, even in sleep. And to Cade's relief, the timber wolf remained on the rocks until he and Susannah were back on the patio before he jumped down to eat when they fed him.

Cade stopped feeding the rest of the antibiotics to Timbers for the wolf no longer looked as if he needed them. He was no longer limping, and looked strong and healthy. Cade was also ready to stop feeding him. Something Susannah objected to strongly.

"You gave me a month, Cade!" she had argued. "You promised!"

"But he's well enough to hunt on his own," Cade had said. "You don't want him dependent on us, Susannah."

"He's not going to be dependent on us," she countered stubbornly. "It's only going to get him back on his feet."

Cade disagreed, but because of his promise, and he admitted, because it was Susannah, gave in regardless. He did however, cut back on the amount of meat they fed the wolf. If Timbers didn't get enough, it was likely he would start looking elsewhere for more. Cade only hoped the animal would look into the wild for food, not to livestock or other humans. It could be disastrous for the animal otherwise.

Thursday morning eased his mind. Susannah was up early. She showered and dressed, then went into the kitchen to make coffee while Cade took over the bathroom. He was just entering the kitchen as she was pouring herself a fresh mug. "Want one?" she asked. It was a rhetorical question as she was reaching for another mug even before he answered.

"I'll be outside," she told him, handing him his.

"I'll be out in a minute," he assured her. "I want to get a sweatshirt." He had barely slipped one on when he heard Susannah's shaky voice.

"Cade?"

He was at the door instantly. Susannah was at the edge of the patio, staring down. He stepped outside to see what had unnerved her. What he found was a dead rabbit. It was still relatively warm. "Well, I'll be," he whispered, his eyes going to the rocks.

Timbers was sitting alertly, his eyes on them and looking almost prideful.

"Well, I'll be," Cade said again. The wolf could hunt. Was hunting, and had left them his kill to prove it.

"Cade?"

He grinned at Susannah. "It looks as if your wolf has brought you a present, maybe to prove he can hunt after all."

The breath went out of Susannah. "You mean *Timbers* left this for us?"

Cade nodded. "Animals have been known to do this; to leave gifts of one kind or another."

"What do we do with it?"

"I'll cut it up and leave most of it for Timbers tonight," he answered picking up the small animal. With another glance at Timbers, he headed back into the kitchen where he went ahead and took care of the rabbit.

Susannah remained outside. She refused to think about the rabbit in the kitchen and instead turned her attention to her timber wolf. "Thank you, Timbers," she called out.

The animal seemed to sit up straighter. Susannah with a grin sat down and enjoyed her mug of coffee. Eventually Cade called her in for breakfast. She cleaned the kitchen afterwards, then again went out onto the back patio. Cade joined her, but tired of just sitting, he enticed her into a game of badminton out in the clearing. There was no net, but they enjoyed the game nevertheless, playing for over an hour. Susannah was hot and tired when they finally called it quits.

"Why don't you go sit while I start lunch," he suggested, having enjoyed the exercise.

Susannah instead followed him into the cabin. "Can we walk down to the creek this afternoon?" she asked as he worked.

"I don't see why not," he returned. They hadn't been down to the creek since last week.

They left right after lunch, Susannah leading the way. She walked them down to the creek, then on up to the cascades where they spent the afternoon. "I love it here, Cade," she said contentedly as she sat with her feet in the cold water.

A warm smile came out of him. "I'm glad. I enjoy coming here as well." He hesitated a moment, then, "How would you like to go fishing tomorrow?" he asked lightly.

"You have the poles?"

"Of course. Did you ever hear of a cabin that wasn't equipped for fishing?"

"Oh, I imagine there's a few around," she said. "I'd love to go fishing," she added.

They left early the next morning with fishing poles in hand. Susannah led the way down to the creek then Cade led her down the creek's banks to the Merriam River. There were several other older fishermen out, but they didn't seem to mind the company. There were plenty of fish all around; Cade caught five and Susannah caught four.

"What are we going to do with them all?" Susannah asked as they walked back up the creek. Nine fish was too many for them to eat.

His hand slipped into hers. "How many do you think you can eat?" he asked.

"About three."

"Good enough. I'll cook six and we'll give the other three to Timbers."

"He'll eat fish?"

"Oh, yes," Cade said. "Wolves eat fish."

She dimpled. "Then I'm glad we caught so many."

"So am I, sweetheart," he said raising her hand up to his lips and kissing it. He froze suddenly, his other hand going to his gun.

"Cade?" Susannah had stilled also.

Cade's eyes were scanning the area. He caught a fleeting glance of an animal; a familiar animal.

"Cade?" Susannah questioned again.

"I think Timbers is following us," he said quietly.

Susannah sent him a quick glance. "He won't hurt us, Cade."

"I know," he said taking her hand again. But he was alert and cautious just the same. Not that he needed to be. Timbers kept his distance as he followed them back to the cabin, then settled up on his rocks.

Cade went directly to the outside storage unit and retrieving a board and a metal stand of some sort, went to work cleaning the six fish they would have for dinner. Susannah, though she didn't help, stood by and watched him do it. "Are we having them for lunch?" she eventually asked.

Cade shook his head. "We'll wait for dinner."

They had sandwiches for lunch. Susannah took her book out to the patio afterwards and read until she couldn't keep her eyes open. It was a mixture of laziness, tiredness, and reading in the sun. Closing her book, she meandered into the cabin. Crawling onto the bed, she took a short nap, surprised to find Cade on the bed with her when she woke. In fact, she was laying half on top of him with his arms around her. She carefully raised her head and his eyes opened. A soft smile filtered across his rugged face. "Hi, sweetheart," he greeted her.

She flushed. "Hi."

His finger came up and caressed her cheek. "You look all warm and cozy."

"I am," she managed to say, her heart suddenly thumping in awareness.

His finger gently raised her chin and without another word, he let his lips take hers. It wasn't a deep kiss, but it was warm and heady and wonderfully lasting melting Susannah clear down to her toes. A sigh of contentment escaped her.

Cade, wanting nothing more but to kiss her again, refrained, kissing her forehead instead as he simply held her. She was in his arms. She had willingly shared the kiss. He would settle for that, for he was too afraid to rush her; too afraid of ruining the tentative relationship they were slowly rebuilding.

"I've got to go to the bathroom," she suddenly stated.

A rumble of laughter escaped him before he could stop it. "That's okay," he said. "I've got to get up and start dinner." He planted a short, quick kiss on her lips and let her go.

Dinner, Susannah decided, was superb. It had been ages since she had eaten fish and even longer since she had eaten fresh fish she had caught herself. Cade merely grinned indulgently when she told him so.

To Susannah's surprise, Timbers also seemed to like the fish. She and Cade watched as he pulled one fish out of the hollow and sat down and demolished it before he went back for the second, then the third. He was still licking his chops as he went for water.

"I think he enjoyed the fish as much as we did," she commented happily.

"I'm sure he did," Cade said drawing her to her feet. "Let's go inside. We need to make a grocery list for tomorrow."

Susannah accompanied him, knowing they were getting low with the food on hand. They discussed menus, writing a list as they went and then drifted into a game of cards that lasted through the rest of the evening. Susannah happily snuggled into Cade as they crawled in bed later that night, contentedly drifting off with another warm kiss on her lips.

CHAPTER TWENTY-ONE

It was another warm kiss that woke Susannah the following morning. Cade was bending over her, already up and dressed. "Coffee's almost ready," he said softly.

"Then I suppose I'd better get up." She yawned.

"Then I suppose you'd better," he agreed with a chuckle. He stood and made his way back into the kitchen as Susannah dashed for the bathroom. By the time she had showered and dressed and returned to the kitchen, Cade was sitting at the table reading the newspaper. He immediately stood and poured her a mug of coffee.

"Feel free to go sit outside if you want," he said as he returned to the table and picked up the newspaper once again.

Susannah gladly did. Settling herself on the bench, she glanced over at the rocks to see Timbers lying on top, surveying his world. Her mind wandered back to Cade and warmth filled her. The man was something; strong, solid, caring, and loving. When he wanted to be.

Did he want to be?

Susannah could only hope so; pray so. For her own feelings for Cade had not changed; they were as strong as ever; stronger even. She loved him, as impossible as the man was at times. But she was leery of him as well; protective of her own heart and feelings. He had already crushed her heart once. She couldn't trust him not to do it to her again. A heavy sigh escaped her.

If only he would apologize for hurting her that first time.

A sudden, sharp yelp from Timbers had Susannah glancing up. She found two older teens not more than a few feet in front of her. Her breath sucked in. She knew instinctively that these were the two teens the sheriff was after; the same two teens who had begun a host of home invasions.

She came to her feet, wanting to cry out for Cade. Instead, she carefully greeted them as she assessed her situation.

The smaller one returned her greeting, moving a step closer. "Nice morning to enjoy a cup of coffee. You home alone?"

"At the moment," she lied, striving to keep her voice even...and loud enough to draw Cade's attention. She took a step backwards. "Is there something you want?"

"You could say so." The teen grinned, moving toward her as he pulled out a knife. "We want you to walk very quietly back into the cabin and do just as we say."

Susannah, in one swift movement, threw the mug of coffee into his face, kicked him in the groin, and dashed madly for the door. Though she had rendered the younger teen useless for the moment, the older one was immediately after her, reaching for her as she dashed inside.

Cade, having seen everything from the window, was ready for him. The moment he entered after Susannah, the frying pan he had been using, came down on the youth's head, knocking him cold.

Susannah, catching a flash of the incident, stopped, looking back at Cade. Her breath sucked in as the first teen was back on his feet charging into the cabin. Cade, his gun already drawn, grabbed the youth and stuck the barrel into his neck.

"You move and I shoot," he told him deadpan. There was no doubt in the teen's mind that he meant it. The boy stilled. Cade removed the knife from the teen's hand. "Now on the floor on your belly," he ordered closing the door, "Hands behind your back."

The boy, suddenly white-faced, shakily complied. Cade handcuffed him, handing his gun to Susannah. "If he moves, shoot him," he ordered. He turned to the older teen. Though he was still out cold, Cade bound his hands with a piece of rope then pulled out his phone.

"Sheriff Ogdon, please," Susannah heard him state. Then, "John, Candlewood. Got a couple of presents for you. I suggest you get over here and put said presents into custody before I decide to shoot them...You got it in one...Right. We'll be waiting."

The phone was replaced in his pocket and Cade reached over and took his gun from Susannah. "You okay?" he asked her.

Susannah nodded. "I am now," she said on a deep breath.

"Good girl." He smiled softly. "You did well, Susannah," he told her, "Very well."

"Thank you. You weren't so shabby yourself." Cade's alertness and quick, solid action in handling the teens surprisingly eased much of Susannah's ever-present nervous fear. He had taken down both teens, singlehandedly, without raising a sweat. She no longer doubted Cade's ability to protect her; to take care of Rico should he show up. The man was all professional!

"Sit down and I'll get your breakfast," he told her laying his gun down on the table. "You might as well eat while it's still hot." With a glance at the two teens on the floor, Cade walked over and served up the omelets, orange juice, and warm applesauce he had waiting.

Sitting down, they began to eat while keeping an eye on the two on the floor. It seemed that they just started when they heard a screech of tires and then a knocking on the front cabin door.

To their surprise, it wasn't only Sheriff Ogdon at the door, but two of his deputies as well. "They're on the floor," Cade told them, letting them in.

John ushered his two deputies forward, then turned to Cade. "Got details?"

"Come on into the kitchen and we'll give you a statement."

John willingly followed Cade, stopping momentarily to check the two young thieves. The older was semi-conscious by now, groaning in misery. "Go ahead, read them their rights and take them to the station," he told his officers, "I'll be there as soon as I get their statements."

Both officers hauled the older to his feet and out of the cabin. Cade turned to the younger teen. "Got handcuffs?" he asked John.

The sheriff pulled a pair from his belt and tossed them to Cade. Cade, digging the key to his own handcuffs from his pocket, removed his handcuffs from the teen and replaced them with the sheriff's. Pocketing his own, he sat down at the table.

John grinned. "Any time you're ready."

"I'll let Susannah tell you how they approached her first," Cade returned picking up his gun and re-holstering it as one of the deputies came back in for the other teen.

Sheriff Ogdon looked to Susannah.

With a sigh, Susannah began. "I was out sitting on the patio with Timbers…"

"Timbers?" the sheriff questioned.

"A timber wolf that's been staying around," Cade informed him. "Susannah's sort of befriended him."

"She befriended a wolf?"

"Yes, she actually has." Cade grinned and explained the circumstances to the sheriff. "He's been no trouble and keeps his distance," he added.

John merely shook his head and looked to Susannah. "I'm sorry. Want to start again?"

Susannah went on and told the sheriff how the two had suddenly approached her and pulled a knife ordering her into the cabin. "I did the only thing I could think of," she said. "I threw my coffee into his face, kicked him where it would hurt, and dashed inside where Cade was thankfully waiting."

John's eyes went to Cade. Cade shrugged. "I happened to notice them approaching Susannah out the window. Saw them pull out the knife and order her inside. Knowing they were coming in one way or another, I grabbed the frying pan and waited behind the door. The first got the frying pan as he chased Susannah into the cabin; the second got a gun in his face. Neither made much of a scene after that. I secured them and called you."

John grinned, sitting back. "Well they certainly chose the wrong cabin this time!"

"Actually the right cabin considering." Susannah said and giggled.

"That's for sure." John looked to Cade. "Thanks, Cade. You don't know how much I appreciate this; to finally get those two punk thieves off our streets."

Cade shrugged. "Let's just consider it a favor for a favor."

"How 'bout I take you and your girl out to dinner tonight to celebrate anyway?" John suggested apparently wanting to do something, anything, to show his appreciation for their help.

"Sounds lovely," Susannah inserted when it looked as if Cade was going to refuse. "What time?"

"6:00 at the Diner?"

"6:00 at the Diner sounds good," Cade agreed.

They walked the sheriff to the door and watched him drive off with his deputies. Cade slipped his arm around Susannah. "Going out to dinner, are we?"

"Yup."

"I take it that includes dancing."

"Oh, yes," she said unable to suppress her grin.

"I see," Cade returned sounding resigned as he hid his own grin. He planted a kiss on her cheek and walked back into the kitchen to clean up. Susannah watched him go with a satisfied smile.

For the rest of the day she looked forward to going out. As the time drew near, she showered and changed, taking her time getting ready. For once, she wanted to look her best for Cade; wanted to turn his head which wasn't exactly easy to do considering she had only jeans and maybe one or two blouses to choose from. Though she was tempted to wear the white jeans she had been given, she settled on her summer outfit instead. She then took her time with her hair and then the touch of make-up she applied. She didn't look like any *femme fatale* but she didn't look bad either, she mused as she looked at herself critically. Maybe, just maybe…

"You ready?" Cade called, dispelling her daydreaming.

"Coming," she said. She took one last glance at herself in the mirror and joined Cade in the front room. He had changed into a new pair of jeans and a clean shirt. He had even shaved, she noted.

"Come on, beautiful," he said urging her toward the door. "If we don't go now, we're going to be late."

Beautiful. He had called her beautiful. Susannah basked in the compliment even as she grinned at him. "So let's go!"

Cade to her surprise, walked her around the SUV and held open the door for her, letting her slip into the passenger seat. He himself climbed behind the wheel and started the Bearcat, driving them into town. John, she noted was just parking his own car when they arrived. The three of them walked into the diner together.

John led them around several tables to one with a reserved sign on it. Removing the sign, he pulled out a chair for Susannah and urged Cade to sit. A waiter was handing them menus almost immediately. They ordered then sat back with a drink each.

"I want to thank you again," John said.

Cade shrugged it off. "Were you able to tie them to the other robberies?"

John nodded. "Several of the victims willingly came in and identified them."

"Will they be charged as juveniles?" Susannah asked.

"Nope. The youngest just turned eighteen this summer. We'll be able to put them both away for quite a while."

"Stupid fools," Cade muttered. He grinned up at his friend. "So now that they're out of the way, are you going to relax?"

"As much as I can."

"Are you kept busy here in Kirtley?" Susannah asked.

The sheriff shrugged. "Not compared to the cities, but we do have our problems."

"Like what?" she asked interested.

John with an amused look to Cade spent the next twenty minutes relegating some of the more comical and adventuresome cases of his job. He only paused briefly when their food was served.

Susannah enjoyed listening to him talk. He had an easy manner and a good sense of humor. "I like him," she told Cade later when John excused himself for a moment.

"So do I." Cade said. "It's too bad his wife is still out of town. You'll like her, too." John had told them that both his wife and teenage son weren't due home for another two days.

"Well, if they're anything like John, I hope I can meet them when they get back."

"I'm sure you will." Cade grinned and pulled her to her feet. "How 'bout a dance? I seem to remember that it was mandatory tonight."

"Absolutely," Susannah said with a happy giggle.

Cade led her onto the dance floor and drew her gently into his arms. It was a slow dance and Susannah easily fell in step with him, savoring being in his arms. They didn't talk as they danced. Instead, they simply enjoyed being where they were; in each other's arms swaying gently to the music.

Cade slowly eased her away as the dance came to an end.

"Have I told you yet tonight how nice you look?" he asked softly.

She dimpled. "No, but I'm willing to let you."

A gentle laugh came out of him. "Then I will. You look very nice tonight, Susannah Brockman; very, very nice."

"Why thank you, kind sir." A rosy flush colored her cheeks.

Cade, with another gentle laugh, led her back to their table. John was waiting along with dessert. Susannah happily indulged in the hot fudge sundae he had ordered for her. She let Cade talk only a few minutes after they had finished before she pulled him to his feet for another dance, a faster one this time.

"Oh, Susannah," he said and groaned.

"Come on," she ordered, dragging him forward.

Despite Cade's obvious discomfiture at the faster dance, he was quite adequate being able to hold his own with the best of them.

"I don't know why you complain so," she accosted him later. "You dance quite well."

"Thank you," he said with a wry smile. "It must be due to the encouragement of my wonderful partner."

"I'll accept that," Susannah said her eyes twinkling.

"You do that," he said and laughed.

Susannah thoroughly enjoyed the rest of the evening. She danced several times with John, and several more times with Cade. Though she enjoyed the faster dances with Cade, it was the slow dances she shared with him that she enjoyed even more. It was a disappointment when the sheriff finally called it a night.

Both she and Cade thanked him for dinner and the wonderful evening and waved him off. Susannah sighed, knowing they were about to go as well.

"Tired?" came Cade's soft voice.

"Well, yes and no," she said.

"Then how 'bout one last dance before we head back to the cabin?" he asked lightly.

"I'd like that, Cade."

Cade led her out on the dance floor and drew her into his arms. Her own arms went up to his shoulders as she laid her head against his broad chest. His arms closed possessively around her, drawing her closer still as his body began to sway gently to the slow music. A feather-light kiss touched her temple.

Susannah closed her eyes, already in heaven. She was where she belonged; in Cade's strong, loving arms, being held close to his heart.

Warm pleasure filled her, warm pleasure that expanded as she simply savored the gentle sway of his body against hers as they moved together...

"Susannah?"

"Hmm?"

Cade wordlessly lifted her chin. His lips touched hers and spread into a warm, soft kiss.

"Oh, my," she said on a sigh as its warmth ran through her.

A gentle, pleasured laugh escaped him. He wrapped an arm around her and walked her back across the floor to their table where he helped her into her sweater, then on outside to the Bearcat.

Though he walked her to the passenger side Cade didn't open the door, not right away. Instead he took her into his arms and let his lips take hers in a warm heady kiss, and then another. Susannah was literally floating by the time he let her go. He ushered her into the vehicle, then slipped behind the wheel and drove them back up the road to the cabin. He kissed her one last time on the porch before he let them inside the cabin. He had meant it to be a warm and light kiss, but his own emotions got the better of him and the kiss deepened instantly, spreading fiery emotion through them both.

Susannah melted into it; into Cade. His arms tightened. The kiss expanded and she pressed herself closer, her heart swirling...

With a shuddering sigh, Cade slowly eased her away. "Come on, sweetheart," came his quiet voice as he unlocked the cabin door and ushered her in.

It was like night and day. He didn't take her in his arms again; didn't take her to bed. Instead Cade flipped on the lights. "How about some hot chocolate before we turn in for the night?" he suggested quietly. He was already heading for the kitchen.

Susannah, still swirling in emotion, didn't notice the quiet change in Cade. Not at first. Not until she had finished her hot chocolate and he suggested she go on to bed without him.

"You go ahead," he told her quietly. "I'll be in later."

Susannah's whole world seemed to crash. He was doing it to her again; shutting her out. Rejecting her. She bit her lip in order to hold back her tears as she changed and crawled into bed. But the tears came anyway; silent tears that cascaded one by one down her cheeks and into her pillow.

Cade, unaware of the tears, meandered over to the cabinet with an inaudible sigh and slipped in a CD, then added a splash of alcohol to his chocolate. He sat and sipped it as he listened to his music. And simply waited. Once he was assured Susannah was asleep, he went in and took the cold shower he desperately needed. Turning off the lights afterwards, he carefully crawled in bed.

CHAPTER TWENTY-TWO

Susannah was disappointed and hurt to find Cade already up when she opened her eyes the next morning. She had hoped to wake in his arms, maybe share a kiss or two. The fact that she hadn't, the fact that he was already up, seemed to verify her growing belief that she was nothing more to Cade than Brock's kid sister; someone he needed to care for and entertain. And if that allowed him a little entertainment of his own...

"Coffee's hot," came his gentle voice from the kitchen.

"What time is it?" she yawned and asked.

"About 7:30. Want coffee?"

"Let me get up and dressed first," she said crawling from the bed. She disappeared into the bathroom where she dressed, then washed her face and combed her hair. Cade had a mug of hot coffee ready for her when she emerged but no kiss. She hid her disappointment.

"Cade, what about Timbers? We didn't feed him last night."

"I fed him," he assured her, "While you were getting ready last night. Why don't you go on out and see if he's around?"

"Trying to get rid of me?" she asked before she could stop herself.

"Not at all," he said, puzzled by her disquieting attitude. "In fact, let me refill my mug and I'll join you."

At least that was somewhat of a concession, Susannah thought. She waited while he refilled his mug before opening the back door. They both settled on the patio bench. Timbers, who had been waiting and watching from his rocks, sat up immediately and gave what only could be considered a welcoming yelp.

"Good morning, Timbers," they chorused, almost in unison.

Cade grinned. "That wolf continues to surprise me," he stated sliding his arm around her. Susannah's heart jumped.

"He surprises me, too," she said. She felt better that Cade had chosen to come out and sit with her, but it didn't quite dissipate her growing fears that the man was simply entertaining himself. "What time is it?" she asked in an attempt to force her thoughts elsewhere.

Cade glanced at his watch. "Time for breakfast." He kissed her temple and stood. "I guess I'd better get in and get it started."

"You want company?" she asked, looking up at him.

"Only if you want," he said.

It wasn't exactly the answer she had been seeking but she took it for a yes regardless and followed him into the cabin. Sitting down at the kitchen table, she finished her coffee as he cooked.

It was an amiable breakfast. Cade drew her out by teasing her with riddles, and Susannah managed to tease him in return. But eventually breakfast came to an end. Cade helped her change Timbers' water then disappeared into the front of the cabin. Susannah, with a sigh, turned to the kitchen.

Finishing the kitchen she went in search of Cade. She found him out on the front porch, apparently working diligently on some report of some kind. Refusing to disturb him, she turned back to the cabin. The bed still needed making. Susannah made it then turned to the rest of the cabin. She dusted and swept the large room, then went in and scrubbed the bathroom from top to bottom.

She was tired by the time she finished. Grabbing a bottle of water from the refrigerator, she picked up her book and went out on the back patio. She knew it really wasn't a wise idea with Cade on the front porch, but for once she didn't care. She didn't want to stay in the cabin and neither did she want to sit out on the front porch with Cade. He was likely too busy to even acknowledge her *if* he even remembered she existed!

Susannah knew she was being both unfair and unreasonable, but her emotions were too scrambled to care. Instead she banished Cade from her mind and concentrated on finishing her book. Cade interrupted her in the middle of the last chapter.

"Sweetheart. Lunch is ready," he told her lightly.

"In a minute," she answered absently, her eyes still in her book. There was no way she could leave it now, not with only a couple pages left to read.

Cade, with a last look at her, disappeared back into the cabin. Susannah followed a mere five minutes later.

Cade placed a plate of tacos on the table and handed her a soda. "Hope you're hungry."

"You apparently are," she said, eyeing the plate.

"You could say that," he said with an easy laugh. "The cabin looks wonderful, by the way," he added.

Susannah merely shrugged as she picked up a taco and began munching on it. "We missed church," she told him.

"I know. I'm afraid I got too immersed in what I was doing."

"Did you finish what you were working on?" she asked.

"Finally," he acknowledged. "I'm sorry about that, sweetheart," he apologized, "but it was something I had to get done."

"That's okay," she said. She reached for another taco.

"You could have come out and joined me."

"I know."

Cade shot her a concerned look, knowing she was brewing, but unable to discern exactly why. There was only one way to find out. "Honey, is there something wrong?" he asked.

"Absolutely nothing," Susannah returned with a false smile that didn't reach her eyes. "So what are your plans for the afternoon?" she asked to change the subject.

"What would you like to do?" he questioned.

"Call Brock," she answered immediately with a touch of defiance.

Cade immediately shook his head. "Absolutely not, sweetheart."

"I want to talk to my brother, Cade."

"Susannah, we've been over this before. Not while you and Brock are under secure protection."

"I'm not asking to *see* him, you brute!" Susannah snapped out, her unjust anger climbing. "I just want to talk to him!"

"It's not safe, Susannah."

Susannah refused to be pacified. "Says you! There hasn't been any sign of Rico anywhere. Not here or back in Denton. So, what harm could there possibly be in one little phone call?" she demanded.

"And what if Rico's just waiting for that?" Cade countered. "Waiting for that one little phone call that will give him a clue as to where we are?"

"But no one's seen hide nor hair of him!"

"Susannah, just because Rico hasn't been seen, doesn't mean he's not still out there waiting and watching and looking."

"And it doesn't mean he is either," she shot out perversely. "I want to phone my brother, Cade!"

"I'm afraid I can't allow that, honey."

Susannah's unreasonable anger intensified. "Right! You called him before!" The man was impossible! He knew perfectly well he could call Brock if he wanted to. He just didn't want to!

"That was while he was in ICU," Cade said trying to reason with her. "And I didn't call Brock. I called the agent that was guarding him."

"So call the agent!"

"Oh, Susannah." He took a deep, frustrated breath. "Honey, it's not possible. For one thing, I don't know who's protecting him now, let alone where he's being protected. And for another..."

"Then call your chief!" Susannah interrupted with a snap. "He knows where Brock is. Have him call Brock and arrange to have Brock call me!"

Cade's head shook. "I can't do that, Susannah." Couldn't. It was unsafe as well as against protocol and he would be a fool to even suggest it to the Chief.

"You mean you won't! You're a brute, Cade Candlewood! An insensitive, horrible brute and I *hate* you!"

Oh, God, he groaned silently. "Sweetheart..."

"I hate you, Cade Candlewood!" she repeated. "You're horrible and miserable and I wish I had never seen you again! I wish they had sent someone else to protect me! Anyone else because I can't stand being around you!"

"Susie..."

"Just go away!" she raged at him.

Cade's jaw clenched. With one last look at her, he turned and slammed his way out of the cabin, the cabin door slamming shut behind him. He angrily made his way to the SUV and yanking the door open he threw himself in and inserted the key in the ignition.

It was the knowledge that he couldn't leave Susannah unprotected that prevented him from turning it and driving off. His head went back and he closed his eyes.

For a long, long moment, he did nothing but sit in numbed frustration. Blast it! She was back to hating him. Why? What had brought it on? He knew instinctively that it hadn't been his refusal to get in touch with Brock. That had only been the catalyst. Could it have been because he had been working on reports all morning? His head shook. No. That wasn't it either. But something had to be the cause. What?

Maybe it was just that she still hadn't forgiven him.

Oh, Susannah, he groaned. *Don't do this to me – to us. What I did happened years ago. Let it go. Give us this chance to start again!*

Would she ever?

She had to! Cade countered. Had to! Because he couldn't face a future life without her; wouldn't. He took a deep, calming breath in an attempt in letting go of his frustrations. Okay, he counseled himself. It wasn't hopeless. These last three weeks had proven it wasn't hopeless. She had opened up to him; had let him get close.

True, Susannah had now closed herself off again. But it just meant that he would have to try harder; be more patient. He had just over two months left; just two short months in which to persuade her to forgive his harsh treatment of her and build back the firm, warm relationship they once had shared…Just two short months in which to convince her to accept both his heart and his love.

His hand went to the door handle, but he let it go. He couldn't rush this. He needed to give Susannah time to cool off; time to get hold of herself and her emotions.

But he needed to be there to protect her as well.

Cade glanced around. He was surprised to realize he could see the entire front yard from where he was. He turned and looked back at the small mirror that had been placed on the far tree years ago. It was filmed with dirt, but still gave him a muted view of the back clearing. Removing his keys from the ignition, he slipped into the back seat of the Bearcat, checked his view once again and then settled more comfortably against its door. A deep steadying breath escaped him as he slowly began to relax.

CHAPTER TWENTY-THREE

Susannah wiped her eyes and glanced again out the cabin's window. There was still no sign of Cade and it had been over two hours now since he had gone storming out. Blast it! Where was he? He hadn't taken the SUV. She had checked over an hour ago and it was still sitting where they had parked it last night. So where was he? Down at the creek? Had he walked to town? Was he with John?

The brute! He was supposed to be here protecting her! What if Rico showed up now?

Susannah wrapped her arms around her stomach and nervously paced the cabin. She was trying hard to avoid acknowledging that this was her fault. That *she* had been the one that had blown up at him; ordered him out.

But it was just that he made her so mad!

And scared, she acknowledged. She didn't know where she stood with Cade. Didn't know if his affections were real or just entertainment on his part. And she was too scared to find out. She couldn't take having her heart crushed by him yet again. The first time had been devastating enough. This time, she feared, would destroy her completely.

She again stopped and looked out the window. He wasn't coming back. Had he washed his hands of her? Called his chief and put in a request for another agent to take over? Her tears started in again over the thought and she found herself curled up on the bed crying her eyes out. Eventually she drifted off to sleep.

It was near 4:00 when she woke; the cabin still empty. Cade hadn't returned. She got up and walked desolately into the kitchen. She wasn't hungry but she needed something to do. She switched on the oven, then pulled two of the larger potatoes out of the cupboard and washed them, setting them aside. Gathering the ingredients, she set her mind to making a meatloaf. That done, she put both the meatloaf and the two potatoes into the oven, then turned and heated water for jello.

She glanced again at the clock once the jello was in the refrigerator chilling. Refusing to let her mind wander to her missing bodyguard, she retrieved her clipboard and determinedly concentrated on finding more words with the letters of *Merry Christmas*. She had found forty more words by the time the oven timer went off.

Not able to eat, she turned off the oven, leaving the meal inside. She put away her clipboard and meandered back into the front room area. Again she looked out the window. Seeing nothing; nobody, she turned to the book case and determinedly went through the books again, looking for something else to read. Finding a book that half-way interested her, she settled in one of the front room chairs. She opened the book to the first page of the first chapter. Not that she could actually read. She simply sat and stared out into the cabin instead… until she heard the front lock turn and Cade walk quietly in.

He merely flashed a glance in her direction and walked into the bathroom, closing the door behind him. Susannah had to fight back her tears of relief. Two minutes later, Cade came back out. His eyes briefly studied her. "Something smells good," he commented lightly.

"Dinner's in the oven," she said quietly, trying hard to keep her distance. She wanted desperately to just throw herself into his arms.

Cade turned with a small smile and walked through the room and entered the kitchen. He pulled the meatloaf and baked potatoes from the oven, then heating a can of vegetables, he set the table. Once everything was on the table, he looked into the front room.

"Susannah?"

She looked up.

"Come and eat, sweetheart," he said gently.

Susannah quietly came to her feet and followed him back into the kitchen. Refusing to let him see how upset his absence had made her, she forced herself to eat. Not even his "Dinner's good," helped. She barely acknowledged the compliment.

Cade didn't give up. He was determined to put some civility back between them.

"Susannah…"

"Is your chief sending out another agent?" she asked.

"No," Cade replied quietly.

So he had contacted his boss! That upset Susannah more than she cared to admit. "You know you had no right to just disappear like that this afternoon," she bit out at him. "You were supposed to be here watching out for me."

"I was watching out for you," he countered.

"Right! You left me alone all afternoon!"

"I was right outside, Susannah, in the Bearcat. I had perfect vision of both the front and back of the cabin."

Susannah's anger shot up instantly. *He had been in the Bearcat the whole time?* While she had worried herself sick!?

"You're a brute, Cade Candlewood!" she stated pushing back her chair and stomping out of the kitchen.

At least she hadn't stated she hated him this time Cade mused, watching her go. With another sigh he stood and picked up the remains of dinner and put them away then resigned himself to cleaning the kitchen. That done, he pulled Timbers' dinner from the bottom of the refrigerator and unwrapped it, then again walked out to the front. Susannah was sitting morosely in her chair, a book in her hands.

"Ready to feed Timbers?" he asked.

Timbers, to their surprise, wasn't out on his rock when they went out to feed him. Susannah put the meat out anyway, Cade as always, just a few feet behind her. Cade then ushered her back to the bench where they both sat quietly waiting to see if the animal would appear.

Timbers arrived a mere ten minutes later. With a welcoming yelp, he turned to his meat and began eating. Susannah and Cade watched him finish off his meal and take a long drink before he nimbly climbed the rocks and settled.

Susannah sat outside with Cade beside her watching as the sun set and dusk began turning into night. Cade finally took her hand and gently pulled her inside the cabin.

"Want to play some cards or a board game?" he asked.

"No," she said a little coldly. "I think I'm going to go in and take a long bath and go to bed." It was exactly what she did. Not that she could sleep.

Instead she planted herself in the middle of the large bed and listened to the music Cade had put on and just waited.

She heard a howl of a wolf off in the distance as she waited. Then an answering howl much closer to the cabin; Timbers. Twice more she heard the wolves howl as she laid there.

Cade eventually turned off the lights and came to bed which is what Susannah had stubbornly been waiting for. She stopped him before he could crawl under the covers.

"What do you think you're doing?" she demanded.

Cade stilled momentarily as he eyed her. "Coming to bed," he replied quietly.

"Oh, no you're not!" Susannah said, claiming possession to the bed. "Go find someplace else to sleep because you're not sleeping here!"

Cade ignored her and climbed into bed.

"Cade Candlewood! I'm not sleeping in the same bed as you! Now go find someplace else to sleep!"

"You go find someplace else to sleep," he said mildly. "I'm sleeping in bed."

Susannah with a huff, grabbed her pillow and the top blanket and stomped her way into the front room area. Cade merely rolled over and pulled the rest of the covers around him, hiding his grin. It was going to be a rocky ride, these next two months, he mused, definitely a rocky ride.

Susannah, with another huff, planted herself in her chair. It could have at least been a reclining chair, she thought glaring at the bed. But it wasn't. It was a big, upright chair that didn't go anywhere. Susannah curled up in it regardless and covered herself with the blanket. Stuffing the pillow behind her head, she lay back against it and closed her eyes. But it was a long while before she actually slept.

Cade, assured Susannah was asleep at last, retrieved her, pillows, blankets, and all, and carried her back to bed.

Susannah stirred in the early morning then snuggled into the warmth surrounding her. It was awhile before her eyes actually opened. She was snuggled into Cade, his arms wrapped protectively around her. It took her a moment or two to realize that she shouldn't be there. She had gone to sleep in the chair. Hadn't she?

Susannah slowly raised her eyes to find Cade awake and lazily watching her. "I see you decided to come to bed after all," he murmured. "Get too cold out there for you?"

"Too uncomfortable," she muttered, not daring to admit she had no recollection of climbing back in bed, only of how uncomfortable the chair had been for sleeping. She removed herself from his embrace and then climbing from the bed, made her way to the bathroom.

Cade was up and dressed by the time she came out. She found him in the kitchen just pouring coffee. He handed a mug to her with a warm, almost tentative smile.

"Thank you," she said quietly.

"Want to go see if Timbers is up?"

She shrugged. "Why not?"

They meandered outside together, settling on the bench, each sipping their coffee. Timbers they noted, was laying on the top rock apparently grooming himself. He looked up as they came out, sat up and gave a short yelp of welcoming. They both greeted him with a grin.

"Do you think he thinks we're his pack?" Susannah asked musingly.

"Apparently," Cade answered with a soft laugh, "Though I wish he could find a true one."

"Is that possible?" she asked, thinking of the howling she had heard the night before.

"Possible, but unlikely," Cade said. "He's really too old to be accepted by another wolf pack." He removed Susannah's mug and pulled her to her feet. "Let's go change his water before we forget."

Susannah willingly went with Cade, knowing there was no way the man would let her do it by herself, especially with Timbers just sitting there. Though Cade no longer expected the timber wolf to come off the rocks when they moved near enough to feed or water him his training kept him cautious and prepared for the unexpected just the same.

"Anything special you'd like for breakfast?" he asked as they picked up their mugs.

Susannah shrugged. "Whatever you want to make."

What he made was a breakfast of pancakes and sausages, with warm applesauce on the side. Susannah enjoyed it in spite of herself. "Are we going down to do laundry today?" she asked quietly as she poured herself another cup of coffee.

Cade sighed. "I suppose we'd better. Want to go down to the creek for a picnic lunch when we get back?"

"That sounds nice," she said managing a smile.

The smile, as tentative as it was, was irresistible and Cade leaned across the table and planted a soft kiss against her lips. "Then let's get started. I'll put the laundry in the SUV while you pick up the kitchen."

Susannah, with a wry shake of her head, cleaned up the kitchen while she finished her coffee. They left for the laundromat when she was done, spending a couple hours washing and drying their clothes, towels, and sheets, as well as visiting the drug store next door between loads. Cade packed them a picnic lunch when they returned and taking her hand, walked her down to the creek, then up to the cascades where they spent a leisurely lunch. Timbers came with them on their outing, settling himself at the top of the Cascades where he could easily view them as well as the terrain around them. He didn't move from his post, not until later when Cade and Susannah gathered up their belongings and headed back to the cabin.

Susannah, still trying to keep an emotional distance from Cade, took a nap when they returned. She slept for an hour, and then joined Cade who was reading in the front. She picked up the book she had started, and went to sit down.

It was then that she saw it; a large book, resting on her chair. *Spirit of the Wild: The Wolf.* She stared at it a moment, then turned to Cade who was watching her with affectionate interest.

"What's this?"

"Just a book I picked up for you."

She turned back to the book, tentatively picking it up as she sat down. Her eyes studied the cover. It held a close-up of a wolf. Its head was pointing upwards, its mouth open as it gave its timbered howl.

"It looks like Timbers," she commented.

"I thought so, too," Cade returned with a touch of a smile.

"Oh, Cade, I do thank you," she said, her hand caressing the book. "I love it."

"If you open it up, I think you'll enjoy it more," Cade teased, enjoying her evident pleasure.

With a flush Susannah slowly opened the book, going through it page by page. Most every page she noted held photographs of wolves; beautiful, wonderful photographs.

"Thank you, Cade," she said again.

"I'm glad you like it," he said smiling warmly. He returned to his book and Susannah continued to go through the one in her hands. She went through it page by page, then returned to the beginning and began reading. She was hardly aware when Cade ambled into the kitchen and started dinner.

Though it was merely leftovers from the evening before, Susannah found herself eating her fill. She cleaned the kitchen afterwards, then with Cade, went out and fed Timbers. They sat outside while the wolf ate then finally ambled back into the cabin. Though Susannah wanted to go back to her book on wolves, Cade refused to let her.

"We're playing a game tonight," he told her gruffly.

"I don't want to play any games," she retorted, looking for her book. It was nowhere in sight.

"Tough," he countered. "You'll play regardless, if you want your wolf book back."

That of course had Susannah's dander back up. She gave in however, knowing she wouldn't get the book from Cade otherwise. Not that she was happy about it. "You're a brute Cade Candlewood!" she groused.

He merely laughed.

They played three games of *Red Rum*, a variant of *Rummy* while they ate the jello Susannah had made the night before. Though Susannah won the first game, Cade won the remaining two which didn't help Susannah's already disgruntled mood. She took a bath and went to bed. Cade followed just a short time later. Susannah obstinately moved to the edge of the bed as he crawled in, just as far away from him as she could. Cade merely grinned in amusement.

"Susannah," he said softly. "You move any closer to that edge and you'll fall off."

Susannah with a maddening huff, ignored him.

CHAPTER TWENTY-FOUR

Though Susannah tried to keep her distance from Cade, it became harder and harder as the days went on. He was gentle and caring, giving her space, yet entertaining her when he could. He often took her down to the creek or fishing or just driving around when they weren't home playing cards or board games or reading together. And yes, he was kissing her whenever he found the opportunity, though the kisses remained gentle and soft and enticingly sweet.

Susannah both loved his attention and hated it. She loved Cade; loved the fact that he was caring and gentle and kind to her. But she resented it as well. She wanted him to sweep her in his arms and kiss her till her toes curled; wanted to know she stirred his senses and touched his soul. She wanted to know he loved her.

And she wasn't getting that. Her resentment and frustrations began to build again and by the end of the week she was back to keeping a resentful distance. If she had been home she easily would have talked to Becky or Gloria about her fears and mixed-up feelings. But she wasn't home. She was here, stuck in a cabin with the man who was causing her frustrations. She had no one to talk to except for Timbers who was too far away to even hear about her troubles, let alone understand them!

If only she could talk to Brock! Brock knew Cade; knew where the man was coming from. He would most likely be able to give her the answers she was seeking, at least maybe enough of the answers. But talking to Brock was seemingly an impossibility for Cade had been adamant about not letting her talk to her brother. If she could only get her hands on Cade's cell phone, she thought. She knew she had no idea where Brock was being secured, or how to reach him by phone for that matter. But darn it! Wouldn't Brock be checking his own phone line once in a while for messages? She could easily call and leave a short message for him to call her. If she kept it that short, there wouldn't be any way to have the call traced, would there?

The question however was moot. She had no chance of ever getting her hands on Cade's cell phone for the man kept it secure in his pocket except on those occasions when he himself was making a call.

Blast it! She'd just have to convince him into letting her talk to her brother. Have to. She determinedly decided to tackle him once again as soon as she finished cleaning up from breakfast that Saturday morning. Cade, she knew was out repairing something on the front porch.

Susannah, with a deep breath, walked out on the porch. Cade sent her a quick smile, but returned to the job at hand. He was apparently repairing the railing that went around most of the porch. She smiled briefly in return.

"Cade?"

"What is it, sweetheart?" he asked looking up.

"I want to talk to Brock," she stated determinedly.

Cade stood up immediately. "You know the answer to that," he returned brusquely.

"But I *need* to talk to him, Cade!"

Cade, instead of arguing about it, pulled her to him and kissed her solidly on the lips. "Go put on some shoes," he ordered letting her go. "We're going into town."

Susannah literally growled, but Cade was already entering the cabin in order to wash his hands. She stomped into the cabin after him. Jamming her shoes on her feet, she stomped back out of the cabin and made her way to the Bearcat. Unlocking it with her key, she slipped inside, relocked the doors and waited. Cade came out a moment later. He unlocked the passenger door with his own key and slid in.

"I beat you into the Bearcat, so you owe me my present," Susannah told him.

"I guess I do," he said gravely, his eyes laughing in amusement.

"A cell phone would be nice," she added as she started the SUV and eased it into the road.

"I'm sure it would."

Susannah ignored his amusement. "So where am I heading?"

"The drugstore."

Great. Considering the drug store was much more than a drug store he could be looking for almost anything in there. Susannah drove on into town and parked just a few car lengths from the drug store's entrance. She followed Cade inside and meandered after him as he took a basket and began gathering the items he needed.

"Anything you need?" he turned and asked.

"A cell-phone," she answered politely.

Cade merely shook his head as he continued through the store. Susannah would have loved wandering through it on her own, but she knew better than to even ask. She was to be within eyesight of Cade at all times when in public. It was a rule he wouldn't allow her to break. At least he allowed her to shop.

She browsed through the book section under his guarded eye, choosing two fictional books that caught her attention as well as a couple puzzle books. Hopefully they would help keep her busy. Cade took her next to the music area, picking up two new CDs, before he finally headed for the counter.

"Home now?" she asked when they had loaded their purchases into the SUV.

Cade hesitated. "Do you mind if I go over and get my hair cut?"

"I suppose not," she said.

"Great." He led her across the street to Toby Green's barbershop. The barber was already busy with a customer so Cade and Susannah sat down to wait. It wasn't a long wait. Within minutes, the customer left and Cade took his place.

Susannah sat a minute or two leafing through a magazine. Tossing the magazine aside she glanced around and came to her feet. "Cade?"

His eyebrow rose as the barber continued to work.

"Is there a bathroom nearby?"

Toby Green stopped working. "There's one in the back," he told her helpfully, pointing to the back of his shop.

Susannah looked to Cade.

"Go ahead," he told her with a reassuring smile.

The bathroom door, Susannah noted as she pushed it open, had a symbol for both men and women. The room itself held a single stall, a sink and mirror, a garbage can. And a telephone. It was a public pay phone, but a telephone nevertheless. A telephone she could use to contact Brock. Susannah stared at it, her heart suddenly thumping.

Dared she? She glanced toward the closed door and back to the phone. Her lip went between her teeth. A moment later, she was digging the change from her pockets.

She would keep it short and simple. She placed the coins into the machine and waited impatiently for the dial tone. Brock's phone rang four times before the answering machine came on. Susannah began her message the moment it beeped.

"Brock. You've got Cade's number. Call me. I need to talk."

It took a mere five seconds. Not anywhere near long enough for anyone to trace the call. Both relief and guilt filled Susannah. She defiantly pushed the guilt away. After all, she had the right to talk to her brother, and nobody could say she hadn't been careful about it.

The guilt, however, didn't quite go away.

Susannah, ignoring it, used the bathroom facilities, and then walked back out to Cade. He was still getting his hair cut. She flashed him a quick, brief smile and sat back down, picking up the magazine she had been looking at earlier. Three minutes later she was coming back to her feet as Cade stood and paid the man.

"Thank you, sweetheart," he said, kissing her gently on the cheek before leading her out of the barbershop and back to the car.

"For what?" she asked guiltily.

"For not minding the stop at the barber's."

Susannah shrugged and climbed into the Bearcat. Facing Cade directly had caused her guilt to climb. He was going to be furious when he found she had called Brock against his orders. But so what? The man had been unreasonable about the whole thing. And she had been careful, she reminded herself. The guilt receded as she drove on up to the cabin.

She backed into the cabin's drive then helped Cade unload his purchases. "So where's my present?" she asked him when everything was inside.

He looked through several bags before he pulled out a small box. "Right here," he said holding it up.

"Are you going to give it to me?"

"Considering you think you deserve it," he said, tossing it to her.

"Of course I deserve it," she taunted, ignoring again the guilt that bubbled up. "I beat you into the Bearcat."

She took the box and opened it to find a watch. It was a sports watch, with a mother-of-pearl face and eleven shimmering crystals marking the hours as well as a day and date. Its band was a durable stainless steel with a safety clasp.

Susannah's eyes shimmered as she took it from its box and clasped it around her wrist. A watch. She finally had a watch again! Glancing up, she found Cade watching her, an almost amused look in his eyes.

"Figured you'd stop asking me the time if you had a watch of your own," he said.

"Thank you," she said in return. "It's not exactly a cell phone, but it will do." *Definitely do!*

Cade laughed, knowing he had pleased her despite her comment. "I hoped so."

Susannah had a hard time not being civil to Cade after that. She supposed her guilt played a little into it as well. She found herself helping him finish fixing the porch railing then playing badminton with him after lunch. They both settled on the back patio to read when they were finished, Susannah starting one of the books she had just purchased. Eventually, however, it grew too hot outside and Susannah went in to lie down. Cade, to her surprise, joined her.

Susannah turned her back to him but didn't move away. Closing her eyes she drifted off with the knowledge that soon she would be talking to Brock.

It was Cade's movement that woke her awhile later. Though she was still turned away from him, his arms were now wrapped around her cocooning her against him. Still feeling warm and cozy from sleep, she turned to him and let her lips meet his.

The kiss brought her fully awake. She flushed and pulled away. "Thank you for the watch," she said in order to hide her embarrassment.

"You're more than welcome," he said lightly. "Want to get up?"

Susannah glanced at her new watch. "I suppose we should." She yawned. "It's almost five."

"I'll go start dinner," he stated letting her go and climbing from the bed.

Susannah sighed heavily. How could one kiss be enough for that man? He should want at least three or four or fifty or more from her before he was satisfied. With another sigh, she crawled from the bed and headed for the bathroom.

Dinner was quiet. Susannah was growing nervous about Brock calling. Though she wanted to talk to him desperately, she was not looking forward to Cade's wrath when he found out that she had called her brother.

And Brock could call at any time.

But Brock didn't call. Susannah told herself that it was too early. He probably hadn't checked his messages today. But he would tomorrow, or Monday at the latest.

But Sunday came and went, then Monday and there was still no call from Brock. By Tuesday afternoon, Susannah was pacing, angry and frustrated at both her brother and Cade. Cade had asked her twice already if something was wrong. Couldn't the brute understand the word no? Maybe he already knew she had phoned Brock and was beginning his torture of her for defying him. Or maybe Brock had already called and that brute had refused to let her talk to him! Susannah wouldn't put it past him, especially if Brock had informed him of her own phone call. She'd murder the brute if he had!

Ignoring Cade who seemed to appear around every corner, Susannah looked for things to do after lunch to keep her away from Cade and her mind busy. She set herself cleaning the entire cabin from top to bottom again. That done, she settled on the bed and tried to read but found it hopeless. She couldn't even get through the first page without going back and re-reading it. She threw the book down and laid back and tried to take a nap, but she was too restless to sleep and too worried Brock's call would come while she was sleeping, and knowing Cade...

Giving up, she sat back up and crawled from the bed. Deciding to go back and work on finding words, she gathered up her clipboard and pencils and slipped outside onto the back patio. To her surprise, Cade was already out there, sitting in one of the patio chairs reading. She hesitated, but sat down on the bench near Cade. He looked up but outside of a brief smile, said nothing. Ignoring him, Susannah plopped her clipboard into her lap and determinedly picked up a pencil. She had given up on *Merry Christmas* days ago figuring she had found all the words that she was going to find, then had gone on to making words from the letters in Brock's name, as well as Cade's. Now what?

Well, she could get a head-start on Becky and go on to *Happy Valentine's Day*. Instead Susannah wrote her own name at the top of the paper. She found nine words almost instantly. She looked for a tenth.

"Still working on *Merry Christmas*?" Cade asked lightly.

Susannah shook her head, not bothering to look up. "Finished that," she told him.

"How many words did you come up with?" he asked.

"463," she said nonchalantly, adding another word to her list.

He sat and watched her a moment, frustrated with his inability to connect with her. He refused to give up. "So tell me," he asked conversationally, "How many words did you come up with out of my name?"

"Oh, about a hundred," she said flickering him a cool look. "Which included such wonderful words as cad, low down, and brute," she added.

"You can't make brute with my name," he stated.

"Oh?" She sent him another look. "I managed it."

"I see." He eyed her another frustrated moment. "In that case, you missed such words as honorable, loyal, and caring," he said evenly.

Honorable, loyal, and caring? Hah!

Susannah glared at him. "Try mean and unreasonable and barbarian!" she bit out hotly. "Those are the words I missed. Not to mention cruel and sadistic and vile and contemptible and –!"

"Susannah. Stop!"

"Why should I?" she cried out, surging to her feet not caring that her clipboard and papers and pencils went flying. "What you did to me–!"

Cade surged to his own feet. "Damn it, Susannah! Stop holding a grudge! What I did happened years ago. It's time you forgave me for that!"

"Why should I? You were mean and cruel and painfully brutal!"

"And you weren't?" he shot back. "There's a name for women who tease a man like that!"

"I never –!"

"You damn well did! There you were, barely eighteen. Beautiful and sexy and bewitching, and so enticingly sweet and coming on to me like I couldn't believe. I wanted you so damn much, Susannah. But by my own word I couldn't touch you!"

"You mean wouldn't!"

"Couldn't!" Cade shot back. "I gave your brother my word I wouldn't touch you; not until you were out of your teens!"

"You...what?" The whole world seemed to still.

He let out a heavy, frustrated sigh. "Damn it. You were sixteen, Susannah, and I was in love with you!"

Sixteen?

Cade's head shook. "Brock knew how I felt and demanded my word that I wouldn't pursue you until you were at least twenty. I had no choice, Susie. You were so young..."

"And you were almost twenty-two," she whispered. Understanding was slowly dawning.

"Yes," he muttered. "So I gave Brock my word and I bided my time, waiting for you to grow up. But suddenly you were eighteen and..."

A hand ran through his hair. "Dear God, Susannah. I never meant to hurt you; to be so cruel. But the pain and frustration of having to deny myself of you, the one thing I wanted most in this world, had me over the edge. I suddenly hated Brock for extracting such a promise from me. Hated you for offering me what I couldn't take. And I hated myself for holding me to my own word."

His eyes came back to hers. "I'm not proud of how I let you down, Susie. I'd give anything to have done it differently; anything not to have hurt you at all. But I did what I did and I've got to live with that. I just wish..."

He stopped suddenly and shook his head. "I'd better go start dinner," he said abruptly, and without another word, turned and walked into the cabin.

Susannah stared after him, her heart pounding. She had been so stupid! Stupid! All these years she had thought...

She shakily entered the kitchen after him. "Cade?"

He flashed a glance at her. "Set the table, will you?" he asked quietly.

Susannah watched him a moment, then did as he asked. Then, with a deep breath, she tried again. "Cade..."

"Will left over chili do you?" he asked sending another glance her way. He had made chili again the day before.

"Left over chili will be fine," she said. She again opened her mouth.

"Then we'll need the cheese and cornbread out," came his comment as he turned back to the stove. "Get them, will you?"

Susannah swallowed hard. The man was doing his best to shut her out. Was he done with her then? Had he decided to wash his hands of her after all? She took a deep, determined breath. "Cade?"

"Let it go, Susannah."

"I can't," she whispered. How could she? She loved him. She couldn't let him go. Not now. With another steadying breath, she stepped closer to him, laying her hand on his arm. "Cade, what *do* you wish?" she asked, her heart in her throat.

"Does it matter?" he countered.

"Yes!" she said tightly, turning him around. "It matters!" Her eyes went up to his, fear and hope and dread all mixing together. "*Please, Cade!*"

Cade stilled as his own eyes searched hers. A solid hope rose. "Susannah…"

"I love you," she whispered shakily.

He reached out and folded her into his arms as relief flooded him. "Oh, Susannah," he said on a breath. "*That's* what I wish; what I hope for. You. Just…you."

"You have me," she told him, burying herself against him. A calming relief was spreading through her; a contented joy. He still wanted her. Still loved her. She lifted her head.

"How touching."

The voice was cold and hard and brought both Cade and Susannah's eyes around. Luis Rico was standing in the back doorway, leaning against the doorframe. A rifle was in his hands; a rifle aimed at them both.

CHAPTER TWENTY-FIVE

Susannah's heart went in her throat as Cade's hands tightened.

"Bout time I caught up with the two of you," Rico said eyeing them both. "Nice trick with the purse, by the way," he added sociably. "You actually had me going for a day or two."

"How did you find us?" Cade questioned, slowly easing Susannah protectively aside.

"Little missy there helped me out," Rico answered easily, pointing the rifle at Susannah. "She finally put in a call to her brother's phone. Not a long message, mind you, just a short, little message that conveniently left me the return number on his Caller ID. It was all I needed. Once here in town, it was easy to find you." The rifle swung back to Cade.

"You know, you're not an easy man to kill, Candlewood. Twice now, you've avoided me. But you know what they say, third time's the charm."

Susannah's heart lurched. *Dear God!*

Cade eyed both the rifle and the man. "Why not just let this all go, Rico?" he suggested, keeping his voice calm. "Get out while you can?"

Rico's head shook, "Unfinished business to take care of. You, for one, then little missy here. Of course, I'm going to take my time with her," he added with an unhealthy gleam of anticipation. "You remember: terror, torture, rape."

It was too much for Cade. With a *"You rotten bastard!"* he charged the man. Even as he charged, he realized he should have kept his cool. But it was too late. Rico's rifle, already raised, went off before he made it two feet. The impact of the bullet sent him flying back against the counter. He felt his head crack against it.

The last thing he was aware of as he sank to the floor was Susannah's heart-wrenching, terrified, *"NO!"*

Susannah's eyes had flown to Rico. An unholy grin was spreading across his face as he eyed her. "Now I think it's time I finish my business with you, little missy," he smirked.

With another terrified, *"NO!"* Susannah bolted over Cade's still body into the front room and out of the front door of the cabin. She dashed madly to the Bearcat, grabbing for her keys as she ran. Unlocking the SUV with the electronic fob she yanked the vehicle's door open and reached up to pull herself inside.

She didn't make it. Rico was suddenly right behind her. He didn't hesitate in grabbing her and pulling her brutally away from the SUV.

"Oh, no you don't," he said. "I've got plans for you."

But Rico didn't have a firm grip of her. Susannah wrenched herself free and bolted away from him. She tore past the SUV, then around the corner of the cabin. If she could make it to the forest trees...

Despite her try, Rico tackled her in the back clearing and she went down before she made it even near the trees. The breath was knocked out of her as she belly-flopped into the dirt with Rico's body following her down. She was vaguely aware of the rifle being tossed aside...of her head bouncing against the ground...of dirt and stone digging into her skin. Still, she struggled to get away.

Rico however, had her easily in his grip. He managed to flip her over pinning her arms beneath her as he straddled her. Susannah continued to struggle desperately to break free. It did little good. Having forcefully constrained her with his own body, he began slapping her, again and again, grinning down at her the entire time; waiting.

Susannah eventually stilled, her chest heaving as she took in one painful gasp of air after another. The rifle, she noted, had been replaced with a knife. Tears welled and spilled over. Rico grinned malevolently as he slowly ripped the buttons of her blouse then took his knife to her bra.

His knife then trailed painfully down the middle of her chest, its point leaving a thin, red, seeping line in its wake. "I'm going to enjoy torturing you...raping you..."

Oh, God!

"NO!" she cried out in new terror as she again desperately tried to fight him off; tried to get away. An ugly laugh came out of Rico as he easily held her down.

"Cade!" she screamed out in agony.

Almost in answer, a dark, compact form suddenly shot over Susannah and directly into Rico, knocking the man back. The knife went flying. A blood-curling scream mixed with a vicious snarling.

Susannah stared in numbed surprise. It was Timbers attacking Rico, tearing into him ferociously! *Timbers!*

She watched in dumbfounded horror as the man rolled from her in an attempt to get away from the wolf, but Timbers didn't let up. Again and again he ferociously attacked the man.

Susannah tried to roll away but found she couldn't move. Rico and the wolf were still too close, their bodies rubbing against her as they fought. Her eyes closed tightly then sprang open as two strong arms began easing her carefully away from the tangled battle beside her.

Cade.

He pulled her safely away and up into his own arms; arms that clamped around her in unbelievable relief. Though he glanced at Rico and the wolf, he did nothing to stop the animal. His concern turned back to Susannah. She was buried into him, trembling uncontrollably. A deep, relieved breath came out of him as he held her. She was alive; safe. His arms tightened.

A moment later silence filled the clearing. The cries and snarling had stopped. Both Cade and Susannah looked over in the sudden stillness. Timbers stood beside Rico's lifeless body, his eyes now trained on the two of them. But it wasn't a wild, vicious look he gave them. It was an almost human look; a look of self-satisfaction and pride…and question.

"She's okay, Timbers," Cade told the animal softly, a shaky timbre to his voice. "Thank you."

Almost in understanding, the wolf's head lowered and with a last look at Rico's lifeless body, he turned and trotted across the clearing and disappeared into the trees beyond.

Susannah looked up to Cade. "He saved my life," she told him in dumbfounded awe.

"Yes," Cade said, his relief still swamping him. His lips came down and took hers. Another kiss followed.

Susannah buried herself into him. "Dear God, Cade. I thought he had killed you!"

"Not a chance," he said soothingly, kissing her temple. "It's what we wear the vests for; protective measures. Unfortunately, it couldn't stop my head from hitting the counter."

Susannah's arms tightened around him. "I'm sorry," she gulped, tears suddenly welling.

"Hey," he said raising her head. "None of this was your fault, Susie. None of it."

"But I led him here!" she cried, "By trying to call Brock!"

"No matter," he soothed as a deep breath left him. "It's over Susannah. Over. He's done for. He can't hurt you or Brock or any of us anymore."

A shudder escaped Susannah. "I love you, Cade. So much. And I'm so glad that you're not dead," she added.

Cade managed to smile. "So am I." His eyes searched her. "Did he hurt you, Susannah?"

"A little," she muttered as she fought back her tears. Reaction was setting in. Her face hurt, as well as her body. And her chest where Rico had taken the knife to her stung.

"I'm sorry," Cade whispered, hugging her to him. He eased back and raised her chin. "I love you, Susannah Brockman. With all my heart, I love you." His lips touched hers once, twice, then deepened into a warm, giving kiss; a kiss Susannah returned in full. A shorter kiss followed.

A deep, shuddered breath escaped Cade. "Go on into the cabin," he told her letting her go. "I need to see if he's by any chance still alive."

But Susannah didn't move. She stood and watched as Cade slowly walked over to the man who had pursued them for so long. He bent down and Susannah saw his hand go out. A moment later he stood and walked back to her. Without a word his arm rounded her shoulder and he led her back toward the cabin.

"Is he...dead?"

"Yes," Cade replied quietly with a nod. Without letting go of Susannah, he pulled his phone out of his pocket and scrolled down to the phone number he was searching for and punched it in. Susannah watched as he waited, then began to talk. "Chief? It's Candlewood. Rico needs a body bag. Did you want to come pick him up, or would you rather I call the local sheriff?" he asked. There was a moment of silence, then, "Yes. About 20 minutes ago," Cade replied into the phone. "No," he drew out after a moment. "Believe it or not, the man was taken down by a wolf...Yes, sir, a wolf. Timber wolf to be exact...Yes, quite definitely... No, Brock's sister is fine. A little bruised and shell-shocked, but fine."

Shell-shocked? Susannah questioned sending a glance in Cade's direction. He merely winked. "Understood. Thank you, sir," he responded. "We'll be waiting."

The phone was snapped off. "They're on their way," he told Susannah.

"What about John?"

But Cade was already on the phone again. "Sheriff Ogdon, please." There was a moment's wait, then, "John? Cade. Just thought you should know, Rico's down...Here...It's not your fault, John. He slipped by me as well. Don't worry about it. All's well that ends well. He's dead, and we're safe....No, the team's coming in to pick up his body...You're welcome to if you want...Right. See you soon."

"Is he coming?" Susannah asked.

"Most likely," Cade acknowledged leading her up the patio step. He escorted her through the open door and into the cabin. "Bathroom," he ordered lightly.

Susannah shook her head. "Timbers needs to be fed," she told him. "I think he deserves it."

"In a minute," Cade answered, "Let's take care of those scrapes of yours first."

He led her into the bathroom and sitting her down, removed the torn shirt and bra she still wore. He cursed as he caught sight of the thin, long cut the knife had left. Warming a washcloth, he gently washed the cut, then the scrapes along her arms and the side of her face. At last he spread an antibiotic ointment over them all. "Want them bandaged?" he asked softly.

Susannah shook her head. "Not unless you think it's necessary," she added shakily.

"I think it would help," he returned reaching into the cabinet for several gauze bandages, "At least these on your arm and the cut on your chest."

Susannah sat quietly as he bandaged her, self-consciously aware that she was wearing nothing from waist up. Cade didn't appear to notice. He handed her several pain-relievers when he finished, then downed several himself.

"Stay here," he said disappearing out of the bathroom the moment the bandages were in place. He came back a moment later with one of her t-shirts. Helping her slip into it, he pulled her to her feet.

"Come on, love. Let's go feed Timbers."

Timbers was not in sight when they went out to feed him. Cade left him several steaks in the hollow where they had been feeding him regardless. "He'll come for it," he assured Susannah.

"I'm sure he will," she said wrapping her arm around Cade. "He's earned it."

"Yes," Cade said, his own arm going around her as they walked slowly back toward the cabin. "He definitely has."

"I can't believe he saved me like that," she commented after a moment.

"I just thank God – and him, that he did," Cade said, his arm tightening. "Are you hungry?"

Susannah shook her head. "Not really. You?"

"Not really," he echoed. "But I think it would help kill time while we wait."

Susannah hesitated. "Want to go to bed instead?" she asked only half-teasingly.

"And have John or the team come waltzing into the cabin in the middle of our lovemaking?" Cade retorted with a shake of his head, "No way." He pulled her to a stop. His hand cupped her cheek bringing her eyes to his. "We'll wait, sweetheart."

"If you insist."

"I definitely insist," he said with a warm smile, planting a kiss on her nose. "Because the first time I make love to you, Susannah, is going to be very special and very private and free of any and all interruptions. You're going to have my ring on your finger and a piece of paper giving me the right."

Warmth spread through Susannah. She teased him regardless. "Do we really have to wait that long?"

"Not as long as you think," he retorted. "As soon as this is cleared up and the team leaves, we're heading for the nearest church and getting married. You want a second, bigger wedding, fine; you can plan it for later. But we're going to bed tonight as man and wife."

Susannah's heart skittered. "Promise?"

"Yeah, I promise," he said pulling her to him and taking her lips with his. The ringing of his phone brought the kiss to an end.

"That should be your brother," he said, letting her go while he dug for his phone. Susannah watched as he flipped it open. "Brock?"

Cade grinned at Susannah. "Alive and safe, Brock," he said into the phone. "Want to talk to her?"

Susannah eagerly took the phone Cade held out. "Brock?"

"You really okay?" her brother asked immediately.

"Yes," Susannah assured him as Cade walked her around the cabin and settled her down on the front steps. "I'm really okay. A couple of cuts and bruises, and I feel like I've been on a roller-coaster, but I'm fine. How are you?"

"One hundred percent better knowing your life is no longer in danger," he said. Then, "I'm actually mending, Susie. Can't walk yet, but I'm actually mending. When are you coming to see me?"

"That you'll have to ask Cade," she said. "Right now we're waiting for your team to come and get Rico."

"Let me talk to him."

Susannah handed the phone back over to Cade. "What is it, Brock?" Cade asked immediately.

"How soon can you get her here?"

"Most likely tomorrow."

"Tomorrow."

"We have one or two things we need to take care of here first," Cade told him quietly with a wink to Susannah.

"Can't the team take care of it?"

"Not this."

"Explain *this*," Susannah's brother demanded.

"As soon as the team leaves, I'm taking your sister down to the nearest church," Cade said solemnly. "In order to exchange a few vows and slip a ring on her finger."

A soft laugh came out of Brock. "I see. About time, friend."

"Yes," Cade agreed softly, his warm eyes still on Susannah.

Susannah's heart jumped with the glance. She loved him. Oh, how she loved him!

CHAPTER TWENTY-SIX

They sat on the cabin's front porch and talked to her brother another fifteen minutes before the sheriff's car pulled in and Cade with a "Got to go," finally closed the phone. John climbed from his vehicle and headed toward them.

"He's in the back," Cade informed him slipping his hand around Susannah's.

The sheriff with a slight acknowledgment headed around the side of the cabin. He was gone a good five minutes before he returned, slightly green. "What happened?" he demanded.

Cade smiled. "Remember the wolf Susannah befriended?"

John Ogdon stared. "You're not telling me..."

Cade nodded. "He came to Susannah's rescue. Saved her life and took care of Rico for us."

"Good Lord," the sheriff said in awe. "And where were you?" he managed to ask looking to Cade.

"Pulling myself off the kitchen floor," Cade admitted ruefully. "By the time I got out there Timbers was already on him. There wasn't much I could do. I managed to pull Susannah out away from them and left him to it."

"Well, he definitely finished the job," John commented with a shake of his head.

"Thank God." Cade stood and pulled Susannah to her feet. "Want to join us for something to eat?" he asked, shooting a glance at his friend.

"Might be a good idea if I stayed around," the sheriff said. "When's your team due in?"

"Within the next hour or so," Cade returned. His hand tightened around Susannah's. "Come on. Let's go find something to eat, and then start closing up the cabin while we wait."

Cade checked the chili that had been left simmering on the stove. He put Susannah to work cutting up the leftover cornbread while he found the cheese in the refrigerator and set it on the table. Susannah added another place setting and a short few minutes later they were sitting down to the warm meal. They talked of little things. John informed them that his wife and son were now home.

"Going to be around to say hi?" he questioned, looking to Cade.

"It's possible," Cade told him with a nod.

They were just finishing when they heard the sounds of a chopper, quite close by.

"That's the team," Cade said, coming to his feet and dashing outside. Both Susannah and Sheriff Ogdon followed him out onto the patio and watched as he directed the helicopter down in the clearing just short of where Rico lay. Four men piled out once the vehicle landed and came to a stop. Bartlett was among them. Cade went out and met them, then took them to Rico's body. Susannah, with a shudder, went back inside the cabin and began cleaning up the kitchen. She wondered vaguely what they were going to do with the leftover food, including the food they hadn't even touched yet.

Deciding not to worry about it, she finished the kitchen, then went through the cabin gathering up both her and Cade's loose belongings and placing them on one of the front room chairs. Slipping outside and purposely avoiding the activity in the center of the clearing, she picked up the clipboard, papers, and pencils as well as Cade's book from the patio and went in and added them to the chair.

Cade suddenly called her into the kitchen. She found his chief and the sheriff already sitting at the table. Cade held a chair out for her then slipped into one as well. Susannah looked up to Bartlett. He smiled warmly.

"I'm glad to see you alive and well and now safe."

Susannah flushed. "Thank you. So am I."

He set a small tape recorder on the table and switched it on. "You don't mind?" he asked, indicating the small machine.

Susannah shook her head. She knew many law officials used tapes now instead of handwritten notes to be sure they got everything down as it was said. Bartlett turned to Cade.

"Alright. Let's get this debriefing over with. In your words, Cade, what exactly happened?"

Cade rubbed his cheek. "Let's just say, I blew my cool," he admitted. He sat back. "Susannah and I had just had a brief, royal argument out on the patio. I finally let it go and came in and started dinner. Susannah followed, and after a few minutes of more talking, we...sorted out our differences and ended up in each other's arms." He shook his head in self-disgust. "The next moment, Rico was there standing in the doorway with a rifle pointed at the two of us. I tried to talk to him out of his revenge, but he was too determined. When he turned the rifle on me I knew he was going to fire. I lunged at him but I was too slow and he was too ready. His bullet sent me back to the counter and I cracked my head. The last thing I remember was Susannah screaming."

He shook his head to clear his mind of that terrifying scream. "When I came to a few minutes later, I heard the commotion in the back. By the time I got out there Timbers – the wolf – was all over Rico. I eased Susannah away from their tangled battle and to safety. A few moments later it was over. Timbers, looking proud and satisfied, looked at us, and then disappeared into the trees. I checked on Rico to see if he was by chance still alive, called you and Ogdon, then took Susannah back to the cabin and cleaned her up. She had cuts and bruises along her face and arms and a knife wound down her chest."

"You have any idea how he traced you here?"

Cade flickered a glance at Susannah but looked back to his chief. A sigh came out of him. "He stated that he traced us through a telephone call that was placed to Brockman's phone."

"I see." Bartlett looked evenly at Cade. It was evident that he was far from happy with the revelation.

"It wasn't his fault!" Susannah spoke out, afraid the Chief was going to lay into Cade. "Cade did everything possible to prevent me from calling my brother. He didn't let go of his phone once and watched me like a hawk. But that first chance I had I went ahead and called Brock anyway. Cade didn't even know I had done it."

"So how did you manage to call your brother without Candlewood knowing?" the Chief asked.

"I…well." She flushed. "We were in town and I had to use the bathroom."

"And there was a phone in the bathroom," Cade finished with a shake of his head.

"Yes," Susannah admitted. She looked back up at Cade's chief. "It was just that I was so mad at Cade for preventing me from talking to my brother and I wanted desperately to talk to him and the phone was right there." She stopped and shook her head. "I'm sorry. I figured if I just left a short, brief message to Brock to call me that the call wouldn't be able to be traced. I didn't even think that the number would be left on Brock's Caller ID. I'm sorry," she said again, sniffing back her tears.

Cade's hand came around hers and he squeezed it hard. "It's alright, sweetheart," he soothed gently.

Bartlett eyed them both a moment then turned back to Susannah. "Okay, Miss Brockman. You're turn. I want to know exactly what happened in your own words."

Susannah sniffed and took a deep steadying breath then with Cade's hand around hers, she explained almost word for word what had transpired in the kitchen. It changed briefly as she explained how she had darted through the cabin and tried to make it to the Bearcat. How Rico had pulled her from the SUV but she had managed to get away again and had headed for the trees in the back.

She stumbled slightly as she described how Rico had grabbed her and threw her down; how he had taken the knife to her. Then with another steadying breath, she told how Timbers had come sailing over her and attacked Rico…and how Cade had miraculously pulled her away.

"If it hadn't had been for Timbers or Cade, I don't know what would have happened," she added on a quiet breath.

"Thank God for Timbers," Cade murmured, his hand tightening around hers. He knew *he* certainly hadn't protected her!

"Tell me about the wolf," Bartlett instructed curiously. "I've never known of a wild wolf defending a man or woman."

"Even I'd like to know about that," John, who had remained silent this whole time, added.

Cade looked at Susannah and grinned. His eyes went back to his chief. "Well, you see…" He began relating to him the story of how Susannah had befriended the injured timber wolf and how it had progressed.

"I think Timbers began thinking of us as part of his pack," Susannah added. "He even followed us when we went off walking."

Bartlett's eyes rose with that but Cade assured him the wolf had never gotten close. "He seemed to have drawn his own line which he never crossed until Susannah was attacked."

Bartlett shook his head and turned back to Susannah. "How are you feeling?"

"A little shook up yet," she said truthfully, "But I'm calming down."

"I'm glad to hear it." He turned back to Cade. "I want you to take her and yourself down to the local doctor's and get yourselves checked over. Then when we get you home, we'll have you both go in for a complete check."

"Actually, Chief," Cade said, "If it's okay with you, Susannah and I would rather stay around here another night or so and drive the Bearcat back. We have a few things here we would like to attend to before we go see her brother."

Again Bartlett eyed them both. A slight smile came out of him. "I see."

"I'm sure you do," Cade said. He came to his feet. "By the way," he told his chief, "I've got that report you asked for, as well as a few others. I'll go get them." Cade left, but returned only a minute later. He handed a folder of papers to Bartlett and sat down again beside Susannah.

The chief eyed the top paper, but put it aside as he scanned through the others. The folder closed and he seemed to let out a sigh as he picked up the paper he had put aside. He looked to Cade.

"You sure about this?"

"I'm sure," Cade returned stolidly.

A deeper sigh came out of Bartlett this time. "I had a feeling it was coming."

"You're a smart man, Chief," Cade acknowledged.

"So are you, Candlewood," Bartlett returned pocketing the tape recorder. He came to his feet. "Well, I believe that finishes it up for now." His eyes flickered to Susannah, then back to Cade. "Go ahead and drive the SUV back. I'll let your partner know you're going to be delayed. And get yourself and your girl here down to the medical center before you do anything else."

"I will."

"I'll take them down there myself," John volunteered with a grin, "Even if I have to arrest them to do so."

Bartlett laughed. "Now that might just do it. Thank you, Sheriff Ogdon." He shook John's hand then held his hand out to Cade. "Congratulations, and good luck to you both," he added sending a smile to Susannah. "I'll process your resignation as soon as your reports are in and you've both been checked out thoroughly back home."

"Not a problem," Cade returned taking the hand offered. "Thank you."

With a finger salute, Cade's chief stepped back outside and headed toward the helicopter. He talked a moment to one of his men then climbed in. A minute later the helicopter's blades were spinning and it slowly lifted off and disappeared out of sight.

Susannah turned to Cade. "You resigned?"

"I resigned," he confirmed.

Susannah threw herself into his arms. "I love you, Cade Candlewood!"

Cade grinned and kissed her, then turned to John.

"You still willing to drive us down to Doc's?"

"You'd better believe it."

"Want to do us another favor?"

"What do you need?"

"A church, a pastor, and two witnesses…tonight," Cade added, winking at Susannah.

John's eyes widened. "The two of you are getting hitched?"

"Yup. Think you can arrange it?"

"Oh, will I!" John returned a wide grin on his face.

CHAPTER TWENTY-SEVEN

To John's credit, he did both. He took them down to the doctor's to have them checked out, and then went in search of the pastor of their church. Having arranged a ceremony for a mere hour-or-so later, he drove them back to the cabin so they could get ready. They had little time for showers, shaving, and make-up, but they both managed.

Susannah, with no wedding dress – no dress at all – donned the white tailored jeans that she had refused to wear around the cabin, and found her knit white top to match it. Though the top wasn't new, and it had a small trim of blue and pink flowers along its sleeves and the neckline, Susannah thought it perfect. It was clean and looked good on her and that was all that mattered.

Cade, too, donned a new pair of jeans. They were either black or dark blue, Susannah was never quite sure. Again it didn't matter. He looked good in them, as well as the crisp, white shirt and darker tie he added.

"Where in the world did you find the tie?"

"They've been here," he replied, "There are a few others if you don't like this one."

Susannah shook her head. "You look perfect just as you are," she said, adjusting the tie.

"So do you." He smiled pulling her gently in his arms and planting a warm kiss on her lips. His release of her was slow. "Ready to go get married?"

"Oh, yes," she said with a soft smile. The smile faded. "What do we do about wedding rings?"

"Being taken care of," Cade said ushering her out to the SUV and into the passenger seat. "I've had a pair on hold down at the jeweler's for over a week and a half," he added. "John's picking them up for me."

212

"A week and a half!" Susannah squeaked. "You were that sure of me?"

"No," he admitted with a smile. "Just determined."

Susannah giggled, loving him more by the minute.

John met them at the church doors with his wife, Maree and their teenage son Justin. Susannah liked them instantly. Justin was a lot like his father and carrying a camera, and Maree was happy and friendly and had brought along her own wedding veil for Susannah to wear. It made Susannah feel like a bride despite the un-bride like clothes she was wearing.

"Well, come on," Cade urged with a grin. "Let's go get this wedding under way."

The wedding was quiet and perfect. Susannah wouldn't have changed a thing. The pastor greeted them warmly. Both John and his wife stood up for them. Justin, their son, took pictures. And Cade, to her surprise, phoned Brock right before the ceremony began, leaving his cell phone on speaker so that her brother could at least be there in spirit while the ceremony took place.

John handed Cade a small box when it came time for the rings; a box that held two matching bands. Both were gold, with two ribbons of shimmering diamonds that crossed in the middle of the ring in the symbol of a kiss. Susannah was literally shaking as she placed Cade's on his finger. But it didn't matter. The pastor pronounced them man and wife and in the next moment, Cade was lifting the veil and wrapping her in his arms for that first magical kiss of their union.

Thanking the pastor and the Ogdons for everything; thanking her brother for bearing with them, they returned to the cabin. Cade, unsure of her feelings regarding it, offered her the option of spending the night elsewhere, but Susannah refused. The cabin had been more than a place of refuge and dangers. It was the place where she and Cade had mended their differences and fallen in love all over again.

"I love you, Susannah Candlewood," Cade had said with an enticingly sweet kiss. Then with a slow, warm smile, he took her by the hand and led her inside where he showed her just how much…

The sun was just hitting the cabin windows when Susannah woke. She was snuggled comfortably against Cade's solid chest, his arms wrapped securely around her. She glanced at the ring now on her finger and a sigh of happiness came out of her.

"Susannah?"

Her heart jumped at the soft rumble of her name. She lifted her head and met Cade's warm eyes. "Good morning," she said.

"Good morning," he returned softly. His hand came up and gently smoothed her hair back. "How's my sweet, wonderful wife?"

"Wonderful," she said with a warm smile. "How's my wonderful husband?"

"Wonderful," he answered with a grin. He raised her chin and planted his lips on hers. The kiss was warm and tender, and tinged with desire. Susannah, with a sigh, settled back against him.

"I suppose we should get up and going."

"I suppose we should," he said as he gently began running his fingers through her hair. "Not that we have to."

Susannah looked up at him.

"Well, your brother did tell us to take our time," he reminded her. "I doubt that he'll expect us for another few days."

"You really don't think he'd mind?"

"I'm positive, sweetheart."

"What about your chief?"

"He knows he'll see me when he sees me." His hand left her hair and lifted her chin. "What do you want to do?"

"Stay right where I am," she admitted with a contented smile.

"Then we'll stay," Cade said, warmth flooding him as he took her lips with his...

They stayed two extra days, using the second day to pack up and clean out the cabin, and to say good-bye to Timbers. Susannah had worried about the wolf, but found she had no need to. For Timbers, when they went outside to say good-bye to him, was waiting on the rocks, sitting proudly; a smaller, lighter wolf sitting beside him. Susannah said a tearful good-bye to them both with joy in her heart.

Cade's arm wrapped around her. "Your wolf is going to be fine, Susannah," he said softly from her side, "Very fine. He's found his mate."

"Yes," she said, "Just as we have." She raised her head and with a warm smile, wrapped her arms around Cade's neck, kissing him with the whole of her love. They were both breathing erratically by the time the kiss came to an end.

"Oh, Susannah." Cade groaned deeply. "I believe we're going to need to postpone our departure just an hour or so longer."

She dimpled mischievously. "I believe so, too."

With a glorious laugh, Cade took possession of her lips once again. Desire and passion swirled through them both. Susannah's heart swelled with a wondrous love as her husband picked her up and carried her back into the cabin.

***

Printed in the United States
By Bookmasters